P9-CNG-849

Tom Clancy's

OP-CENTER

THE BLACK ORDER

TOM CLANCY'S OP-CENTER NOVELS

Op-Center

Mirror Image

Games of State

Acts of War

Balance of Power

State of Siege

Divide and Conquer

Line of Control

Mission of Honor

Sea of Fire

Call to Treason

War of Eagles

Out of the Ashes

Into the Fire

Scorched Earth

Dark Zone

For Honor

Sting of the Wasp

God of War

ALSO BY JEFF ROVIN

The Hindenburg Disaster

The Transgalactic Guide to Solar System M-17

The Madjan

Dagger

Starik (with Sander Diamond)

The Red Arrow (with Sander Diamond)

Cat Angels

Vespers

Stealth War

Fatalis

Dead Rising

Tempest Down

Rogue Angel

Conversations with the Devil

Zero-G (with William Shatner)

Tom Clancy's

OP-CENTER

THE BLACK ORDER

CREATED BY

Tom Clancy and Steve Pieczenik

WRITTEN BY

Jeff Rovin

ST. MARTIN'S
GRIFFIN
NEW YORK

This is a work of fiction. All of the characters, organizations, and events portrayed in this novel are either products of the author's imagination or are used fictitiously.

First published in the United States by St. Martin's Griffin, an imprint of St. Martin's Publishing Group

www.stmartins.com

Designed by Omar Chapa

The Library of Congress Cataloging-in-Publication Data is available upon request.

ISBN 978-1-250-22234-3 (trade paperback)
ISBN 978-1-250-81772-3 (hardcover run on)
ISBN 978-1-250-22236-7 (ebook)

First Edition: 2021

10 9 8 7 6 5 4 3 2 1

Tom Clancy's

OP-CENTER

THE BLACK ORDER

PROLOGUE

Philadelphia, Pennsylvania
January 15, 11:18 p.m.

In the two years since retiring as commander of Naval Support Activity Philadelphia, Captain Richard "Atlas" Hamill had been dedicated to three things.

The first and most important was his wife, Sophia. They had recently celebrated their forty-second wedding anniversary, and their love and friendship were "eight bells strong," as he put it. Hamill had met the Texas native when he was stationed at Naval Station Corpus Christi. That was where she gave him his nickname, after the moving van he had stopped beside to give her their first kiss.

Hamill's second great passion was hunting, which he did every weekend during season. Absent sea air he required country air, the smell of leaves alive or rotting—he did not care. He ate what he killed, and always thanked God for His bounty. During the off-season he kept fit by walking the Western Pennsylvania woods.

The captain's third passion was spending at least several

minutes a day in the company of his neighbors, the dead ones: the towering ghosts of Independence Hall, the birthplace of the nation that the captain loved and served.

Whenever he was in the city, whatever the weather, the sixty-year-old walked two blocks from his Spruce Street town house to the historic compound. His knees never failed to weaken as he stepped on that holy ground. Even when he had the flu a year before, Hamill had dragged himself to the rooftop of his four-story home to gaze upon the iconic building. His wife, her gray hair whipping in the wind, had gamely helped him up the steep staircase—to argue would have been futile—then hustled him back inside before he could catch pneumonia.

"I thought I heard the Liberty Bell up there," he had said, smiling in his feverish state as she tucked the comforter under his chin.

"I hit my head on the door helping you," Sophia had replied. "Now we are *both* hearing things."

In all the years he and Sophia had been together, the captain had never confided that it was more than love of country that compelled him to lay eyes on the landmark. It was a sailor's superstition that bordered on obsession. Richard's father, Captain Martin Hamill, was XO of the USS *Yorktown*. He had refused to board the aircraft carrier for its decommissioning until his lucky silver dollar flipped heads up into his left palm. He had done that every time he'd boarded for the past quarter century. To the elder Hamill a successful flip meant he would not go down with his ship.

Martin Hamill lived to be eighty-nine, his wife, Carol, ninety.

On the day of the decommissioning, the coin flip had accomplished one thing more. The ceremony that had transferred the *Yorktown* from active duty to the Atlantic Reserve Fleet, the "Mothball Fleet," gave them their permanent home. After the event, the elder and younger Hamills had decided to walk for a while and let their emotions settle. They took an out-of-the-way turn and strolled onto Spruce Street, right past the For Sale sign outside the corner building. Martin Hamill bought the four-story town house that afternoon.

Richard Hamill did not become overly superstitious until his mandatory retirement after thirty-eight years. That was only his "public" retirement, as the retiree called it, because he had immediately gone to work as a consultant for the Office of Naval Intelligence. Major Becky Lewis of the Transnational Threat Department remembered him from a logistics conference years before and booked him a train ticket. She recalled him having spoken about his love of hunting, and it was not Hamill's years in the navy that interested her but his unique knowledge of the game lands throughout the state—and fellow hunters. Hamill had recently celebrated the twenty-fifth anniversary of PAVE—Pennsylvania Venison, a loose collective he had cofounded and which helped feed veterans suffering hard times. Hunters dropped off food at his home, and he brought it to veterans in his station wagon. His own kills were among those hand-delivered to the group.

Now, most days, Hamill was busier than when he had been running the supply and support services for naval operations at NSA Philadelphia. His reconnaissance for the Office of Naval Intelligence was dangerous work, as it turned out. Much more dangerous than bear or bobcat. His job was to circle ever closer over five hundred acres to a target that his handler only suspected was real. Its possible existence was something she surmised based on information from "Taikinys," a debriefed arms dealer. The gun-and-explosives runner had kept using the words "black order," though neither Major Lewis nor Atlas Hamill had ever heard of such a thing. Initially, she had taken those words to describe a secret purchase agreement. But then she wondered if it might be part of a name. Just yesterday, when he returned from his latest "walk in the woods," as he downplayed his activities to Sophia, he began to have a feeling that he was not just looking and watching but being watched. A hunter's instinct, nothing more, which he communicated to Major Lewis.

If Sophia knew how risky the work was, she would have dragged her husband to safety, just as she had put her small arms around him and hauled him to and from the rooftop. All he had said, in passing, was that if Sophia ever needed anything from the navy she should press two on speed dial. She, of course, was number one.

Well, he thought, *America was born in danger and would always face such challenges.* Philadelphia's native son Benjamin Franklin had risked his life just by showing up for meetings and affixing his name to an immortal document. *Should I do less?*

Just a half hour before, after walking to Walnut Street to

remind the Founding Fathers that yet another American presidency was soon to begin, Captain Atlas Hamill lay on his back and shut his eyes. He did not lament his fears but welcomed them. He was proud and content thinking about the few tourists who had stood with him in the cold, amidst the skeletal winter trees, looking up at the bell tower, its famed contours set emphatically against a gibbous moon.

He was somewhere between wakefulness and sleep when a bus growled three floors below, on the corner of Spruce and South Third. Sophia had never liked the sound and the faint whiff of fuel, but it made her husband smile. Both had a comforting, almost narcotic effect on the system. Diesel was in the noses of most seamen. Functioning machinery was in their ears. This was especially true when they bedded down in bunks stacked three or four high. At lights out, the olfactory and auditory senses were undistracted.

Sleep came just as the point of a knife stung the throat of Captain Hamill, its straight edge going deep under his Adam's apple and causing blood to gush into his windpipe. He gasped, the flood burbling as it poured into his windpipe and rose in his throat, backing into his mouth.

Sophia Hamill woke when she heard gurgling and wheezing sounds to her right. It was faint enough so that she thought, at first, a homeless person was regurgitating in the street. Then she was aware of it being closer, much closer, and rolled toward her husband. She saw his dark shape trembling violently against the glow of the clock on the night table.

"Richard!"

The woman jerked upright, her right arm flinging out to find the light switch.

She was pushed back by a masked figure who was looming above her, his weight on her chest and shoulder pressing her arm deep and helpless in the mattress. She reached up with her left arm to push back, and he smacked it away with his free hand. She snaked it up again, and he struck it again, harder. Fully awake and terrified she looked up, saw her attacker silhouetted against a portion of the ceiling that was lit by a streetlamp just below the window.

The woman screamed with violence that rocked her entire body. The hand on her shoulder jerked to her mouth. A leather glove, pliable with age, trapped the cry in her mouth, causing her cheeks to expand. The attacker's fingers closed tightly and gripped her jaw. He leaned his weight on her mouth, jamming her head into her pillow even as her husband flopped freely, weakly to her left. She was now aware of blood soaking her back starting at the shoulder and creeping down along her ribs. The sensation was warm, wet, and impossible. Her eyes were wide as she sucked air and the smell of leather through flared nostrils.

The killer was not oblivious to the death rattle of the man beside her and the blood spilling with weakening spurts from the dying man's wound. He simply did not care. The intruder had committed an execution, not a murder.

"The devil is not as black as he is painted."

He had withdrawn the gory knife with his right hand, the hand that had rapped her left arm hard. He moved the double-barrel fixed blade hunting knife over, put the point against the widow's left side. The pinch of the blade was in line with her racing heart. Her chest struggled against his weight as it expanded, hard and fast with each short, sharp breath; her breath, along with her small struggles, made the corpse beside her rise and fall grotesquely. The rapid beat of her heart caused the blade to pulse. The man on top of her could feel it throb through the metal.

The killer gazed down through a black ski mask. It was good to feel the random strands of wool on his lips, his own hot breath warming his cheeks, his hair damp with perspiration despite the cold. The smells here were unfamiliar, yet the mask brought back the past. The feeling of service blended with the more satisfying sense of power. He took a moment to savor it, as he always had.

The Iranian bomb maker in Basra. The young war widow on her way to pick up a suicide vest in Tikrit. The Iranian spy in the Green Zone who gave him a gift: the location of an American hostage, who was liberated that night.

Every one of them had been a personal triumph of surveillance and bribery, stalking and eavesdropping, and finally isolating and killing. Civilians would never understand the balance of patience and urgency an undercover operative required in-country.

The others did.

The killer saw the pinpoint gleam of her eyes directly below his own. Those eyes were large and frightened, and they widened even more as he pressed the tip of the knife a little harder.

He smiled under his mask. It was a look of terror, open and pleading.

The man waited a moment before lowering his face closer to hers. She was just an animal now, afraid and without dignity or shame. The light in her eyes died as his head blocked the source. He spoke, his voice a whisper, his breath warm on the woman's cheeks.

"You will deliver a message, Mrs. Hamill. Nod if you understand."

Sophia Hamill nodded obediently, more from horror than understanding.

"You are to tell your husband's employers that the war has begun. Inform them that those who move against us will die, whether it is one or one thousand. Is that understood?"

This time she did not nod. The command did not make sense.

The man leaned closer, his full weight on the hand pressing her back. "Mrs. Hamill, will you communicate what I told you, or must I write the message in your husband's blood?"

The woman tried to replay the words, to process them. Comprehension did not make it through her terror.

The man relaxed his grip on her mouth but did not raise his hand. "One last time, you are to tell the people your husband worked for: the war has begun. The war has begun. You will tell them that, yes?"

This time the simple phrase stuck. The woman nodded vigorously.

In a single, fluid movement the intruder drew the knife

from her side, raised the hand that held it, and brought the steel hilt down on her forehead.

The woman let out a grunt as she felt an electric shock race from that point around her skull. She squeezed her eyes shut and saw circles of rusty red that slowly turned to black.

With the woman unconscious, the intruder went back to the dead man's side of the bed. He turned on the light and snatched up the man's cell phone. It was locked.

That wouldn't matter, Poole had said. The manufacturer's theft-deterrent software could be tricked into entering recovery mode with signals from cloned servers. A new password could then be furnished and used to access everything stored on the phone.

"I hope so," the man muttered.

Checking to see that the woman was still out, the man went downstairs. He removed his ski mask, changed into the clothes he had left on a chair, and exited by the front door.

Upstairs, after what may have been seconds, minutes, or even longer, Sophia realized that the man's hand was no longer on her mouth. She drew a long breath, felt it fill her lungs, and yelled it out until her chest had deflated and her face had twisted into something barely human.

Driven more by instinct than thought, she pushed herself from the bed. Her forehead screamed with pain and she fell stiff-armed against her night table.

She felt her phone. She had to call—

No, not 911.

Just a few days before, Atlas had put a number into her phone. Someone at the navy. Someone he said she should turn to if she ever needed anything. Sophia asked him why, and he said that there had been security concerns, nothing to worry about, but to call if anything—*anything*—happened out of the ordinary.

Her finger shaking, Sophia unlocked the phone and pressed the saved number.

Sobbing and fighting back nausea from the blow to her head, she heard a woman's voice, sobbed out her name, then did the only thing she was capable of doing.

She screamed.

CHAPTER ONE

The White House, Washington D.C.

January 16, 7:55 a.m.

"It takes some getting used to," Admiral Chase Williams, retired, said quietly, sitting forward in a plump armchair in the small West Wing office.

The only other man in the room, Deputy Chief of Staff Matt Berry, stopped packing items on his desk and looked at his companion.

"For whom, you or me?" Berry asked.

"Both. I just never thought of you moving from the West Wing to the private sector."

Williams's voice was flat and the words, like the man's attitude, were noncommittal. It was rare for Williams to be neutral about anything. The director of the National Crisis Management Center—informally, Op-Center—was an athletic six-footer with a commanding presence, even in repose. He had a perpetual squint that came from a lifetime on or near the water. Though his eyes were not hard, his ability to make tough, at times, impossible decisions and to do it correctly had earned him the respect of subordinates and colleagues alike.

Berry was standing beside an open backpack and holding an inauguration flag in one hand and a deep blue Camp David coffee mug in the other. A head shorter than Williams and over a dozen years younger, Berry was unintimidated. He frowned at the other man.

"It's a jump," Berry admitted. "Especially for a cynic."

"You're a helluva lot more than that, Matt."

"A mega-cynic?" Berry suggested.

Williams frowned. Unlike the rumpled Berry, he always tried to see all sides of a discussion. It was not just their different natures but their different careers. For Williams, it was the result of having worked in arenas where orders carried risks for others. The first was as an admiral, a combatant commander for both Pacific Command and Central Command. The second was as the director of Op-Center. Now, it was as a covert team leader for the pared-down Op-Center.

"You know what Angie accused me of yesterday?" Berry went on. "She said I look at the dark side of everything. Not just government and people but my own life."

Angie Brunner was the attorney heading the transition team of President-Elect John Wright. The former Hollywood studio head was credited as being the architect of the campaign of the Pennsylvania governor, and Wright had named her as the next presidential chief of staff.

"A bit out of her line of expertise, I would think," Williams said. Again, diplomatically.

"The fact is, we are irredeemably programmed. Which route did you take driving from the Watergate this morning?"

"The usual. Why?"

"Was there anything different?"

Williams shrugged. "A ten-minute delay on 66."

"Right. There was a fire early this morning at the Columbia Apartments, hot fire, blew the windows all over the streets. You waited. I would've cut around State Plaza."

"You would have saved about a minute. *And* given in to impatience."

"A venial sin, yeah. The point is we're different." Berry shook his head disapprovingly. "I'm going into the private sector because, unlike you, I can't wait for the ideal situation to turn up. You, my friend—you got lucky with Black Wasp."

"That I did," Williams agreed. And there was not a day he did not thank God—and Berry, and the president—for that opportunity. When Op-Center was downsized, President Wyatt Midkiff—through Berry—offered Williams a one-person, three-soldier operation based at the Defense Logistics Agency. It was not his dream position. A basement office in the sprawling but austere McNamara Headquarters Complex rich with the recycled air of deep state and black ops. It was the worst possible spot for a man who loved the sea. But there was a stain on his record—more importantly, on his soul—that he had to wipe clean. And he had. With the blood of a terrorist.

Berry smiled triumphantly, took a step back, and resumed putting the personal contents of his desk into a backpack.

"I'll tell you this, Chase. I won't miss the political games. How long have we been without a vice president?"

"October 17."

"Nearly three months, and Bustercluck was three months before that. No, sir. I will take a think tank disagreement over that scale of smear and rancor any day."

Berry was referring to the impeachment of Vice President Newman Clark over a ten-year-old senatorial campaign finance abuse. It was directly after the worst of COVID and the news media drank deep of innuendo and hearsay. The Senate was somewhat united in his removal but refused to approve his replacement unless—by nomination or by the president's death—that replacement was Speaker of the House Buster Kahn, a member of the opposing party. Midkiff had supported his VP to a point, but not the railroading to name a career insider. The electorate agreed. Kahn's own bid for the presidency had not survived Super Tuesday.

Berry finished packing. There had not been much to take. Apart from a few mementoes there had been a backup personal tablet. Christmas cards he had received from members of the Midkiff administration, reminders of the few friends he still had. Pens branded with the names and logos of various government agencies, evidence that he had once been a player. A box of M&M's from Air Force One with Midkiff's gold-embossed signature on the box.

Evidence that he had been that closer to power, officially deputy chief of staff but in fact acting chief of staff. His predecessor couldn't take it, and Berry had not wanted the title and the target that came with the title. But he had the power. Chase Williams was evidence of that. The admiral's predecessor at Op-Center was founding director Paul Hood. When Hood was diagnosed with ALS, he stepped aside, and Berry pushed for Williams to take his place.

The sixty-one-year-old watched in silence as Berry took a moment to look around. He understood his companion and, his comments notwithstanding, he admired the man's intuitive grasp of situations—national, international, and Berry's own.

Though Williams had offered a counterpoint to his friend's actions, he did not judge them. Berry had not been asked to remain in the administration by the president-elect, nor had he expected to be. Governor Wright and President Midkiff belonged to different parties, different ideologies, and different generations. The new, younger commander in chief wanted more Pennsylvanians and fewer Washingtonians for his inner circle. Of course, Wright was not yet born when Jimmy Carter made that same mistake with fellow Georgians. And he obviously had not studied history. When wagons are circled like that, good and bad ideas alike remain inside.

But Wright would have to make his own mistakes or show everyone else how it was done. Right or wrong, one of the other decisions the president-elect had made was to retain Williams, Op-Center, and Black Wasp intact. Wright was navy, and fraternity never hurt. It helped that Op-Center—and Black Wasp—had two wildly successful covert missions in the bag.

Williams knew it was not necessarily Chase Williams that Wright wanted. Rather, the idea of having a small, secret, personal army—one he could always "blame" on his predecessor if it were outed—had apparently appealed to Wright. The admiral was simply convenient.

Berry zipped the bag. He did it slowly, almost reluctantly.

"And so it's finished," Berry said.

"I hate to say it," Williams said, "but being surrounded by federal vipers brings out the best in you. A think tank or an ivory tower may not suit you."

"You're not wrong. I already feel the withdrawal symptoms. But—and this is greed piled atop cynicism—the high six-figure salary was a powerful inducement, and I can parlay that to TV gigs."

Berry shouldered the bag. Williams rose. Both men looked around. The framed pictures had been taken down the night before. The place looked as impersonal as the White House freight elevator. Unlike the Oval Office, there was no history here.

So close, yet pay grades away.

"One more question," Berry asked quietly. "The cash we've got in your office for off-book operations. Did you ever wonder if I intended that to be my own personal retirement fund?"

"I did," Williams admitted.

"If I asked, would you give it to me? Part of it? Any of it?"

"Are you asking?"

The man was silent for a period bordering on the uncomfortable. The tension broke when the first notes of Beethoven's Fifth sounded on Berry's phone.

"The answer is 'no,'" Berry said before reading the text.

"Well, my friend, the vipers are active. The president wants us both."

Williams was not surprised that Midkiff knew he and Berry were together. The president's executive secretary as well as the Secret Service were copied with the name of every visitor and who they came to see.

Berry set his backpack on the desk, and their breakfast plans at the Retro Hot Shoppe were put on hold. He extended his arm, and Williams left first. They walked briskly along the West Wing corridor that was full of other employees with boxes and backpacks, with creased, youthful faces Williams did not recognize. Some were going, a few were coming, and all was chaos. When the two men reached the Oval Office they were waved in by Natalie Cannon. The supernaturally efficient woman had made no secret of where she was going in four days: to her family's horse ranch in Silver Spring, Maryland. Only her loyalty to her longtime boss, Midkiff, had kept her here for eight long years.

Berry had intended to ask Williams if Natalie's plans were "interesting" too—he could not resist pushing and probing—but there was no time. Not when they saw the face of the president. For the past few days, Midkiff had been relaxed, openly sociable. That look had been wiped away, as if by a flood.

"Close the door," Midkiff said flatly. He was looking at the monitor on his desk.

"Mr. President," Berry said. "Good morning" did not seem appropriate.

"Please sit," Midkiff said in response. "Harward and Hewlett will be checking in shortly. I held off bringing you in because we know so damn little."

The president was referring to National Security Advisor Trevor Harward and Homeland Security Secretary Abraham Hewlett.

Berry sat in one of the two armchairs facing the desk. "Where are they?" he asked, concern rising along his spine.

"Naval intelligence." He regarded Williams. "There's been a murder. It's someone you know, Chase."

Williams was suddenly oblivious to settling into the other armchair. Williams's mind went automatically to the people he had worked with closely at Op-Center before the downsizing. He thought of the terrorist he had assassinated in Yemen, of Iranian sleeper agents taking revenge. He had been closest with Deputy Director Anne Sullivan, who had landed at the State Department. And visual analysis expert Kathleen Hays, who had flowered at Op-Center, had gone to the National Reconnaissance Office. Williams knew where they were working, but they were not privy to his whereabouts. He was heartsick waiting for the president to continue. It had only been moments, but it felt far longer.

"Last night, around eleven, Captain Atlas Hamill was stabbed to death in his bed," the president said.

The name was clearly unfamiliar to Berry, who looked at Williams. The admiral did not react outwardly. Inside, he was sick.

"Who was he?" Berry said.

"He used to run Naval Support in Philly," Williams said in a soft monotone. "He retired a couple of years ago, fed veterans in need."

"I'm sorry, Chase," Berry said.

The admiral and the captain had interacted with some frequency at both United States Pacific Command and United States Central Command. Hamill was an honorable man and a crack logistics officer. Williams had tried to get him for PACOM, but Hamill did not want to leave his home.

Williams sat silent, staring. Typically, death came along a familiar path, the line of duty or an accident. This news, this method, was so unexpected he could not yet rouse himself to ask who or why.

"Actually, Chase, it appears that Captain Hamill was not retired," the president continued. "He was collecting his pension, but he was also working off the books for the Office of Naval Intelligence. In fact, Mrs. Hamill had the number of her husband's contact there on speed dial and called that number instead of 911. The matter went on immediate internal lockdown."

"What did Atlas Hamill have to do with naval intelligence?" Williams asked.

"I'll get to that in a minute. There's something else. The man who entered the home told Mrs. Hamill to deliver a message, which is probably the only reason she's alive." Midkiff put on eyeglasses and read from the monitor: "He said, 'Those who move against us will die,' and then he told her, 'The war has begun.'"

"Forgive me for asking, but what was the woman's mental state?" Berry said.

"It's a fair question," the president said. "She was hysterical, of course. But I'm told that before she was sedated, she seemed to have total recall of the event and damn near everything the intruder said. She didn't imagine any of it."

"What about the ONI?" Williams asked. "I just don't see the connection."

"All we know, at present, is that ONI has him listed as a Contact Only Asset."

Williams registered surprise.

"That's going to slow things down," Berry remarked.

A Contact Only Asset was a confidential source, meaning only the "handling" officer knew their function. Williams and Black Wasp were the same. In their case, the contact was Matt Berry working on behalf of the president. To get to a "Contact" at ONI meant getting approvals through a chain of command. More often than not, COAs acted not only outside channels but outside regulations. That was the reason most people in government referred to the acronym by another name: Conceal Our Assets. Even the president was kept out of the loop.

"Red tape and secrecy are why I sent Trevor and Abe over there now, to try and cut through the hedges," the president said. "Allen Kim is also in contact with the FBI field office trying to secure footage from surveillance cameras in the area." Midkiff held up his secure phone with a series of texts from the FBI's deputy director. "The Philadelphia PD initially pushed back on that request. Within an hour of the call from Mrs. Hamill, there were three ONI investigators out of Lakehurst at the Spruce

Street town house, looking for evidence, and four masters-at-arms arrived from NSA Mechanicsburg—"

"Not Philly?" Berry asked.

"Not Philly," the president confirmed.

Naval Support Activity Mechanicsburg was a sister facility located 110 miles northwest of Philadelphia. The navy had wasted no time removing as much direct responsibility as possible from NSA Philadelphia.

"Everyone had instructions to refuse admission to the town house not just to local authorities but to everyone except a very small number of specifically authorized personnel," the president continued. "The police still haven't been told there was a murder. The remains of Atlas Hamill were claimed by a doctor from the Office of the Armed Forces Medical Examiner at Dover Air Force Base. They're looking on the body, and at the town house, for fingerprints, of course, along with fibers, hair, spit—anything. Special Agent Dave Wildman, who runs the FBI field office, told the PD that the bureau is also in the dark—which Kim says should at least get police to cooperate with them."

"Under what, the shut-out agencies act?" Berry asked. "They can share traffic control duties?"

"That's pretty much it," Midkiff said. "I told Kim who is not cleared to inform anyone below and only the director above."

"How did we survive eight years of this?" Berry wondered aloud.

"Love of country," Williams replied. "The same as Captain Hamill."

The comment sobered the querulous deputy chief of staff to silence.

"What does Vice Admiral Nathan have to say about any of this?" Williams asked.

"I spoke to him just before you walked in," Midkiff said. "He said the ONI was as much in the dark as everyone else. He said his people would cooperate fully with Trevor and Abe. Ordinarily I wouldn't count on that—"

"But the director can't run out the clock until the twentieth," Berry said. "Not a lot of time to find someone to blame."

"Is there anything else about Sophia Hamill's condition?" Williams asked. He had heard enough of politics.

"Mrs. Hamill was not seriously injured, at least physically."

"Was she in the bed at the time?"

The president nodded.

"Is there family?" Williams asked. "She's going to need that."

"No kids, as you probably know, and no one else has been told. ONI security took her to NSA Philadelphia, where she's under guard. That's the way it's got to be for now. Hewlett pointed out that she may be expendable now that the message has been delivered."

"Something's cockeyed about all this," Berry said. "We had a retiree on a secret mission that did not seem to have much heat. Now, overnight, it's become a war. How did the ONI not know?"

"Matt, you know as well as I do that we can get intel about China's Xinjiang electronic warfare compound faster than we can from some of our own agencies. Let's see what Trevor and Abe dig up."

A weary silence filled the room as Berry decided to check emails on his tablet and Williams looked around the Oval Office. He thought back to the first time he had come here as a newly minted admiral. He had felt privileged then, the location a shrine to freedom. Now the luster was tarnished, even if his personal idealism was not blunted. As he looked around clear-eyed, the walls and doorjambs showed their age. Seams were visible under the paint or jambs, and furniture was nicked depending on the sunlight.

Still, the place meant something. He seemed to recall that Atlas lived near Independence Hall and had the same feeling about that sacred ground.

The president's desk phone buzzed.

"It's Trevor," Midkiff said and thumbed it on speaker. "Matt is with me—go."

The president did not mention Williams because, as far as anyone knew, Op-Center had been shut down.

"We don't have much, but we pried something out of ONI. They believe that Captain Hamill was investigating something called the Black Order."

"Is that an ONI designation or—?"

"It's what the group calls itself, Mr. President," Harward said. "There was a request just yesterday from the COA handler, pushed through Hopper Information Services Center, to investigate the name. The response triggered a shit storm that shot up to the vice admiral and back down within six minutes. I've got the answer here: 'HISC . . . 9:01 p.m. . . . check ordered by U.S. Fleet Cyber Command reveals the Black Order showed up on the dark web in an overlay network that had its own distributed hash table."

"Overlaid on what?" the president asked.

"The ONI," Harward replied, pausing a moment to let the implications register.

"How were they discovered?"

"HISC did a deep dig when the name *didn't* show up, because the handler knew it had been in the files of a gunrunner named Taikinys. Someone reached up from the dark web and expunged it. Investigators found the Black Order on the far side of a choke point called Canadian Hemlock. It was something big, tangled in every ONI database, and growing everywhere outside the sunlight."

The news was stunning. Someone outside the Office of Naval Intelligence had constructed a copycat network that hid within the infrastructure of a major intelligence framework. For how long, and revealing what, they had no idea. Clearly, it had exposed Atlas Hamill.

"It's got everyone spooked," Harward went on. "IT guys here had to leave the building to text or call with sensitive information. I'm outside right now. They don't know how many linked systems have been compromised. Vice Admiral Nathan expanded the blackout, ordering that until they were sure the overlay had been removed, everything at the ONI be done face-to-face, or in handwritten notes couriered between offices."

"ONI PROP," Berry said.

The president looked quizzically at his deputy chief of staff. Williams was glad. He had not heard the term, either.

"Paul Revere Operation Protocol," Berry said. "If an entire system is vulnerable, you go old-school with the investigation. Nothing communicated, except by mouth or handwritten, and only on a need-to-know basis."

"Trevor, you're saying this Black Order has been able to access ONI files across the board?" the president asked.

"It's actually worse than that, sir. It's possible that they poured into every system linked to ONI—base security, harbor, and waterway cameras at every port in the free world and many outside of it. Through those, they may have gained access to other security systems. Whoever designed this, I'm told, was a genius. Someone told me Mossad has learned about it—probably their own dark web spies—shut all of our intel sharing systems down, and is looking for Black Order fingerprints in their system."

"But in all of this shutting down and checking for tracks, there is no indication whatsoever what Hamill was doing for them?" the president said. "Is that possible?"

"If they know, they aren't sharing. They're angry and in damage control at the same time."

"Do I need to get the vice admiral in here?" Midkiff asked.

"Honestly, sir, I'd feel better if he were working on this matter instead of lying to you."

Harward would not have been so blunt before the election. Now, he was actually doing his job instead of sucking up. But there was another dynamic, one Williams hoped was not in play. In the waning days of any administration, information was capital, and it could be used to preserve fiefdoms. Someone like Trevor Harward might not hesitate to deploy whatever he gathered or knew or suspected to bargain his way into some other appointment with the new administration.

It's a stinking business, Williams told himself.

"It's Matt. Who is the handler? I assume they're being questioned."

"They say they don't know."

"The ONI doesn't know," Midkiff said with disbelief.

"Sir, they say sequestration is the only way to prevent leaks."

"That was before. Wouldn't that person have come forward after hearing about Hamill?"

"Not if they were part of this," Berry pointed out.

"Some people here are saying that same thing," Harward said. "Couple of people have called in sick, one was simply a no-show and is being checked on. But if it's not one of them, then they're hiding in plain sight . . . maybe even using access to cover the Black Order's tracks."

Berry did not have to ask, again, how they survived eight years of this. His expression said as much. Williams refused to allow himself the luxury of headshaking.

Williams grabbed a White House pad from the coffee table, passed Berry a note.

Berry read it. "Trevor, did Atlas Hamill leave behind a trip manifest or auto license they can track, see where he went, who he saw?"

"They won't know that until they can find him in the system. He doesn't show up anywhere except on inventory and requisition documents from NSA Philadelphia."

"Jesus, is there *any* way we're up to speed?" Berry asked.

"Yeah, you want to take notes, see what any of our IT people can make of what the Black Order 'genius' came up with?"

"Sure," Berry said, activating his phone recorder.

The others heard paper rustling. It was the NSA director checking handwritten notes.

"Okay, the Black Order fingerprints consisted of variable-length numbers. Cryptology has been working on deciphering it, but the two investigators were more interested in getting through the DiffServ and IP Multicast layers to locate the site layer—frankly, they lost me. But they found a spot where a 'packet format,' those bundled numbers, piggybacked onto an ONI data stream."

"And that spot was Hamill's former command?" the president guessed.

"Yes, sir," Harward replied.

"That's why outside personnel were brought to the base," Berry said, shutting off the recorder. "Inside job."

"We have to at least consider that," Harward said.

Williams suspected that the technical information was going to be of no use. Anyone smart enough to construct that bridge would be smart enough to blow it up.

"I don't know why I'm asking," Berry said, "but what about Captain Hamill's cell phone, personal computer—"

"Laptop and tablet are en route to ONI. They found a cell phone on Mrs. Hamill's side of the bed and took that too."

"Has anyone scheduled a debrief of Mrs. Hamill?" Berry continued.

"We don't know. I'm told that she's out now. It was either

that or restrain her. The only other information she offered is that the killer wore a ski mask, but that's no help. It wasn't just to hide the killer's face, but—it's winter. A lot of people have ski masks. We could get surveillance footage, look at dozens, maybe hundreds of people and be wrong. And if he took it off, we would have no way of knowing it was him."

"Any idea how the killer got in?" the president asked.

"If they have any ideas, sir, no one's shared them."

There was conversation on the other end of the call. Harward seemed to be swearing. He came back on the line after nearly a minute.

"They have the identity of Captain Hamill's handler," Harward said. "They found his name and contact numbers, and only that, were on her computer."

"How did they know what computer to go to?" Berry asked.

"It was the one who didn't show up for work today," Harward replied. "Major Becky Lewis. She died in a fire at the Columbia Apartments early this morning."

CHAPTER TWO

Fort Belvoir North, Springfield, Virginia
January 16, 7:55 a.m.

Every morning for the past two months, Major Hamilton Breen awoke in his room at the officers' quarters and did something he had not done for most of his thirty-eight years: he put himself through a regimen of squat thrusts. He didn't cut corners. Each squat was deep. Each thrust was full extension. He set a web metronome on sixty beats a minute and did 150 without stopping.

He counted along, as he was doing now, facing the drawn shades so he would not be distracted.

The regimen was partly for the exercise, of course. During the four months prior to squatting and thrusting, since he first came to Fort Belvoir, the major had never been motivated to train. He had not been on an actual mission. His daily routine consisted mostly of watching a console or monitor while the other two Black Wasps trained. And his pre-transfer habits were of a sedentary nature. Breen was a former professor at the Judge Advocate General's Legal Center and School on the University of

Virginia campus in Charlottesville, Virginia. He had been happily teaching, counseling the JAG corps on investigations and working on cases, and enjoying his commitment-free relationship with American history professor Inez Levey. For recreation, he had always preferred motorcycles to stationary bikes and had no patience for treadmills or rowing machines. When he walked, it was inside a courtroom.

The previous summer, his life changed. That was when the army officer had been "asked" to leave the wood-paneled halls and ivied walls he had occupied for most of his career. The trip was just 105 miles northeast, but the journey was far greater. Breen, along with Lieutenant Grace Lee of the U.S. Army Special Operations Command, Airborne, and Marine Air Ground Task Force sharpshooter Lance Corporal Jaz Rivette, had been seconded to a top secret, multiservice force code-named Black Wasp. The three later learned that they were the latest rapid deployment unit attached to Op-Center. They were continuing a fabled legacy that began a quarter century before as the original Striker morphed into JSOC—Joint Special Operations Command—and had finally become Black Wasp, the smallest, most eclectic, and most mobile incarnation of the team.

The contraction was only fitting. Op-Center itself had undergone changes. It had been downsized from an organization hundreds strong and headquartered in a two-story building located near the naval reserve flight line at Andrews Air Force Base, to just one man, Chase Williams. The admiral worked—they were told, for they had never been asked to visit—at the Defense Logistics Agency. The change was tactical, but that had not been the reason for it. Op-Center took the fall for an intelligence miss that resulted in a deadly attack on the Intrepid Sea, Air & Space Museum in New York City. Williams's team *had* missed it—along with every other intelligence agency. The reason Op-Center took the hit was because it was their successful operation against Iran that had triggered the counterattack.

The Washington community believed that Op-Center had been de-chartered. Only a few people close to the president—and now, to the incoming president—knew that Op-Center still existed, in name, in the person of Chase Williams. And only two people, the president and Matt Berry, knew that Black Wasp was a part of that enterprise.

At times, the secrecy and segregation gnawed on Breen. He was accustomed to talking with teams of attorneys, service personnel who were on trial, opposing counsel. Unlike courtrooms and classrooms, where he litigated or taught—"Prosecuted or persecuted," he once jokingly described it—Breen's present assignment did not afford the luxury of long analyses. Grace and Jaz were kids, the latter younger than his students. And Chase Williams was an admiral, stoic even when he said "Good morning." Accustomed to commanding hundreds of professionals, Williams had his own issues with going undercover and working in relative isolation.

For that reason, as important as a physical workout was, the squat thrusts gave Breen mental pause. It provided a brief but essential distraction from what an expert witness, psychiatrist Lorraine Powell, had once referred to as "the nattering monkey brain." Living in every human skull, the monkey had just one function: to chew over questions that resulted in more questions instead of answers.

"It's one thing to reflect on a matter," the medic had said during a deposition. "It's quite another to obsess, especially when change is not possible."

Quieting the chatter had proven to be necessary being a member of Black Wasp. Initially, Breen had been appalled by the aggressively unconstitutional nature of the team. He still was, to some degree. They were not just off the books, paid for by the services from which they were "on extended leave," they operated outside international law—entering countries illegally, torturing for information, and worse. One of the reasons President Midkiff had hired Breen was because his conservative ethics and legal experience were supposed to be a moral compass for the team. But Black Wasp had no command hierarchy, his rank meant nothing, and his views were not always shared by the others. One, the summary execution of a terrorist in Yemen, had put an early strain on his relationship with Chase Williams. Intellectually, Breen understood how a public trial would have been a nightmare for families of the terrorist's victims, a forum to advance a vile cause, and it would have ended in much the same way. But it would have come after due process, not the fiat and vengeance of one man.

The murder had one positive effect: it strengthened Breen's resolve to stand up for his beliefs. The second mission, to South Africa, had been more balanced. Breen had learned to assert himself, and Williams had learned to listen—at least a little.

He finished exercising, continued to think about nothing

except showering, and went about the rest of the morning routine. Six days a week, upon leaving his quarters, Breen typically met with Grace and Rivette, both of whom had longer and more ambitious morning rituals than his. Lieutenant Lee trained in a variety of Chinese and Japanese martial arts for at least an hour while the lance corporal headed to the shooting range. Afterward, they drilled together in reconstructions of entire towns complete with "dummy" terrorists and hostages. These were used by other units to practice door-to-door searches.

Except for the solo drills, the rest of the routine did not happen this morning.

Each member of Black Wasp had been furnished with a dime-sized Secure Page Alert Device. Breen wore his SPAD on the underside of his wristwatch. When the SPAD vibrated, Black Wasp members grabbed their go-bags and reported at once to the base's officers' club at 5500 Schulz Circle. The Georgian revival–style structure was little more than a staging area, a convenient place to wait while transportation was arranged. Actual briefings and planning took place en route to the target where the environment was secure.

Dressed in fatigues and limber from his exercises, Breen changed into civilian clothes and jogged over; he was coming to like the rush he got from exercise. He was the first to arrive. There were only two other officers in the club, both lieutenants, sitting separately. They saluted as he moved by; here, even Black Wasp members honored protocol.

The major was followed ten minutes later by Grace and then Rivette, who was moving to music he had been listening to while firing an assortment of handguns and rifles. The fatigues of the two younger members were still damp with the sweat of their workouts.

"Good morning, sir," each had said upon arriving.

It had been two months since their last mission. Breen had enjoyed having half his day free—and safe—but the younger members had been eager to get back in the field.

Grace was twenty-six years old, stood five foot two, and wore her black hair tufted on top and buzzed on the sides. Her eyes were dark brown, but their intensity made them seem almost black. She approached with her characteristically light, quick stride. She had explained many times that her energy, her chi, made her physical self buoyant. The others respected her skills without entirely understanding them; but when she fought, she did seem capable of flight.

Four years her junior, Rivette had a short cut with a surgical part; he did not bother shaving and didn't really need to. But he took great care of his hair. He walked with a quick, swaying gait in time to the music he was listening to. His walk made him seem carefree. He wasn't. The San Pedro, California, native forced himself to stay loose, more often than not succeeding.

"When you tense, you telegraph you're gonna do *something*," he once explained. He said that "chill" was a quality the drifters, grifters, and gang members on the riverfront all had in common.

Rivette had discovered his proficiency for firearms at age ten, when he stopped a bodega robbery with the owner's handgun. The police department enrolled him in a junior marksmanship program where he excelled, thanks in part to his street training to stay loose.

Breen was reading his tablet. The others got orange juice from the modest breakfast buffet. They sat in a trio of antique salon chairs clustered around a small, Edwardian-style tea table.

Sitting, Rivette reached into his shirt pocket, tugged out his phone, turned off the music, and removed his earbuds.

"Any ideas what's up, Major?"

"There's an embarrassment of riches from Azerbaijan to Zagreb," he said, flicking a finger at his tablet. "I just don't know which is ours."

"Same sewer, different day," Rivette said, chugging his orange juice.

"Do you really believe that?" Grace asked Rivette.

"Since we still got jobs here, it's true."

"When you were a kid, didn't you ever look out at the Pacific Ocean and—"

"Get all soultronic?"

"Excuse me?"

"See rainbows and butterflies? Nah. Sometimes I thought about Japan because I dug the idea that there was another Japantown, but bigger. Mostly when I watched the sea it was because I earned a buck an hour looking for boats. They brought the sailors and rich folks from Marina del Rey or Santa Barbara that my cousins rolled or sold to."

The SPADs buzzed twice, meaning that Williams was on his way. Grace sipped her juice from a straw.

"Didn't anything inspire you?" she asked. "Did you ever go to church?"

"Yeah, when my grandma made me. Mass sometimes, Confession a lot." He smiled as he thought back. "Y'know, there *was* something I liked. The organ. I liked the way it made my hands vibrate when I put them on the pew in front of me."

Grace made a face. "That's it? The music didn't do anything?"

"This music does." He shook his phone at her. "Lieutenant, I *never* heard a song with 'hallelujah' that I wanted to download. Anyway, I heard the tunes you listen to, J-pop and K-pop. That's just chirpy birds. And what do you call those dishes?"

"They're not dishes, they're Tibetan singing bowls. I also listen to Sibelius and Scriabin. Depends on how I feel, how I move."

"Whatever. We each got our own style, right?"

Grace regarded her teammate like he was a target. "I know what I have to do."

"That's how you sound when I'm winning at Chinese checkers."

"We both win if you give this a shot."

"Give what?"

"Wherever we're going, let's swap phones for the trip. You listen to my playlists, I'll listen to yours."

Rivette frowned. "Bad idea, if you want your phone to get there alive."

"You won't even try."

"Your life depends on me, you don't want me thinking how much I hate 'Girls Who Luff' or the dude who sings it."

Grace returned to her drink. The major had continued to scan intelligence updates as the cultures clashed. He did not judge their views. These two believed every word they said and, like every action they took in the field, they backed it with the passion and certainty of youth.

It was nearly 9:00 a.m. when Chase Williams arrived. Even though he was retired, the admiral always wore his uniform when he came to the club. The team did not see Williams between missions; only Breen met with the Op-Center director, here, once a week, to provide status updates on training. But while Williams was a commanding figure, he lacked the taut urgency characteristic of their previous meetings.

Rivette looked at him with his sharpshooter eyes. "You gonna miss me, Lieutenant?" he asked Lee.

"What are you talking about?"

"The commander looks like a man from HROM. The kind who says, 'You didn't cut it, kids.'"

Human Resources and Organizational Management was the U.S. Marine Corps division that managed personnel. It was the division that sent Rivette to Fort Belvoir. Unlike the broader Manpower & Reserve Affairs, HROM handled high-performance units.

"Uh-uh," Grace said. "It's something else."

"How do you know?"

"No executioner brings his tablet to a hanging."

Breen agreed with Grace's assessment. Though Williams was not toting his go-bag, the dissolution of Black Wasp would not come with documentation. They had been processed here through the Directorate of Human Resources, Human Capital Program Management, for "training." That was where orders or forms would be found.

The trio stood and saluted. Williams returned the salute, and Rivette grabbed a chair for him. The young man clearly was not yet reassured.

"You're traveling light, sir," Rivette observed.

"My gear's in the car," Williams said as he sat.

Grace saw relief spread across the features of the lance corporal. *Like sunset on the Pacific,* she thought. The woman was glad too. The universe would not place her in a position to restore balance and then wrest her away. The Tao, the way, did not operate by whim.

Breen knew from Williams's comment that wherever they were going they weren't flying from the fort. They would go from here to the airfield to preserve security. If they were staying local, that suggested either the upcoming inauguration of John Wright or the military officer who had died that morning in an apartment fire described as "suspicious." The major had looked the victim up on the active duty roster of the U.S. Navy: Major Becky Lewis was naval intelligence. Unless there was a specific threat against the president-elect, that seemed a more practical application of Black Wasp.

Unless that's how Wright intends to use us, as a shadow for the Secret Service, Breen thought unhappily.

The major told his monkey brain to climb another tree. Yet it persisted, wondering why the president would be directly concerned about Major Lewis.

Williams leaned in slightly as he looked at his team.

"Two ONI agents have died within the last few hours—one, most likely both, were murdered. We are driving to Philadelphia to investigate the one we know was a homicide. I've forwarded the deceased officer's records; you can read it in the car."

Breen went right to his inbox.

"Captain Richard Hamill," he said, looking at the file tab. "Not flagged—"

"He was not an asset of the president or anyone working with him."

Williams proceeded to tell them about Captain Hamill and what little was known about the home invasion. He would discuss the Black Order when they were in the van. He also shared something about the traffic patterns in the neighborhood, which he had downloaded to his tablet. That information was mostly for Breen, who had an eye—and mind—for patterns. There were graphs from the Department of Transportation regarding demographics, passenger points of origin by city block, and other data about the riders. Included was ridership around the neighborhood of naval facility.

"In case someone left there, fulfilled the mission, then returned," Williams said.

"A betraitor," Rivette said disdainfully. "Not just a rat, a rat who comes back for more."

"Is there any evidence that this was an inside operation?" Breen asked.

"Not yet, though the widow is being guarded by MAs from off-base."

That word "widow" left an unnatural taste in Williams's mouth. It underscored the fact that Atlas was gone.

"A sensible precaution," Breen said, reviewing the traffic file. "Surveillance?"

"Currently a turf war between the Philadelphia police and ONI."

"Like being in a courtroom without a judge," Breen said. "But it doesn't look like the assassin came from and returned to the base, at least not at that hour and not directly."

"The guards at the gate?"

"We have to assume they're unreliable, based on what you said. No, forensics. There is no such thing as a fully sanitized crime scene. They will scour the base for a match to anything that shows up in the Hamill house. A killer who has planned for war would not have risked departing from there, or returning. Was there surveillance at the home? The ONI should have had access to that."

"Not that we're aware, and ONI has closed ranks around this."

"So we have nothing about the crime itself, other than what you told us," Breen said.

"Which is why we're going to Philly," Rivette said.

"That's right."

"You said there was a warning left with the widow. Not just about war but about killing anyone who interferes," Breen said. "Bravado or possibility?"

"You'll read what little backstory we have on the road. But it appears credible."

Rivette and Grace shared a brief look that transcended their different backgrounds, interests, and skills. Breen noticed it, and a phrase from a previous war, the American Revolution came to mind, the words on the Gadsden rattlesnake flag:

DON'T TREAD ON ME

CHAPTER THREE

Philadelphia, Pennsylvania
January 16, 9:01 a.m.

When the Free Library of Philadelphia first opened in 1894, it was jammed into three small rooms in city hall. It wasn't until 1927 that the majestic Central Library opened on Logan Square, a site that is now, as the Parkway Central Library, the nexus of dozens of local branches and annexes.

Chuck Boyd loved working in that repository of knowledge. The forty-two-year-old had grown up in a particularly impoverished section of South Philadelphia, where his library was whatever books he found in recycling piles on the street. That was where he discovered textbooks and contemporary authors; no one threw out Shakespeare or Walter Scott, it seemed. He spent a dozen years repairing and then driving a city bus, where he was always friendly with his passengers. He hoped, one day, to be in a position to help some of the less advantaged—and himself—by taking night classes at the Community College of Philadelphia. Receiving a bachelor's degree in HR management, Boyd landed a part-time position at the Free Library's Office of Adult

Education as a program administrator. Working tirelessly at both jobs, he placed several of his graveyard shift riders on new trajectories, and within two years he was named OAE director. He was the only full-time staffer. The operation was as lean as its director.

It was a wonderful job and a stimulating environment. Boyd was especially pleased with the many community residents who came in to help. A surprising number of local businesspeople gave money, but a few also donated time. One of the most dedicated and enthusiastic volunteers was Burton Stroud, a square-jawed former army Ranger who had a very successful home security business. Stroud spent several early morning and late evenings a week matching program graduates with jobs at the level of family-sustaining employment. Stroud was typically at his desk before Boyd, reading through employer emails—there were tax breaks for working through OAE—and searching the web for daily job postings.

Stroud was there bent over the office laptop when Boyd walked in. The man was engrossed in something and did not look up. That was usually the case with Stroud. Boyd could tell he was concentrating; the army veteran had an old burn scar on his right cheek. It was about the size of a palm heel and reddened, as now, when he was caught up in something. Stroud never talked about the injury, and Boyd never inquired. The man had served in Desert Storm, and Boyd assumed it was a combat injury.

Boyd entered quietly. The other four desks were empty. The gunmetal desks were set in a row along the large windows, and

Stroud was at the farthest. There was a chair beside each desk for those who came seeking a brighter future. Except for the computer, a phone, and an iPad, Stroud's desk was bare.

The steam heat hissed as Boyd unwrapped his scarf from the lower part of his thin face. He hung it on a coatrack, beside Stroud's cashmere coat, and smoothed his full gray mustache.

"Good morning, Chuck," Stroud said, finally looking up and smiling.

"Good morning, Burton."

"It surely is January, eh?"

"A bit brisk," Boyd admitted. "The guard mentioned that you were here unusually late last night."

"One of my people didn't get off work until eleven. I wanted to be here for him."

"You're a good soul," Boyd said.

"Just paying it forward. In fact, I'm chatting with someone right now who has two potential students."

Boyd stuffed his gloves in his pocket, hung up his coat, and entered his small cubicle to the right. He put his shoulder bag on the gunmetal desk. A sofa and a small end table were the only other furniture in his work space. Boyd went to the single-cup coffee maker on the table. Stroud had already used it—three times—Boyd noted from the plastic containers in the wastebasket. The office smelled pleasantly of hazelnut. He put in a single-brew packet.

Boyd leaned out the door as the machine sputtered to action. "How was the traffic on Walnut?"

"Fine. Why?"

"I was on the bus when I got an alert from the SEPTA app that said Spruce Street was closed."

"Oh? What happened?"

"Some kind of residential break-in."

"I didn't hear. What was it, a homeless person? I've seen them sleeping in the bus shelters."

"They've been doing that since I started driving, poor souls. I suppose it could have been anyone. But it got me wondering. Does your business pick up when people hear about things like this?"

"A break-in? There's an uptick, sure. People always want information, security in a panic. There will probably be a line at the shop when I get there."

"And they call you because they see your ads everywhere."

"In that business, you have to be synonymous with comfort and safety. But their interest usually subsides when they hear the cost of installation and monitoring, or that they'll have to keep their cats or dogs somewhere they won't trip the motion detectors."

"I didn't consider that."

"The dirty secret is, dogs are the best security as long as you don't mind them barking at trucks and pedestrians."

"I don't think they would be welcome here." Boyd grinned.

"Which is why everything from the rare books below to the stacks above are under the protection of Stroud Safe at Home."

Boyd nodded graciously. Stroud had donated the security

system, and it kept Boyd energized, the things he could learn from the people he worked with, about life, business, and just paying it forward.

The percolating water stopped trickling, and the director half turned to his office. "You know, I just have to say it again, Mr. Stroud."

"What's that?"

"How much I appreciate the work you do. All of my volunteers, but you in particular. You truly care."

Stroud renewed the smile. "More than I can put into words, Chuck."

The director returned the smile and followed the smell of fresh coffee. When he was out of sight, Stroud's thin smile twisted into something framed by cross, knowing lines. The scowl was not directed at Boyd. The director was a decent man, devoted to his job and to the less fortunate. Stroud's frown reflected the cauldron boiling in his soul, a condition Burton Stroud had endured for too many years. He had kept it down as long as he could, as long as there was still a chance at righting the course.

He had overlooked the friendly fire that had injured him in Iraq, the result of some pothead who misdirected an MK-77 incendiary bomb on an Iraqi trench that, at the time, had a Ranger exploratory unit. Two men died, so Stroud had to consider himself fortunate. He had tried not to dwell on the rise of Occupy, of Antifa, of left-wing violence directed at stifling free expression. The course would self-correct, he hoped.

He prayed.

Then the nation had an election. The new president and

Congress, the new governors and state legislature, all tipped toward youth and radicalism. The winners not only hated the nation that had endured for nearly two and a half centuries, they were committed to remaking it—into something "Truly Democratic," as John Wright's slogan promised.

Voiceless, their votes, too, were rendered useless by campus and internet voting drives, the traditional citizens of a once-shining nation no longer had options other than one.

One option . . . and a timetable. *His* timetable.

Stroud turned to the office computer and finished archiving the messages he had exchanged with Christopher Sarno. They were the reason he was in the office so late and now so early. The messages had started coming in at 10:33 p.m. In the event of Sarno being discovered and interrogated, they provided a cover story. It was OAE work, with other members of the Black Order as the potential clients. Philpotts had gone so far as to enroll in classes to broaden his career opportunities.

He reviewed them to make sure there were no gaps in the timing.

11:10: opened some doors
11:18: two prospects look good
11:30: man unemployed woman accepted
11:38: interview over
12:13: at Jung's Synch for a drink

The language was innocent by design, the first three sent while Sarno was still inside the Hamill's Spruce Street town house. Jackson Poole's embedded override of Stroud's own home protection codes—a key Poole had baked into every navy system—had worked, and the door had opened silently as planned.

The messages were fine. He archived them. A second set of messages had come in this morning as Stroud was sitting there. These were from Dee Dee Allen, a former Delta Force lieutenant. They accomplished the same goal of creating an innocent-seeming electronic trail, crafting the same story. She was visiting a friend in Washington. They were at dinner. They hung out together. She left to go to her hotel and sleep.

All true, as far as they went. The communiqués informed Stroud that her mission, too, had been successful. The morning news corroborated that fact.

But the emails did more than provide cover for the two "recruiters" and for Stroud. The time stamps commemorated the end of an old day in America. The emails marked the precise beginning of a plan that had gone operational after more than a year of planning, when it became apparent that Wright would be the next president. Though these sets of emails were just the preliminary maneuver to the war itself, they were no less important than the first shots at Concord and Lexington.

And the Free Library did more than provide an office computer. They offered a secret sanctuary to Burton Stroud. His home was one hub of operations. The Homestead was another. The office of Stroud Safe at Home was a constant buzz of walk-ins, staff drama, salespeople vending new security systems, learning about new devices and brand extensions. This OAE office was a retreat, a pod of giving souls doing good work, a place to think.

No, a place to act. The world would be a very different place when he returned tonight, before closing time.

Stroud turned to his tablet to conduct business for Stroud Safe at Home. There were inquiries from Washington Square and the waterfront district, both of which abutted the crime site. Walk-ins were sure to follow, probably at lunchtime, after details of the attack became known and people had time to ruminate, to be more fearful than economical.

He would let the office handle the first wave. Right now, he had other work to do. Jackson Poole must get into position, though Stroud would not be using the same military language he used with the others. The man was a passionate civilian, neither a booster nor participant in military exploits. He could not be pushed. And while the ONI might not be the most fleet-footed behemoth in the intelligence superstructure, there were others off the grid who would be looking into this; some fiercely, since it involved "their own." He remembered those irrational, go-get-'em souls from Desert Storm. Stroud did not yet know who or what they were, but their paths would likely cross very soon.

And then he would deal with them too.

Lines from Dante's *Vision of Purgatory* passed from his memory to his lips when Christopher Sarno had neared Thirtieth Street Station. The words had emerged as a whisper, which carried the faint hint of scotch.

Lo! there the cliff
That circling bounds it! Lo! the entrance there,
Where it doth seem disparted!

The drinking had been enough to justify sitting at Synch's for several hours. It had taken the high off the kill, tempered his euphoria, but it fell well short of leaving Sarno inebriated. That was the kind of behavior that could undermine the closing-out phase of the mission. In his experience, that was where most military operations went south. The heavy lifting done, one member of a team—just one—relaxed, got sloppy, and others paid the price.

Not me, not now was the one mantra Sarno had that wasn't from the fourteenth-century Italian poet to whom he was supposedly, distantly related.

Dressed in a gray greatcoat, the Rome-born assassin had entered the station. It was not as comfortable as the orange jacket he wore when he worked as a deliveryman for Stroud Safe at Home—a useful cover—but it was certainly warmer. The coat had a floppy hood, but Sarno did not wear it. The night had been frigid, but the cavernous station was warm, and concealing his features would have drawn the attention of the police. That was why he had removed his ski mask. Reports of a killer wearing such a garment would target other men out on a frigid night, wasting the time and resources of law enforcement.

Instead, the rangy killer wore a green knit cap with a white pom-pom on top. It was seasonal, jaunty, and matched the Philadelphia Eagles scarf pulled round his neck. He lowered the scarf with a finger as he walked through the great hall—just enough to appear like any man coming in from the cold. But the cap rested a little low, nearly to his eyebrows, covering his unusually high forehead, the scarf still raised just enough to cover his strong chin.

What Sarno wore and how he wore it were an added layer of precaution. After three days of surveying his route, Sarno knew where the surveillance cameras were and had avoided them in the street—not because he was concerned but because the woman in the bed might have noticed *something*, and that *something* might show up in surveillance.

He practiced sensible precaution here as well, maneuvering along the shadowy right side of the benches, turning to gaze into dark storefronts, pausing at the only open shop, a newsstand, that peddled every candy, sugary beverage, and Chinese-made trinket in creation—but no news.

The world has changed too fast, the sixty-three-year-old had reflected.

When he was a kid, thirty cents would get him a comic book and a 3 Musketeers candy bar. Now that bar was of a size to induce a sugar high, and there wasn't a comic book to be had for under four bucks. He remembered when commuters here were reading newspapers or *Sports Illustrated*. After that they were struggling with sudoku. Then everything was subsumed by texting and FaceTiming and playing games and emailing. If anyone even noticed the old, gorgeous travertine facing of the nearly ninety-year-old station, he would be shocked.

He hated it all. The tech devices were not the problem. They were just an outward manifestation of inner rot. Stroud had his political agenda, which Sarno shared. But his own need was bigger. *The hottest places in hell are reserved for those who, in times of great moral crisis, maintain their neutrality.*

They *all* had to be stopped, every lazy, entitled kid, every deviant, every drug user. Both of his former wives had called him an anarchist, and maybe he was, at heart—

Stop!

He forced his mind and emotions back on track. He was high from the kill, but he had a job to do; several, in fact. He had not slept in thirty hours, but he was feeling loquacious after two scotches.

It had been either that or coffee; the bars were darker. After the killing and the delivery of the message, Sarno had moved around for several hours, unmasked, visible, riding buses and popping into some of his favorite night spots. There were not many all-night spots in Center City, but there were enough. Downtown Philadelphia was certainly livelier than when he had been a failing student at Drexel University.

That was how and where Sarno got to know Burton Stroud. They were in the same European literature class. Stroud was a native Philadelphian and a criminology major. Sarno came from Western Pennsylvania and was studying military science. With nowhere else to go at night, they would debate history while drinking scotch or rum they had snuck past the dorm monitor. They drank less these days because the work required a clear head.

At least, clear enough to get me to the house.

Sarno had not gone directly to Stroud's place in Germantown, because authorities would be watching trains, highways, and waterways. Again, it was not an essential delay, just prudent. Stroud had deemed it best to stay in town at least until dawn. That way, if Sarno were caught, it would not be at the house, and Stroud and the others would be able to help.

It was also important to be seen by people, if not surveillance cameras, in the hours after the action. Innocent men had nothing to fear. They talked, they listened, they engaged. That had been Sarno's modus operandi when he was an active field agent with the CIA Special Activities Center. A dozen years in Lebanon and Syria taught him that there is no such thing as "looking" suspicious. Either you were guilty of something or you were not.

Sarno had finally made his way through the busying station. People were just trickling from their suburban enclaves, from the "circling bounds," pouring into cabs or streaming their way around the ever-present construction along the Schuylkill River. He wondered how Dee Dee had made out; it was about that time, according to the big station clock. But he did not want to take out his phone, check the news, be distracted.

The man increased his pace, wanting to get home before exhaustion overcame him. He walked briskly toward the SEPTA regional rail, rushing against a tidal hash of footsteps and cell phones. He wished he could put in his noise-canceling AirPods, but he needed to be able to hear in case the clump of shoes or boots came from behind him. He did not have the hunting knife he had used on Hamill, the one he had used to dress so many deer and boar. And Iranians operating in Iraq. That, along with the mask and his beloved old hunting gloves, had been dropped in a garbage truck. He'd watched from a short distance away as they were crushed under egg cartons and banana peels. But he had taken off his coat before going upstairs—so Mrs. Hamill would not see it—and was still wearing the black jogging suit she had seen. Until he could dispose of that garment, he did not want to be stopped. Though he had a Glock in his pocket, the police had guns too.

Sarno boarded the 9:21 for the half-hour ride to the Germantown station. He was the only one who got off at the old, stone-walled, open-air stop. Climbing the stairs, he walked along streets lined with bare, old trees. His pace slowed, exhaustion finally catching up with him as he neared Lincoln Drive and Harvey Street. The town house was owned by Burton Stroud, a gentrified antique residence where they used to have their late-night talks. The only difference between then and now were the many electronic upgrades for security and communication and the dead man's switch.

When Sarno arrived, he emailed Stroud at his OAE address:

10:15: bedtime

That let Stroud know that Sarno had reached the house. If he thought he had been followed, he would have added:

Am keeping one eye open.

The assassin would sleep and then, at one, Stroud would join him. By that time, Dee Dee would have returned to her base in Washington—for security reasons, he did not know where that was. The group's cofounder, Mark Philpotts, along with Eiji Honda, would video in from the West Coast. Even Gray Kirby was expected to make the conference—hopefully safe and headed home. Jackson Poole would not be present. He had only one function, apart from survival, but it was *the* essential task spread across many theaters of action, and Stroud did not want him to be distracted.

Sarno went to his second-floor room, sat on the bed, and took off his shoes. He used the small adjoining bathroom, then let the satisfaction of a job well done wash over him as he collapsed backward. His last thoughts, before he fell into a fast, deep sleep, were, *"In that book which is my memory, On the first page of the chapter that is the day when I first met you, Appear the words, 'Here begins a new life.'"*

CHAPTER FOUR

Fort Belvoir, Virginia
January 16, 9:34 a.m.

Amtrak would have been easier, but they needed to be mobile when they reached Philadelphia, and the weapons would have been a problem. Rivette liked to travel heavy. The lance corporal had brought his Colt .45 and a Sig Sauer 9mm handgun, along with two weapons he had picked up on the team's mission to South Africa: a Vektor SP1 semiautomatic with a fifteen-round magazine and a Russian AS Val assault rifle. The overhead racks of the Acela were not designed for his gear.

"If there's a war, you do not want me underdressed," he said as Grace watched him load the van. She carried nothing but a butterfly knife worn in a sheath under the big sleeve of her left arm.

Within fifteen minutes of breaking up the officers' club meeting, Williams and the Black Wasp boarded a large Ford Transit Op-Center had at its disposal.

Three years old, the vehicle had originally been part of Aaron Bleich's "Geek Tank," the IT division of Op-Center. Bleich had based the design on the International Space Station.

To keep the foundation from becoming outdated, the van had a basic frame, electronically; the tech was mostly plug-ins. All that remained were basic CYT—cover your tracks—tech in the dashboard to obscure and confuse what he called "bar-code" tracking: basic toll booth, parking lot, and laser speed guns, anything that might expose the Geeks to interference. Bleich did not have those devices running constantly—"Disrupted signals also get the attention of law enforcement"—but were available as needed when the van went where it was not supposed to. His team had also set up the TRAC system: Tank Recon and Correlation, interlocked social media analytics, and threat analysis vectors that helped to predict future trouble spots. The team still used that to create their drill scenarios.

Williams had never quite understood the casual hours, dress, and pop culture tastes of the millennials in the Tank, but he had respected the unorthodoxy of their problem-solving. Accepting them had made it easier for the admiral to bend when it came to Grace and Rivette.

The base Logistics Readiness Center, Transportation and Maintenance, at Fort Belvoir was more old-school than Bleich. Sergeant Major Olivia Stewart had already fitted the vehicle with Pennsylvania tags to disguise its point of origin. It was a formidable van, though a downgrade from the fleet of vehicles Op-Center had maintained during their tenure at Andrews Air Force Base. Williams was fine with that. That Op-Center itself had been a pared version of the fleets he had commanded.

As long as our team has the tools and depth we need, the outside can shrink, Williams thought.

Williams was behind the wheel, and Major Breen was beside him, reading his tablet. Grace and Rivette were in the back reviewing the thin file that Berry had collected on Captain Hamill.

While alert for news and any updates from Matt Berry, the major was deep in research.

"There's no historical antecedent for the name Black Order, as far as I can tell," Breen said after they were well under way.

"Does there have to be?" Williams asked. "Most of the groups we watched at Op-Center arose from specific events."

"True, but virtually every movement, lawless or not, has a historical root, a genesis going back to the Sons of Liberty in the American Revolution. This one just 'appeared.' Also, I've checked the history of the Naval Support Activity base, the biography of the captain—nothing jumps out that would presage a home invasion, a tactical murder, or an ideology to support the killer's stated threat of war. Yet these are all part of a plan. Geopolitical plans have philosophies. Decoding the name might help understand them, and I'm not finding anything that fits."

"What are some of the historical names that don't fit?"

Breen consulted his list. "The Black Guard, an army of West African and Moroccan slaves in the seventeenth century. Black Friday, the U.S. gold market crash of 1869—"

"The Black Panthers," Rivette said.

"A good example, albeit different in that it was partly rooted in black nationalism," Breen said. "The point is, there are dozens of names with 'black' and also 'order,' but none together."

"What about the individual words?" Williams asked.

'Black' could be night, darkness, fear, or race. 'Order' might mean a group or a sequence—"

"Or a command," Breen said.

Williams frowned. "Yeah. Overlooked the obvious."

"But yes, if you start pairing synonyms you get something like 'fearful command' or 'dark group,' which are generic and no help. We've still only got a group, size unknown, with an agenda we don't know, who sat around and came up with an intimidating name."

"Which could be nothing more than that," Grace suggested. "Because of their savagery, the Chinese 'Tong' combined with any name evoked fear in New York in the early twentieth century."

"I get the scary name; my gramma uses them in her voodoo. But the thing I'm *not* getting is why Major Lewis picked a retired logistics guy to work as a spy. I mean, a guy with a GPS could've done that job, or someone from her own group."

"Secrecy," Grace suggested. "Maybe she knew the captain from a conference or project, thought she could trust him. I don't imagine there were many people she felt she *could* trust."

"Because of leaks?" he asked.

"Because of her past."

"Not following," Rivette said.

"Major Lewis founded the Lucinda Project at Annapolis, an off-site LGBTQ support center. It's in her bio under 'activism.'"

Rivette checked. "It doesn't say the last part, about it being LGBTQ."

"That's because the armed forces had to purge descriptors

about sexual identification from service records," Breen said. "Only the registered name of an organization could be recorded."

"Women at Bragg talked about it, knew what it was," Grace added.

Rivette made a face. "I like my world. It's simpler."

He rested his hand briefly on his empty hip holster, then reached for his grip behind him. He began to clean his guns, one at a time, using an unscented scrub so a target would not smell him coming.

What Grace had said was an education for Rivette but also for Williams. The admiral had not known that about Major Lewis, and it was useful information. She was not afraid to be independent or go around the upper brass. That might help to explain her approach to this mission: do it the directest way, not necessarily the navy's way, perhaps not even the safest way. He was glad, just then, for the open-idea policy.

Williams's phone pinged.

"It's Matt," he said. Grace leaned forward between the seats as he punched the call on speaker. "We're all listening, Matt."

"Good, this is for everyone. The apartment fire was one hell of a thing. It was caused—you're not going to believe this—by an exploding arrow."

It took a moment for the team to process the information.

Rivette did not look up from his guns. "I believe it."

"No one manufactures them," Williams said. "It had to be handmade."

"That's what the ONI is saying, but there's not much left of the device. Looks like someone attached an incendiary grenade to a shaft, pulled the pin—which has not been recovered—and let it fly from an adjoining building."

"Dude could've been up to 150 or more yards away," Rivette said.

"A rooftop facing the window, exactly 148.7 feet," Berry said. "Good get. The shooter gained access by knocking out the security guard with gas that also obscured the security image, then blowing the doorknob with a blasting cap—not from our military, either. The tail end of Cyrillic letters survived."

"Russian," Williams said.

"No one thinks Moscow is behind this," Berry said. "They don't do splashy hits."

"But a knife hunter and a longbow hunter did," Breen thought aloud.

"Who said that?" Berry asked.

"It's Hamilton, Matt. I'm just thinking out loud."

"Well, that occurred to me too. Pull that threat. What are we looking for, outdoorsmen with a political agenda or just looking for kicks?"

"They didn't kill Captain Hamill just for kicks," Breen said. "There was also a message to deliver."

"The Black Order could be outdoorsmen or survivalists or both," Williams said.

"Maybe they don't like hunting laws or waiting periods," Grace suggested.

"If that's true, they'd likely target forestry personnel or infrastructure," Breen told her. "That seems too modest a goal with two murders as a prelude."

"I agree, so what *does* this tell us about a next target?" Berry asked.

"Damn good question," Williams said. "They eliminated the two people who were apparently spying on them. If we take them at their word, war next—"

"With the form, arena, and goal unknown," Berry said.

"Do we know if any ordnance is missing from NSA Philadelphia?" Breen asked. "A war requires weapons."

"We don't stock Russian blasters," Berry pointed out.

"I could buy those from Turkey online," Breen said. "Not something you'd steal."

"Well, I'm hoping ONI checked," Berry said. "I'll ask. They seem willing to answer questions that require a simple 'yes' and 'no,' so that should be easy."

"'Territorial integrity,' they call it," Williams said. "Makes me wonder what ONI was sending in their daily briefs when Op-Center was at Andrews. Did we only get low-grade intel while they kept the highly classified material to themselves?"

"I can answer that if you want to take this private, Chase."

That surprised him. "No. Go ahead."

"Wasn't Op-Center selective about sharing intel? Didn't you withhold data from January Dow?"

Dow was with the INR, the State Department's Bureau of Intelligence and Research. She was an aggressive, political creature who helped orchestrate the end of Op-Center as a broad-based intelligence operation.

"I did do that," Williams said. "I was concerned about giving sensitive information to someone who put ambition above results, might have buried or swapped it."

"That's Washington," Berry said. "Everyone deals with the vipers their own way. You're going to Philadelphia to collect data that, frankly, I may or may not share with ONI. At least, not until we're sure the Black Order isn't on the inside."

Williams was silent. Berry was not wrong about any of that.

"Meanwhile, ONI has not been able to oust the District of Columbia fire department from what's left of Major Lewis's apartment," Berry continued. "The FBI was able to get people on the scene, and I'll hear from Allen Kim if there's a wall safe, handwritten notes, anything."

"Understood," Williams said. "Hopefully, the FD will—"

"Hold on," Berry said. "Something from ONI, and it's more than just one word." There was a short, pregnant silence before Berry continued, "Okay, this fills in some blanks. ONI want to know if anyone has picked up anything about weapons being sold, traded, or stockpiled in Western Pennsylvania."

"Hunting territory," Williams said. "That explains Atlas Hamill's involvement."

Berry continued, "After he read about Lewis's death, the gunrunner Taikinys contacted the ONI and said that what triggered this whole investigation was the delivery of arms and explosives to various spots in that region where cash was waiting."

"Not people?" Williams asked.

"Not people. This is not a business deep with trust."

"I get that, but why would this Taikinys rat out a client?" Rivette asked.

"Seems that Taikinys was a concealed asset himself," Berry said.

"Double-dipper," Rivette said.

"A frightened one at that. If the Black Order is eliminating people who have knowledge of them, he's afraid he'll be next."

"Did he say where he made the drop-off?" Williams asked.

"Won't give us that," Berry said. "He piggybacked on cartel trucks—not people you want to piss off."

"Do we know what kind of weapons they got, and how many?" Williams asked.

"Over the course of eighteen months, Taikinys delivered an assortment of grenades, Ruger 10/22—"

"Takedown semiautomatic . . . affordable," Rivette said.

"Good to know," Berry said. "Not necessarily well-financed. There were also Colt 6920s—"

"Also inexpensive semis."

"And a variety of handguns. Firearms total thirty-seven pieces."

"Good-sized platoon," Williams said.

"Plus the knives and bows and arrows and whatever else they could have picked up legally," Breen said.

"I guess we don't need to know about NSA Philadelphia inventory," Berry concluded. "You're up to date. I'll call if the D.C. fire department finds anything."

Berry clicked off. Breen was already analyzing the new data.

"We've got a picture forming," he said. "Lewis finds out about Black Order from Taikinys and very generally where they're based. The dealer would have avoided telling her what he sold them, lest ONI leapfrog over him and try to choke his supply at the source. Based on his information, she might suspect survivalists. No imminent concern. She approaches someone she knows, someone who knows that region, to look into it. And not *just* someone: someone who's retired."

"Why did that matter?" Rivette asked.

"Captain Hamill would have been exempted from the SAFE provision for married operatives," Breen said.

SAFE was Spousal Agent Field Exemption. If an unmarried agent of equal qualifications were available for a mission, he or she was the one who went.

"So what, she put him in danger without telling him how much so his lady wouldn't talk him out of it?" Rivette asked.

"I think it had more to do with internal secrecy," Breen said. "Major Lewis would not have had to get an agent exemption from her superiors."

"Lewis used him," Williams said.

"He appears to have gone willingly," Breen pointed out.

"Hey, we used that bus driver in Yemen—remember?" Rivette added.

"Jaz, don't," Grace cautioned.

"I'm just saying, not judging." He went back to cleaning his guns. "Bet I know today's headline," he said. "THE HUNGER GAMES KILLINGS."

"You just keep on going, don't you?" Grace said.

"Thinking out loud, like everybody else. You obviously don't know about TKs—thrill-killers. This is exactly what they do. The whole thing could be some nasty medieval cosplay. Anything's possible."

Williams did not immediately dismiss the idea, and it chilled him—the possibility that this was nothing more than a video game that had moved into the real world. A new generation of assassins and terrorists might have no greater ambition than to mimic the actions, ethics, and dress of a TV show or film or online adventure was somehow more frightening than the notion of violent ideologues or psychopaths.

"You know, there may be a connection at that," Breen said.

"To what?" Williams asked.

"To what we were talking about before, outdoorsmen. That could be how they picked up on Captain Hamill."

"That group he founded that fed venison to needy veterans," Williams said.

Breen went to the dead man's file. "PAVE," he read. "Pennsylvania Venison."

"I don't know. Atlas was used to keeping secrets. His work for ONI was not something he'd drop in a conversation."

"No. But they would know where he traveled. If you've got an enclave with an arsenal, you establish a perimeter. Something with eyes and ears."

"What about membership in gun or hunting clubs?" Williams said. "Maybe these people had human eyes and ears, alert to anyone who went traipsing in their neighborhood?"

"There's nothing in his record. Hold on." Breen typed on

his tablet. "Pennsylvania . . . Philadelphia . . . Scranton . . . the Poconos . . . there are about a dozen hunting clubs."

"Given the weapons, worth checking the membership rosters," Williams said.

"I'll bet those are locked," Rivette said.

"Why would they be?" Williams asked.

"They'd be doxed to death," Grace informed him.

Breen tried a few of the lists. "You're right. Access is denied."

"Wouldn't they have dark-webbed their names anyway?" Rivette asked.

"Removed them from the rosters?" Breen asked.

"Yeah."

"No. There may be printed lists from the late 1990s and earlier. Filter out the deceased, and anyone who's missing from the online list but is present on the printed list is automatically a suspect."

"Printed," the lance corporal said laconically. "Guess it's not totally useless."

"Missing details aside, this is starting to point a direction for us," Williams said. "Major Lewis engaged Atlas to nose around in Western Pennsylvania. Either he got close enough to see something or to be seen—possibly both. The question is, can we find that too?"

"If we can find out where he went, I'm happy to go look," Rivette said.

"We're talking about five or six hundred acres," Breen said, still looking through the hunting clubs. "For us to try and duplicate

Captain Hamill's path, without even knowing where the cartel dropped the weapons, is probably not the best use of our time. Might also put us in a gun battle we don't want right now."

"Wait, something doesn't make sense," Williams said. "I see how they found out about Atlas. But what about Major Lewis?"

"The dark web—" Rivette said.

"Couldn't have been," Williams said. "None of this information was in the system. Major Lewis covered her ass."

"Not in *that* system," Breen said, looking back at a page in Hamill's file. "But it was probably in another. The house inventory—there was one cell phone, and it belonged to Mrs. Hamill. The intruder must have taken the captain's phone. The captain's contact would be on it."

"I thought those were mostly unhackable," Grace said.

"That's what the makers want you to think," Rivette told her. "My cousins did it all the time."

"It's not a mistake an experienced field would have made," Breen went on, then stopped and regarded Williams. "Sorry, Chase. I didn't mean to—"

"No, you're right. This was not Atlas's game." He shook his head. "That's on Lewis."

"She obviously did not realize the gravity of the Black Order," Grace said.

"All of this is useful, but we need more information," Breen said. "Philadelphia first."

Williams and the others all concurred.

The car was quiet again as Breen read up on Naval Support Activity Philadelphia, and Williams mentally replayed the conversations with Berry—the one about January Dow and the earlier one about vipers.

The admiral loved serving his country as Atlas had, as everyone in the van did for different reasons and to different degrees. But he did not possess the fire in the belly that Berry did for the vipers, and he did not like hypocrisy, in himself more than in anyone else.

Maybe I should consider leaving with Wyatt Midkiff, he thought. *Turn this over to someone with a cleaner slate.*

There would be time enough for that.

Right now, they had a war to stop.

CHAPTER FIVE

New York, New York
January 16, 11:48 a.m.

Gray Kirby was going to enjoy today, a day that local activists had promoted with zeal that approached the Second Coming. Ironically, it would be a day to remember, though not for the reasons they expected.

At the heart of the online and in-person lovefest was one of the most eagerly awaited panels at the Broadcast Entrepreneurs' Convention: an appearance by Global Voices Network founder and chairperson, Rachel Reid. The heir to the Reid Jet fortune, Rachel had founded the GVN in 2015 to create platforms for underrepresented ethnicities and genders who were working in new telecommunications media. The service was an out-of-the-gate success, earning critical and consumer accolades. It lost money, a lot of it, but that did not seem to matter to billionaires with causes.

The fact that the panel was also a nexus of protest, drawing fire from groups like Traditional Ethics of America and the Sensible Morality Community, barely got media coverage. Moderation was the new conservative fringe.

The event was being held at the sprawling, glass-ceilinged Javits Center on the west side of Midtown Manhattan. Reid had flown from Atlanta the night before and was staying at the Wagner Hotel in Lower Manhattan. The hotel was situated on the harbor with an unparalleled view of the Statue of Liberty—an icon Reid's supporters decried as too white, even though she was green. The location also offered a short, direct run up the West Side Highway to the conference venue.

Rachel's stay at the hotel had not been announced, but credit card reservations had been easy for Jackson Poole to hack via Stalkyourex on the dark web. Gray Kirby had driven a rental car from Philadelphia two days before and had taken a room at the Marriott a few blocks north of Rachel's hotel. There, he had shown a false Canadian passport—the same one he had used until just a few months before when he retired from the Department of Homeland Security. The name Leopold Kramer was a "miser": it would show up on select visas and passenger manifests, but it would return nothing to anyone who checked deeper. No one at Homeland Security would recognize the name, which was the point of having it. Fewer people, fewer chances for exposure.

It felt good to be back in business, not just on the street but working for like-minded people, risking everything for strongly held beliefs. On the Department of Homeland Security books, Kirby had been a field supervisor in the Countering Weapons of Mass Destruction Office. In reality, the business major had been responsible for stopping those attacks by eliminating the attackers. He was the one who knew about Los Verdugos, their route, their goods. Before earning his master's degree from Princeton and joining DHS he had served as a Seventy-Fifth Ranger Regiment sniper. On his own, from a Ranger demolitions expert, he had learned to construct EFPs—explosively formed penetrators; specifically, directionally focused charges. In combat, he had learned that it was often necessary to flush out a bunker, basement, or foxhole before you could pick off the occupants. He did not want to call for support and wait, so he learned to do it all himself. "Mr. One-Stop Shopping" the other members of his unit had nicknamed him. It was a respectful epithet.

Not like the names that come from the mouths of too many spoiled youth and social justice panderers, he thought. Names like "Nazi" and "fascist" and "Neo-Confederate." Most of these people did not realize how dangerously like Hitler's brownshirts *they* were.

The Wagner Hotel was adjacent to One West Street, a thirty-seven-story building completed in 1911. That proximity made things easier for Kirby. The old tower afforded an open rooftop that looked directly down at the entrance to the hotel. Kirby had made his way up there the night he arrived. It had been simple; he pretended to be a food deliveryman at dinnertime, when deliverymen were plentiful and the overwhelmed concierge routinely shooed them in without calling tenants. Kirby got off on the thirty-sixth floor and took a single flight of stairs to the roof. The door was unlocked due to fire department regulations that mandated 24-7 rooftop egress. There were no cameras; crews working on the aging façade had disabled them so they could not be seen smoking up there.

Braced against a bitter cold blowing in from New Jersey, Kirby had gone to the west side of the roof. Reid's hotel was framed by the Hudson River and the harbor, the pinpoint lights of ferries and barges surging through the night. Unseen, the sniper watched as guests left the hotel. He did not like the angle. Targets were only in the kill zone for two or three seconds before reaching curbside and the cabs there. That was enough time for two shots, but there were variables. Few guests had their heads uncovered as they made their way from the lobby. A hat with a brim would obscure his view. Kirby did not like to estimate his targets. Also, Rachel would have at least three or four bodyguards maneuvering her, possibly blocking her at a key moment. There was another reality. Being just a few blocks from the World Trade Center, the area was heavily patrolled by police helicopters—even at night.

And there was a final problem. Anticipating that he would only have a short window to take Reid down, he had brought a Cobra rapid-fire sniper rifle. Given the amount of pavement, asphalt, and the car-bomb-resistant planters, there was likely to be ricochet, collateral damage.

This vantage point was a no-go.

The Javits Center offered different challenges. There was no convenient aerie looking down on the target area, and there were also several routes she might take to get inside. Tracking her from the ground, a shot would be difficult—especially since he intended to survive. Hundreds if not thousands of fans, supporters, and GVN Zombies, as devotees were called, would be swarming the convention center awaiting her arrival. Thick circles of media would be clustered around them, watching in all directions. If he were caught and "Leopold Kramer" IDed at DHS, that could lead to exposure for the rest of the group. As soon as he showed up in a trench coat—to conceal the Cobra—that in itself would cause police security cameras to automatically single him out. The moment he reached into the folds to withdraw the weapon, counterterrorism officers would move in. Their shouts, the urgent rippling panic, would snap Rachel's security detail into action.

Kirby would never get out alive, and he put the chances of making the kill at just under half. Neither was acceptable.

Fortunately, the veteran operative had considered these and other potential challenges before he left Philadelphia. There was a third option—the most challenging and also his favorite—and that was the one he chose. Before retiring the night before, Kirby had notified Jackson Poole. The IT master liked that plan best because it was inside Lower Manhattan's famed Ring of Steel, an interconnected system of public and private surveillance.

And he would be safe in Philadelphia if things went south, Kirby thought.

But that was all right. It was a story as old as civilization. Not everyone was a warrior, just as every warrior was not an astrologer or ironworker or cook.

Kirby had awakened early that morning. He dressed in a suit and tie, a gray fleece vest—a color that looked misleadingly blue to some eyewitnesses, black to others. He pulled on North-Flex Cold Grip winter gloves and a New York Yankees cap. The logo was sewn on loosely, hanging literally by a few threads.

Wrapping the Cobra in his trench coat for transport, he went to his rental car at the nearby Rector Street garage and put the items in the trunk. Returning to the hotel, he grabbed the gym bag he had brought. No one at the Marriott would have seen his car or its Pennsylvania plates. No one at the garage would have heard of Leopold Kramer. It was a perfect disconnect.

He walked through the lobby. Guests with luggage siphoned all the attention of the staff. He stepped outside and crossed the footbridge to the Hudson River. The sun in the Middle East used to bake and enervate everyone in his unit; here, it warmed and energized Kirby.

By the time he strolled down the Hudson River esplanade to the Wagner Hotel, Kirby looked every inch a trader from nearby Wall Street going for a lunchtime workout.

As he neared his target, a breeze from the harbor brought the smell of salty sea air. The Atlantic Ocean was visible beyond Coney Island, the sunlight glinting white on the blue-gray waters. Reaching the hotel, he stopped in the parklike meridian across the street, put his silent smartphone to his ear, sat on a cold bench, and waited. Rachel always departed a hotel five to ten minutes before she was due to speak. She was invariably late and, just as invariably, that caused excitement at the location to swell.

Kirby ignored the hucksters clustered like hyenas on carrion, trying to flag down cars to sell inflated tickets to Ellis Island

and Lady Liberty, even to the free Staten Island Ferry. They were useful enough as a distraction. Their aggressive voices, bright red jerseys, and pointing, windmilling arms insisting that cabs drop fares where they could sucker them—all of that would draw pedestrian eyes away from him.

At five minutes before noon, two big men—one a transgender, Kirby had read—emerged from the hotel lobby with Rachel Reid between them. To Kirby's eyes she trailed clouds of sanctimony along with her two watchful companions. Her white shearling long coat and wide-brimmed felt hat were as radiant in the clear sunlight as they were hypocritical, having cost—he had also read—more than either bodyguard earned in a year.

Kirby loathed the woman at first sight, even more than when he watched her self-righteous videos. He had hated ISIS, the Taliban, but that was geopolitical and tactical; this was visceral. He had to prevent himself from moving against her too early.

His target was not the woman but a white stretch limousine at the curb. The vehicle had been sitting there long enough for Kirby to confirm what he had anticipated. The car had local livery plates and was not riding low. Rachel was slumming it: she had a rented conveyance without heavy armor plating. Kirby was not surprised. He had seen similar vehicles in photographs of the woman as she pontificated her way around the world. The private jet was indulgence enough. The woman was not, after all, the president of the United States. A separate aircraft for an armored car would have been too much.

Besides, this way she could score points for hiring local. "Investing in your neighborhood," as she put it in her speeches.

One of the bodyguards moved a few paces ahead of Rachel. He motioned away the female chauffeur, who had been standing by the back door on the passenger's side. The driver hustled around the rear of the vehicle, then made her way toward the driver's side.

Kirby ended his "call" by texting his go-code to Stroud, one of two he would be sending:

00:00

Gray Kirby propelled himself from the bench like a star player in a playoff game. He walked briskly between a line of waiting cabs and crossed the street to the car just as the driver was shutting her own door. When he was just steps from the vehicle, near enough to catch the notice of the second bodyguard, Kirby did two things in quick succession.

First, he drew his trusted Browning Hi-Power 9mm handgun from inside his vest and put a bullet through the bodyguard's forehead. The man's sunglasses flew in a high arc as he fell backward, blood spraying from both sides of his skull. The second thing Kirby did was jerk the index finger of his left hand, the hand with the gym bag. He had tied a line of speaker wire around the base of the finger. Inside the grip the wire was threaded through eight cylindrical Scalable Offensive Hand Grenades. He heard a series of clicks as pins were pulled.

As the assassin had expected, the moment the first bodyguard went down his companion bent behind the car for protection, his arm around Rachel, pulling her with him and toward him. The guard could not see the meridian on the opposite side.

Beyond and around the theater of attack, the shot had caused a moment of frozen concern followed by panic. The hotel doorman swore and radioed for security and then 911, the cabbies dropped behind their dashboards with terror-alert instincts, and the few pedestrians in the vicinity ran, hard, some dropping groceries but not phones. Other people dragged madly barking dogs behind them. Like a herd of startled hippos, the ticket vendors looked over, then bolted into Battery Park to the relative safety of the trees.

Meanwhile, Kirby was moving toward the vehicle. He bent as if he were bowling and slid the bag under the back of the car—under the back seat on the driver's side. The powerful explosives were on a five-second timer. They stopped within inches of where Kirby had been aiming.

By this time, the bodyguard had pushed Rachel into the limousine and climbed in beside her. He drew a handgun from a shoulder holster and barked at the driver.

"Go, *go*!"

The chauffeur did not need prompting, but the car did not move. Kirby used one second of the five-second countdown to shoot the woman in the left temple. The point-blank impact caused a spray of skull shards and clumps of brain to become airborne to her right, followed by her arms doing a swan dive in that direction. The rest of the driver's body followed, sprawling into the passenger's seat. Her shearling splattered with gore, Rachel finally screamed.

The bodyguard threw himself on top of Rachel, also as expected. Now she was doomed. From behind the smoky glass the bodyguard's eyes sought the gunman. He saw Kirby backing away, the Browning still in his hand. The security man seemed to be weighing whether to continue shielding his employer or to exit the idling car and give pursuit.

That process consumed the remaining four seconds.

Kirby was between the first two cabs when the powerful explosion rocked Little West Street. He threw himself behind the second cab and watched around the dinged fender as the roar, smoke, and fire rolled in all directions. It cracked the windows in the front of the hotel and on the blast-ward sides of the cabs. Shrapnel peppered the vehicles and the lobby with loud, ugly chinks and clangs. Several squirrels and pigeons dropped straight to the pavement.

Crucially, the blast did one thing more. The powerful detonation heaved the driver's side of the vehicle more than two feet off the ground. The force was not enough to turn the car on its side. The limousine teetered on its two right-side wheels, balancing like a stunt vehicle, before flopping back down with a bounce and a grating crunch of metal. The hard landing popped a back tire. All of the windows cracked on impact, jagged chunks of glass crashing to the asphalt and shattering, the two back seat occupants flopping up and down like crash test dummies.

Even as the limousine was settling to earth, Kirby ran toward the car. He was peering inside as he approached, undistracted by the panic around him. Both occupants were bloody but alive. The blast had torn ragged holes in the bottom of the limousine; he could see through the broken window that Rachel's legs were useless, unrecognizable lumps of ripped flesh and haphazard angles of bone. The bodyguard was struggling to right himself like a big dog that had been hit by a car. His left arm was shredded, though he did not seem to realize it as he used it to try and push himself into a sitting position.

Kirby had seen his fellow soldiers do that. Rage rose in him, demanding release.

The assassin shot the guard, first in the left eye and then in the right. Some Afghans believed that the dead man could never, now, find his way to paradise. The man dropped across Rachel's lap. She had winced at the pop of the shots but was too dazed to process it—it or the shot that went into her heart, ending her life.

There was new noise behind Kirby, but he knew what it was and did not turn until he had put two more bullets into Rachel, making sure she was quite dead. The sound came from the cabs. Though their chassis were torn and windowless, and several tires had been punctured, the vehicles tore away. Even as they clanked north on bare rims, Kirby had already tucked the gun in his vest, and he began running east across Little West Street and then West Street, where drivers were just realizing what had happened and were slowing, stopping, or thumping over the meridian to head north toward the World Trade Center.

Kirby finally heard a great many sirens as he fled, all of them pouring toward the hotel from the north and east. Police were also running toward the hotel from their beat on State Street. Kirby knew from his time at DHS that the NYPD counterterrorism division drilled here frequently. He also knew he had less than a minute to disappear. There was also a police department mobile unit stationed permanently at the Museum of Jewish Heritage on the western side of the hotel. It would be at least a minute before those officers, too, arrived on foot. Since there was an active shooter, they would approach with caution. That bought him a little more time.

Within half a minute, Kirby was running along Liberty Place and merged with other panicked lunchtime pedestrians—none of whom had been in a position to see him. With no one paying attention to just another frightened pedestrian, he reversed his vest as he walked, showing bright blue now. He ripped off the Yankees logo from his cap, stuffed it in a pocket, and turned the hat around as he headed for the subway stop on Rector Street—along with dozens of others who were looking to get away, to go anywhere that wasn't there.

Before a minute was out, police converged on the hotel. It was a good response time, Kirby thought, but not to stop him. He and others were already pushing through the turnstile toward the platform.

Their voices floated around him with self-absorbed predictability.

"I was here on 9/11 . . . just eating a hot dog when . . . I knew there'd be another terrorist attack . . . may be others . . ."

No one asked if anyone had been hurt. Kirby wished he had worked killing a platform of narcissists into the plan.

The northbound subway was still running, and as the One Train pulled in, Kirby boarded with the rest. Chatter in the car was hushed, frightened, and confused. There were sobs. People were talking, and only the passengers continuing from South Ferry were listening, asking if they shouldn't get off.

Kirby took no pains to conceal himself. If Poole had done his job, there had not been a surveillance camera functioning between Bowling Green, the Hudson River, and the Manhattan terminal of the Staten Island Ferry.

Within one minute the subway had reached Cortlandt Street. Kirby was the only one in his car to get off. He climbed the stairs, emerging in front of Century 21 on Broadway. He turned back south and approached the parking garage from three blocks to the north; police would not be looking for a man in a blue vest headed back toward the crime scene.

As he walked, Gray Kirby texted Burton Stroud the second word, the one that said he was getting into position for his second assignment, if it was required:

Score!

CHAPTER SIX

Philadelphia, Pennsylvania
January 16, 12:07 p.m.

The towers of Philadelphia loomed large when Berry called the van for a third time.

A second call, an hour earlier, had failed to add information that might open new avenues. Berry reported that Captain Hamill had not belonged to any hunt or gun clubs.

"Most of the groups are strong on pro-gun, pro-rights activism, and that doesn't seem to have been the captain's strong suit in retirement," Berry had observed.

"Understandable," Williams had replied. "When you belong to the navy, all the other clubs seem like poor runners-up."

"Which brings me to the one exception—the Pennsylvania Venison charity. We found an interview where Captain Hamill talked about where he did most of his hunting. He mentioned Sproul State Forest and Allegheny National Forest. That's 476 and about 802 square miles, respectively."

"That's still a lot of terrain," Breen had said.

"Well, we don't know how much of it he actually covered

over the years or, more importantly, while he was working for Major Lewis. I talked to Drug Enforcement, and they gave me the route the cartels are thought to use through that region. Unfortunately, that's no help. They come in at night by small plane and use the trees and geography of the Appalachian Plateau for cover."

"They file a flight plan, surely," Breen had said.

"Of course. They're airborne before DEA hears of it and clean when they land. Amazing what can be done with a simple, low-tech operation."

"We know that," Rivette had muttered.

When Berry was finished, Breen had said, "Not quite a bust for verifying Taikinys's story, but not much guidance, either."

"What about satellite surveillance of the area?" Grace had asked. "There must be signs of habitation."

"There are, mostly cabins that are rented during hunting season and unoccupied the rest of the year," Berry had said. "We're checking the paper trail, but there are over three hundred residences with some fifteen hundred renters during that period."

"Tax records?" Breen had asked.

"We're collecting names, but someone who can hack the ONI can certainly erase their files at the IRS."

The third call from Berry came after an hour had passed in relative silence, each of the four rereading the files or—in Rivette's case—listening to music and still cleaning his guns. As much as Williams relied on Rivette's marksmanship, the lance corporal depended on Major Breen telling him anything he absolutely needed to know.

Berry was already agitated when Williams thumbed the phone.

"You remember that feeling after the second plane hit the Twin Towers?" Berry said. "The sick realization that we really were under attack?"

All four members of the team were instantly alert. Breen switched on a news feed.

"The war," Williams said.

"We don't know what it's about, but it has apparently started."

"Christ," Breen said as he saw the images from New York.

Breen held up his tablet with photos from the scene. The two in the back craned to see.

"The victim was jet heir Rachel Reid," Berry said. "The woman wasn't simply gunned down in Lower Manhattan. She was blown up and shot several times, along with her driver and two bodyguards."

"Blown up how?" Williams asked.

"Her limo was parked outside a hotel, took what looks like a bag of explosives that got delivered, with a short fuse, right under Ms. Reid's seat."

"The perps?"

"Perp—singular, according to sketchy reports."

"One person caused the blast and fired all the shots?"

"That's right. Then got away clean."

"How is that possible?" Williams asked. "That is a heavily trafficked area, no subway for blocks around. I've been there for Fleet Week—"

"Eyewitnesses? The killer chose wisely. Where's everyone looking? Not at the buildings or the park, they're looking at the Statue or their cell phones. Add to that, once the shooting started, observers ducked, hid, or fled. The cabbies right outside the damn hotel ducked and *then* fled. A dog walker took cell phone video of the immediate aftermath and got one of his animals run over by a fleeing cab, the phone knocked down and shattered. A tourist walked into traffic on West Street trying to get video—got clipped by a car making a U-turn. Most of what she recorded was the sky."

"Where was hotel security?" Breen asked.

"Safe."

"What do you mean?"

"They were stuck in the elevator thanks to automatic lockdown procedures when there's an active shooter."

"Well, what information *do* we have?" Breen asked as he typed on his tablet. He was not reading but searching.

"We've got—let me count—five people who say that the assassin looked like a businessman. One of those is the concierge, who assumed he was a local. He was apparently on the phone on West Street before the attack, and the five agree he was carrying something, though they can't agree whether it was a backpack or a shopping bag or possibly a gym bag. The coming plastic bag ban has created havoc for 'If you see something, say something.' Everyone is carrying big, empty bags for groceries."

"Whatever it is, you'll probably find it came from Walmart or Whole Foods," Breen said. "Something so common we'll be looking at store surveillance for months."

"And it was packed with explosives, which we already know were provided by Taikinys."

"You're reaching the same dead ends as we are, just faster," Berry said. "All of that's bad, but this is worse. The attacker did not just get away, he got away 'invisible'—surveillance was knocked out, just as with Captain Hamill and Major Lewis. Actually, let me rephrase that. It was surgically cut. Part of the Ring of Steel is the public WorldCam. Two sites there: from the harbor toward Battery Park and from the Hudson toward the esplanade. A third, a camera at the foot of the Canyon of Heroes looking up Broadway. Surveillance on all three went down, in unison, at the scene and along the probable escape route."

Breen stopped typing. "Didn't anyone at the NYPD notice?"

"Yes, Major. But there's not much you can do in ninety seconds. The blackout lasted from about thirty seconds before to one minute after the attack."

There was a grim silence. Grace broke it.

"So these are not just hunters. They're certainly military."

"But whose?" Rivette asked.

"What about forensics?" Breen asked, resuming his typing.

"The NYPD and the FBI field office are getting the grenade fragments, fabric from the gym bag, bullets—but you already know where that leads us."

"The explosives would have had to travel to New York by private car," Breen said.

"How do you know it was a car?" Rivette asked. "Back in LA, we used boats."

"The Wagner Hotel is just a few blocks from the marina

at the World Financial Center," Breen said. "According to their website, no one registered to moor there in the last twenty-four hours. No private helicopters landed at the east- or west-side helipads in that same period. Trains rattle too much for detonator caps. That means they had to be driven into Manhattan—"

"Gonna stop you there, Major," Berry said. "First, do you know how many vehicles enter Manhattan every day?"

"Two hundred and ninety thousand," Breen said, reading from his tablet, "and one of them was our man. That's why most big cities have a SmartTag system that sees everyone who comes in, then searches databases and tracks them if necessary—"

"Second," Berry cut him off, "New York is required by law to erase SmartTag data the instant a vehicle is tagged as 'clean.' Civil libertarians on the force, *hired* by the damn force, insisted on it."

The major recalled the legal challenges to the Metropolitan Transportation Authority's Surveillance Technology Oversight Project in 2020, the facial recognition technology on subway platforms that directed transit police to cars where registered sex offenders and suspected terrorists were located. The courts deemed them invasive spy tools and ordered them discontinued.

"Fine," Breen said. "Have them check surveillance from downtown parking garages before the cameras went off. They may not have connected the dots yet. Captain Hamill was looking into *someone* in Pennsylvania. If they concentrate on just Pennsylvania license plates, they may get lucky."

"I'll suggest it, but I guarantee it will trigger a turf war between the NYPD, the Port Authority of New York, and the state police like it did even after 9/11. The perp will be long gone before the question is settled."

A line from a comic strip Williams loved as a kid, *Pogo,* came to mind. "We have met the enemy and he is us."

"Wait a sec," Berry said. "Something just came in from the NYPD, I'm reading it now—Office of the Chief of Counterterrorism says, 'Alert, not for release, blah blah . . . a concierge and a receptionist at the Marriott Downtown on West Street saw a guest fitting the general description of the attacker. Business clothes, charcoal or dark blue vest, carrying a gym bag, wearing a Yankees baseball cap. He left the hotel walking south. They say his name is Leopold Kramer, Canadian. He has not returned to the hotel. Paid with traveler's checks. Officers from counterterrorism are checking his room now.'"

"They can't really expect to find him," Breen said. "That man, Leopold Kramer, was seen because he wanted to be seen. The resources are being devoted to a ghost."

"Assuming this Leopold Kramer is a misdirection," Williams said, "that brings us back to what Grace suggested."

"Which brings NSA Philadelphia back into play," Breen agreed. "Do you think you can get in legitimately?"

"Probably. The name and uniform may have traction. Bucking the ONI is less precarious than insulting an admiral, especially if you don't know he's retired."

"The good news, if you can call it that, is now that Black Order has had their Fort Sumter, we expect to be getting an ultimatum," Berry said. "The president is hoping he can reason with them."

"I don't think that will be their tack," Breen said. "It will more likely be a threat of escalation."

"What's the difference?" Berry asked.

"An ultimatum is a red line. Give us a billion dollars, or else. It's simple, clean, yes-or-no. An escalation is open ended, and these people seem to have bigger objectives than ransom. The words they gave to Mrs. Hamill, if she reported them correctly, were that anyone who 'moves against us will die.' That suggests a process. Anything they don't like will be met with violence, not a new deadline."

"That's not good," Berry said.

"That's why they called it a war," Rivette observed.

"If you're right, then I don't know what the president will do," Berry said. "These bastards told us a war was coming over a dozen hours ago, and the Office of Naval Intelligence was not prepared to move. The shit thing is, they're still best situated to handle this—that is, except for Black Wasp."

"What do you need from us?" Williams asked.

"Right now, we need whatever information you can get and by any means necessary. Stop short of kidnapping Mrs. Hamill, but—hell, if you think that'll help, do it. We have to stop this. We'll clean up any messes later."

Williams and Breen knew what that meant: they'd be disavowed by the Oval Office and take the full blame. It was the price of doing business.

"I'm going to talk to the president about what Hamilton just suggested," Berry said. "Talk to you when either of us has something."

The call ended just as Williams was turning onto Exit 22.

Breen sat reflecting in silence on the territorial self-sabotage of the system. That was one reason he loved the courts. There was the dispassionate guide of case law and the singular rule of the judge.

"Major, I know you don't like speculating, but who the hell is the target of all this?" Rivette asked.

"I'm wondering that too," Grace said. "What is it a war *on*? The wealthy?"

Breen shook his head. "An attack on Wall Street, just a few blocks away, would have made that statement more effectively."

"So, Rachel Reid—women's empowerment?"

"Closer to the mark, Lieutenant," Breen said. "This was not an attack on the media. This was a massacre directed at *her*, an assault on an ideology. In this case, social reform."

"If you're right," Williams said, "and the nation has gone from rhetoric to open revolt, then the Black Order is correct. This *will* be war—a second civil war with a lot of soldiers willing to take up arms on both sides."

"That many people can't be insane," Rivette said. "Even gangs are smarter than that."

"This has been simmering for over a decade," Breen said. "Whatever you think of the motivations, when you tear down statues and symbols that are dear to a large section of the population, your feet are set on a path to confrontation."

"'Invisible,' he called the killer," Grace said. "How do we anticipate the next attack?"

"Anticipate it from Philadelphia no less, without any kind of high tech like the bad guys have," Rivette added.

"We have to get ahead of the Black Order using electronic intelligence tools ONI doesn't have," Williams said as he guided the van toward Independence Hall.

"Like?" Rivette pressed.

"You always counter electronic intelligence with human intelligence," Williams answered. "That's a big, linked resource greater than any web."

CHAPTER SEVEN

Philadelphia, Pennsylvania
January 16, 12:44 p.m.

The alert eyes of Burton Stroud shifted between the three computer monitors on the large mahogany desk. The events unfolding before him were a thing of beauty and anticipation. Like a playwright who had watched his brainchild go from idea to keyboard to opening night, he was waiting for reviews—though he knew what they would be.

He had a great cast and a world-class stage.

And your tech crew. Mustn't forget him.

Of course, Stroud knew he had one advantage leading up to opening night. He was small and nimble instead of bureaucratic and clumsy. Just the handling of Captain Hamill showed how effective intelligence work *could* be. Not overcrowded and hamfisted as he was watching things play out now, but tactical. If Jackson Poole did not routinely overfly the woods with drones, and conduct facial recognition if he did see anyone, they would never have known about the naval officer. Once he was identified, and his calls monitored, the ONI operation against him was unearthed. It remained only to obtain Hamill's phone to get the name of his contact.

Eventually, the Black Order would get around to the only man who could have informed the ONI of a hostile presence in Western Pennsylvania: Taikinys. They would not even have to do that themselves. They would simply inform the cartel that had risked exposure doing business with him.

And then, one day, a new war will target them, Stroud reflected. One could not repair and restore America without eliminating drugs. The kind that cities enabled by passing out free, clean hypodermic needles. Money that should be spent on science and education was going to cartels by way of healthier addicts. The world was mad.

But that was for another time. He had known that to attack his own nation he would have to be swift, organized, and ready to blow up not just people who fostered corrupt values but also watch and, if necessary, take down electronic systems more powerful than his. He was sorry the ONI dark web shadow had been uncovered. Immediately before Sarno's incursion that morning, Poole had—with a keystroke—disengaged the Black Order from their dark web operations pertaining to the ONI. All he left were trails that led nowhere, forcing investigators to waste a few essential hours pursuing dead ends and burned electronic bridges. Even the best IT professional could not follow a road that had been blown up along with the encryption and the private cloud that contained it.

All that remained of the dark net were the now-isolated hacks into municipal surveillance and communications systems.

Working in the sophisticated electronics setup in the basement of Stroud Safe at Home, Jackson Poole had crafted those hacks to be triggered and terminated on a precise timetable that the assassins were obliged to follow.

He was blind now, but so was the other side. Which was fine. The shadow had served its purpose. It had given them access to the systems they had required. The operating plan going forward was targeted aggression and careful oversight. Those had been Stroud's two guiding principles prior to founding the Black Order, even before he had joined the Rangers. Growing up in Pennsylvania, he was nine when a fast-spreading nocturnal wildfire took out the entire block, including his home.

The fire department had committed their resources to containment first. That doomed that which he cared about most. Stroud got out of the house on his own, but his mother went back for their important documents—the passport her husband needed for work, birth certificates, a pair of photo albums. She turned the hose on herself before rushing back inside, trying to hide her anxiety behind the smile she left with her boy.

A life was lost for papers, all of which burned with Norma Stroud.

Burton Stroud Sr. was a journalist who had been on the road covering the 1980 presidential campaign. The elder Stroud was in St. Louis; his newspaper, the *Atlanta Times,* chartered him a flight home. Whenever the story was told in adult whispers, it killed Burton Jr. that the words "rushed home" were used to describe his father's actions. What the boy remembered was sitting alone in an emergency room for seven hours while the second-degree burns on his face and arms were tended to.

The matter might have ended there for Burton Jr., with the clinging ghosts of loss and fear, save for the official findings. A joint investigation by the Riverside County Fire Department and the Department of Social Services determined that the blaze was caused by illegal immigrants who had been camped on a hillside, smoking. Burton Jr. knew about Smokey Bear and his warnings. It seemed ridiculous to him that a cartoon animal should be the face of something so grave. The boy wanted a bear that would use its size and claws to rip the flesh from the three men who had started the fire and suffered nothing more than deportation.

The Mexicans were sent home. The Strouds *had* no home. The situation and its resolution were grotesque.

Burton Jr.'s father was made an editor, and the two moved north to Granada Hills, where the boy lived a life that teetered between withdrawal and acting out. Psychiatry that could not resurrect his mother, and laws that had failed him had continued to fail the nation. As soon as he was able to enlist he did so, wanting to do nothing more than to protect the republic from those who cared nothing for American citizens or laws. Concurrent with that journey, he also sought an outlet for aggression that refused to die.

More than forty years after Stroud's loss, both goals burned even brighter in his soul. Everything he had done since the age of eighteen—his career as a Ranger, his computer studies at Drexel University, the founding of Stroud Safe at Home, and finally the establishing of the Black Order two years before—had pointed to this day, this beginning.

This war.

Stroud was at home in Germantown, seated in a bedroom that had been converted into a tech center. The hardware included a powerful 120-watt desktop jammer. It impacted all frequencies in the 130–2700 MHz range, meaning no one inside or outside the house could hear what went on inside this room.

Secure from eavesdroppers—even random, contactless identity thieves that were not targeting him as such—Stroud was on a new platform. Poole had created a pared-down clone of Linux crafted to limit network services and exposure. It was also unrelated to the dark web setup. In a few moments, when he videoconferenced with the rest of the team, the footprint would be like a pane of glass in profile: thin, clear, virtually impossible to find unless you were looking for it. And even then it would still be difficult to crack.

Forging and obliterating footprints on the web was just one cornerstone of the Black Order playbook. Stroud had built the organization on the five tactics of ancient Greek warfare: progress, regress, remain, anticipate, fix. Every situation required one of those actions.

Stroud was also surrounded by people who shared absolutely his beliefs.

"No one is innocent who willingly supports our oppressors," Stroud had said at their first full meeting. "There will be casualties. We must make the support of anti-Americanism come at a price none will pay."

There was no objection or complaint. With one exception, every member of the Black Order possessed a level of zealotry that anesthetized fear, transcended Christian morality, and understood the need for extreme shock and awe to secure results.

Stroud had a team of seven soldiers, all unmarried, to start a revolution that would remake a nation. The cowards who wanted to seize their guns, soil their Constitution, fracture their nation, had to come to a hard and permanent stop. The members of the Black Order all recognized, with regret but without dispute, that their acts had to be violent, even horrendous, to accomplish that goal. When they had all gathered for the first time, only Jackson Poole expressed any hesitancy.

"There's not a lot of us to fight a war," he had said. "How do we win?"

The remark was cautious but not fearful. Otherwise, Stroud would have removed him.

No one, especially the outspoken Gray Kirby, jumped in—yet. They gave Stroud the opportunity to respond.

"We win because our numbers are not known to the enemy," Stroud had said. "Every time the left speaks, we win supporters. Every time Hollywood opens its privileged mouth, we win more. Those actors who trust their emotions to tell stories. That's not how real people survive in the real world. When those children emote against us, we multiply."

"There does not have to *be* a lot of us, not to start," Gray Kirby had then said with the passion that was his hallmark. "It took only a handful of colonials to attack English soldiers at Lexington and Concord—their *countrymen,* I remind you—and start the American Revolution. In 1914, a single assassin with one bullet killed Archduke Ferdinand of Austria and ignited the First World War. In 1958, Fidel Castro and a handful of supporters hid in the mountains of Cuba. A year later Castro was running the nation. We will achieve no less than these people did."

"All true, but it's more basic than that," Stroud had said. "We have social media."

"Yes, the media will help," Kirby had said. "But we must furnish them with shock upon shock. In the 1920s, the Purple Gang in Detroit scared even seasoned bootleggers and extortionists. Their tool was simple: ruthless violence. Even the Mafia was afraid of them. Our acts are not driven by greed but by patriotism, and while we send Marxists into hiding we will bring more heroes to the front, more Americans who honor tradition."

"Thank you, Gray," Stroud had said.

Neither man had to remind them that they would not even have to take his case to the media. They were already there. So engrossed was Stroud with the flood of information on his devices that he jumped when Christopher Sarno walked in. Though the assassin had not slept for very long, the man seemed not just fresh but invigorated when he entered the room.

"My God," Sarno said, looking over Stroud's shoulder. "Kirby did it!"

"He did. So did Poole. The New York operation was a complete success."

"Congratulations, Chief."

"To us all. You were the first soldier in the field. Congratulations on that."

"Thanks, Burton." Sarno continued to look at the screen. "Four dead. The target and who else?"

"The members of the Reid party, as we allowed for, and the chauffeur, as we expected. No one else was seriously injured other than those who fled into traffic."

"'Through me you go into a city of weeping,'" Sarno said.

"There will be plenty of that," Stroud said. He turned and regarded Sarno, his careful eyes searching the man's face. "How are you?"

"Me? I'm fine. Rested."

"I don't mean physically." Stroud indicated the monitor. "Blowing people up, shooting them is different from getting close and cutting a throat. Any repercussions?"

"Emotionally? Nothing. You've been in those situations. You know."

"That's why I'm asking," Stroud said. "You train the body and spirit for a mission, but the mind is less obedient in the moments before sleep."

"I slept fine. Before that I drank fine. That man should have stuck to hunting deer."

Stroud smiled approvingly. "Just making sure."

"Man to man, right? You're not my boss outside the store."

Sarno's voice had an edge, and Stroud had to stifle his own instinct to remind him whose house he was living in, whose food he was eating, whose cause he had grabbed to serve his own joy of killing. After years in the field, constantly alert and living in a warren like a beast, Sarno had a touch of the Neanderthal. He did not understand that psych profiling was a form of debrief, a baseline measurement, not a critique. Stroud had to step gingerly.

"Fraternal concern," Stroud said evenly. "I'm just checking."

"Nothing has changed, and nothing will. I'm in till we win."

Stroud smiled approvingly and made no further comment. The former CIA agent had his priorities straight, at least. The war was what mattered now.

Sarno pulled over a wooden chair and sat. He did all of it soundlessly, a habit he had adapted in upstairs apartments and attics wherever he worked. If people knew you were home they might be reluctant to talk. Or if they wanted you dead they would know exactly where to shoot.

Sarno pointed at a news feed on Stroud's smartphone. "What are they saying in the media?"

"Shock, fear, lamentations . . . and very little information about who did this. If the authorities know anything, they are not sharing it."

"Too early for a press conference, I guess."

"That'll be at six."

"Wanna bet?" Sarno laughed.

"Right now it's the usual posturing from local and national law enforcement and politicians and statements from actors about the sainted Rachel Reid," Stroud said. "Mourning as performance art, like Gaelic keening, right down to the stock words and phrases—'appalling,' 'bring to justice,' 'prayers to the victims' families.'"

"Has either president spoken?"

"Wright issued a statement—'condemning in the strongest terms,' that's another big one—and Midkiff is going to address the nation at eight."

"Right there shows how little they have," Sarno said.

"Predictable as the seasons, which is why they are playing catch-up. The president needs time to canvass foreign as well as domestic intelligence services."

Sarno's eyes continued to move between the screens. The one in the center was Stroud's command console. The cable news was in a small box on the right-hand bottom. The rest of the screen showed small red *x*'s beside over thirty lines of code. Stroud had deactivated the ONI overlay and explained to Sarno that as long as each of these digital trip wires did not register green checkmarks, the path to Black Order was inviolate.

The other two monitors were for conferencing. The screens would become active as each operative checked in. Despite knowing that everyone was safe, Sarno saw Stroud experience a few minutes of anxiety before the screens became active—drumming a finger on the desk, sitting back then forward, shallow breathing. Sarno had survived in the field because he had learned to note countless human traits and tics and what they meant. An itch evoked a quick, reflexive response; people who scratched their ear or forehead casually were signaling. A man who did not look up from a bistro table at a beautiful woman was either gay, a saint, or watching someone else.

At the appointed time, two faces appeared on each monitor. Dee Dee Allen and Gray Kirby were on one side-by-side split screen, Dee Dee in her hotel room, Gray in his car. Former

Marines Mark Philpotts and Eiji Honda were together at the Piedmont 22 Hotel in Atlanta. They had once joked that as a Black man and an Asian they were only there for diversity. Dee Dee was a woman, and gay. All of that had nothing to do with the outrageous fascism of inclusion. Stroud hoped that many other people of color and from different backgrounds would join the crusade. Neither Philpotts, Honda, nor Dee Dee could stomach the notion of imposed equality. They were here because they merited places on the team.

Philpotts had been the first to join Stroud. Their chance meeting—Philpotts called it "fateful"—occurred at a gun show in Harrisburg, Pennsylvania, in 2019. A Newark, New Jersey, native of African descent, Philpotts was working as a guard at the Three Mile Island nuclear facility near Harrisburg, and the men talked unhappily about the temporary ban on AR-15s. The embargo was the result of several mass shootings. Philpotts blamed the media for demonizing weapons instead of advocating the treatment of unbalanced citizens.

"A dollar's worth of gasoline allowed a jealous boyfriend to kill eighty-seven people at the Happy Land club," the security guard had said. "Nobody pushed for a ban on matches."

Stroud had agreed not just wholeheartedly but passionately. The two went out for coffee—Stroud did not drink alcohol—and discovered that they had military experiences in common. Both had been deployed, in different branches of service, in Unconventional Warfare and Direct Action operations. Their divisions took combat into enemy-held, politically sensitive regions where high-profile or officially acknowledged forces dared not venture.

The men shared war stories and kicked around their grievances. They were angry about the state of things in America. They were not just angry about the uninformed and reactionary hatred of guns but about the fury turned against gun owners by the population at large; against supporters of the Second Amendment; and, by extension, against the framers of the Constitution.

Over the next few weeks, by Facebook Messenger and in Philadelphia, the men discussed the larger topic of saving America and American exceptionalism. Born and raised on the streets, Philpotts was quicker to burn than Stroud. That was why he worked as a guard. Anyone pushed him, he had a responsibility to push back, hard.

"How far do you think you'd go to protect your inalienable rights?" Stroud had asked in a face-to-face meeting.

"I don't 'think,'" Philpotts had said. "I know. I killed for America. I wouldn't even do that for God."

It was Philpotts who brought Eiji Honda into the mix.

An electrical engineering student at the University of Pennsylvania, Eiji was the grandson of a kamikaze pilot who had disgraced the family by failing to complete his mission. Eiji's father, Akihiko, had come to America to study and to escape the shame—and stayed. He married an American woman, became a citizen, and opened a restaurant. Akihiko said that America had saved the Honda family. Eiji felt honor-bound to repay that service.

During their time in the Marines, Honda and Philpotts had watched as the nation that they and their comrades fought and bled for edged toward a precipice.

"I'm not sure who is the clear and present danger," Honda had said. "The Taliban or the radicals who want to shred, not unite."

Honda was ready to do whatever was necessary to preserve the nation that had saved his family.

During the second of his two tours of Iraq, Stroud had met Taikinys when the man was brought in for interrogation—and released—and learned about IT wunderkind Jackson Poole, an outside consultant with the navy's Information Technology Division, Software Applications. During Poole's half dozen visits to Iraq, he had stayed as deep in the Green Zone as possible. Stroud interacted with him on electronic surveillance of hostile targets. Poole was a self-professed geek, not a hero, patriot, or ideologue. Stroud actually pegged him as a borderline sociopath, happier with software than with people.

Poole was Stroud's first hire when he opened his business. The thirty-year-old turned out to be manageable—even content—as long as Stroud gave him respect and responsibility. For extra pay and a chance to screw with society at large, he was happy to join the Black Order. His functions there were designed to limit his interaction with people, save for Stroud and one or two contacts at the base for which they were ostensibly working.

Stroud waited until Poole was fully on board to tell him there would be fatalities.

Poole had actually shrugged. "Everything I do is electronic with self-destruct built in," Poole had said. "My ass is covered."

Sarno was the next person to join. Stroud and the retired CIA field agent had reconnected when they had come to Stroud

Safe at Home looking for a job; he found, instead, a purpose. It was Sarno, in fact, who had suggested the name for the unit. While overseas, he had read Dante to remind himself that hell was not one place but many, each with its own circles, its own sins, its own tortures. He called those nine circles the Black Order, a reminder that any situation could easily degrade into something darker.

The designation also aligned with Stroud's admiration for the Purple Gang.

Dee Dee was more of a challenge. The ex–Delta Force lieutenant was now an Uber driver whose specialty was assassination with cyanide-tipped arrows. Stroud had become aware of the forty-six-year-old when she had won a National Field Archery Association competition in freestyle bow hunting. He had hired her to use her skills to try and get around security he had been engaged to install at the Philadelphia Zoo. It wasn't that he expected anyone to hunt caged tigers. Rather, Stroud was interested in exposing his systems to the kinds of stealth tactics they had never faced. He was forced to develop new motion detection systems to detect the speed and low profile of an arrow.

Asking her to join the team, Stroud was clear about what was required.

"If the big, neon warning is, 'You'll have to kill noncombatants,' my response is, 'Three couriers, including a boy, died when I took out the head of the ISIS Financial Council.' We're facing a theocracy of hate, and I'll do whatever is necessary."

Gray Kirby was the last person to become a member of the Black Order. Stroud and the hedge fund manager had been seated at the same table during a fundraiser for long-shot conservative presidential candidate Reynold Stevens. The former sniper was filled with rage at the prospect of John Wright becoming president and the wealthy being trashed louder than ever—"going back to George Washington and Thomas Jefferson, which shows just how diseased people are." He openly lamented having no recourse but to watch the country deteriorate for four to eight years.

"That may not be entirely true," Stroud had told him.

Before the night was over, Kirby had enthusiastically committed himself to the Black Order.

And now they were gathered for the first time since H hour. Whatever anxiety Stroud may have been feeling had evaporated, replaced by pride and gratitude.

"Welcome," he said. "To begin, to Joe beside me, to Dee Dee, and to Gray I say well done. Exceptional jobs, each of you."

Dee Dee and Gray thanked Stroud in unison. Sarno pursed his lips and nodded, ever the lone operator.

"We pass the mission to Mark and Eiji with complete confidence and mutual purpose."

"And trust that we're not going to let these bone bangers show us up," Philpotts teased.

Stroud smiled. "That too."

The slang referred to a recruit so inept they could not handle a weapon and had to resort to beating an enemy with a bone.

"Let this momentum carry us forward with confidence but not overconfidence," Stroud continued. He looked at the two on the right monitor. "To that end, Dee Dee, Gray, was there anything unexpected, tactically or personally? Anything that might help Mark and Eiji . . . Gray, in case there is a floater mission? You can private message me if you like."

Each member of the team was proud, and none of them was likely to publicly acknowledge second thoughts, guilt, hesitation, or any of the qualities that sometimes surfaced as post-traumatic stress.

"There is only one thing I want to say," Dee Dee told him. "It pertains to the mission I just completed and to what just transpired."

"Go ahead."

"I don't think any of us wants to kill, and that was my feeling this morning. But what became clear at the moment I fired, as you've been telling us all along, the goal is *that* important. It's greater than any of us or any of our targets."

"They're object lessons," Kirby murmured.

"Exactly," Dee Dee said. "I felt proud, Burton. I *feel* proud. I am proud of your leadership, and I want to remain one hundred percent proud of the team."

"I was going to say the same thing," Gray Kirby remarked.

Applause would have been vulgar, but Stroud nodded approvingly. The others silently admired the sentiment. Sarno looked down, then back at the screens. He was feeling something unexpected and new: envy.

Stroud took on greater gravitas as he regarded the group.

"Gray, move on to your next position. Dee Dee, proceed to the Homestead through Philadelphia, as discussed. If you are needed, I'll text. We will reconvene, all of us, at 9:00 p.m., when

I will have a much clearer picture of our next steps. If for any reason it is unsafe for me to return here, or use this system, log onto the darkcabbage.com system and wait for the email that will come as soon as possible thereafter. If you do not hear from me by 6:45, you know what to do. All of you."

"Continue the war," Sarno said, more to himself than to the others. "With payback."

"Let's pray it does not come to that," Dee Dee remarked.

"That is true," Stroud agreed. His eyes and his voice hardened. "But remember this. There is no room for sentimentality. Yes, bestow compassion where it is practical and appropriate, but nothing more. Americans have shown they are willing to negotiate with anyone to make the pain stop. We must make the pain so great, so lasting—we must be ready to hit the enemy as hard and as often as necessary—that they will beg for it to cease. Remember: the duration and extent of the war is not on us. The amount of blood we shall spill and the destruction we *must* cause is on those who have oppressed us."

"A war of liberation," Philpotts said.

Stroud smiled, and his eyes shifted to the former Marines. "Mark, Eiji—good luck and Godspeed."

"We won't let you down, any of you," Philpotts said, his strong jaw twisted into his self-assured, almost cocky grin.

Stroud thanked them and ended the feeds. There was a thick silence in the room.

"Think I'll make a sandwich," Sarno said. "You want anything?"

"I'll get something later, thanks. I have some media requests to turn down—can't have my voice on TV until we're finished, obviously—and then I'll go to the store. I'm told there's been a thirty percent bump in walk-ins."

"Everyone's scared," Sarno remarked.

Stroud frowned. "Everyone's always scared, Christopher. They have been since I was a kid. The Soviets and the bomb, the anarchic streets during Vietnam, gas rationing, recession, 9/11—times are always dangerous."

"Sure, but this is different."

"I was about to make that point," Stroud said. "We've become Nazi Germany, people afraid of not just security risks but social dangers. Saying the wrong thing, using the wrong neologism. Stroud Safe at Home won't help them. But we will."

"Damn right," Sarno said.

He left to eat and Stroud turned the system off, save for the burn program for which only he and Poole had the codes. Once activated, the program would render the physical devices in the house unusable; the destroyed programs would still be safe at the Homestead.

The Homestead, he thought with longing. It was a special place. A training ground, a sanctuary.

The Stroud family had purchased fifty acres in Western Pennsylvania for cash in 1968 and had set up a series of dead-end corporations to own the deed and pay the taxes. It was a nondescript building with a series of heavily fortified underground bunkers, all of them designed to warehouse supplies, train men, and provide sanctuary from the nation's domestic enemies. During the Second World War, munitions had been stored there. The remote location prevented it from being repurposed as underground facilities were in so many other states.

One day soon they would all be safe there, secure in the compound . . . and, more importantly, living in the nation they had saved.

CHAPTER EIGHT

Philadelphia, Pennsylvania
January 16, 1:01 p.m.

Chase Williams remembered when muddy things were clearer. One stood out, from about four years before.

He was in the White House situation room, having just phoned in General Diane Karl, the supreme allied commander in Europe—whose face dominated the screen at the south end of the room. The only other people present had been President Midkiff and Trevor Harward. Karl, a thirty-year veteran of the trenches, was supernaturally prepared for the meeting. It would be a crisis averted, though at the time no one knew that.

He could still see her steady voice, her strong gaze, her economical words.

"We have satellite and ground eyes confirming that Russian forces are deploying throughout Belarus," she had said. "Their advance is continuing, and we have reliable sources in the Kremlin assuring us that it will be stopping where the NATO Response Force and its Very High Readiness Joint Task Force are located."

She told the men how close those forces were to the Belarus border and what U.S. troops were available on the ground in Europe as well as at sea in the Baltic or elsewhere.

"There are also readiness issues with NATO, specifically their transport aircraft. The report I received just before Admiral Williams called said they were looking at ground transport options."

"'Readiness issues,'" Midkiff had replied. "What they are looking at is their dependence on Russian energy sources."

The result of the extended video teleconference was that the president decided to take no action at that moment. He ordered another session six hours hence—by which time the Russians had, in fact, stopped all forward movement.

In the second video teleconference Karl had suggested that it was all a test to see how the United States and NATO would respond. She was right. Putin retreated the following day, having learned nothing.

Williams was relieved that an international showdown had been averted thanks to good intel from multiple sources, a reluctance to default to force, and cool, considerate heads.

Right now, Black Wasp has only one calm head—Major Breen—and none of those other qualities.

It was not exactly a crisis of faith that Williams was facing, but he was not as certain of his approach as he had made it sound on the off-ramp. The navy fraternity *was* strong, as he had said. The question was one of ethics.

You murdered a terrorist out of hand; yet you question the morality of pressing sailors to reveal secured information, he thought.

His world, at least, had truly gone off its axis.

The van rolled toward a roadblock. The streets were still closed to vehicular traffic, the barricades and only the barricades under the control of the Philadelphia Police Department. Breen had read that the PD had gone to court to regain control over the protection of their own citizens. It would take another few hours for that matter to be argued, adjudicated, and then appealed.

Two masters-at-arms were standing outside Captain Hamill's Spruce Street town house. The two were stationed on either end of the home about twenty feet apart. They carried sidearms and commanded a complement of three corpsmen who stood on the other sides of the residence.

Pedestrian traffic was sparse in the cold daylight, and even the rubberneckers did not linger. Chase Williams would be the exception.

The rest of the team waited in the van on Sixth Street as Williams went to Spruce on foot. All were silent. Breen was looking at windows around the site, noting who might have had a view of the building. Rivette was busy trying to figure out ways of getting into the house. Grace was studying the guards and their posture, patterns, attentiveness.

Williams looked around as he walked, exploring the immediate neighborhood. He spotted two sedans with ONI stickers parked a discreet distance away. When he neared the town house, he glanced about for possible ways the intruder could have gained access to the property, to the home. Along Sixth Street, all the town houses were joined, one roof connecting to the next. Because Atlas's house was last, there was only one adjoining roof. A metal sailor weathervane was attached to the chimney, facing toward the other rooftops. There was furniture on the roof, meaning a deck of some kind, and ingress. It represented an easy access, visible only to any neighbors who had been out there on a frigid night.

One of the police officers standing beside a streetlight watched Williams as he passed. The blue navy uniform, like the others that had been there, was instantly toxic to the other blue line. Understandably—Williams was presumed to have jurisdiction on their turf. With fraternal concern, he hoped the masters-at-arms were prepared for blowback when the courts let the PD in.

Williams approached the master-at-arms nearest him. She saluted, all the while giving him a stern, unfamiliar look.

"Good afternoon, Lieutenant Trayne," Williams said, returning the salute, reading her name tag, then stopping and looking up at the façade.

"Good afternoon, sir. I'm sorry, sir, but I have been instructed to admit no one without—" Suddenly, she stopped. "Excuse me. Are you Admiral Chase Williams?"

"I am," he said, leaving out the "retired." Right there, he knew, he had crossed a line.

The young woman's critical gaze and matching expression softened. "I'm sorry, I was not informed you were coming. This is truly an honor. I trained under a recruit division commander who had your picture on the wall of his office."

"The officer was—?"

"General Lester Savage, sir. Said he was part of the security detail at CENTCOM during his second shore tour."

Williams laughed. "Yes, Les Savage, a *very* good man. We had a chaplain, of all people, who used to tease him about being 'Less' Savage than the rest of the team. The general had to work twice as hard to prove he wasn't."

"Yes, sir." Trayne smiled back for the first time. "Those were the general's exact words."

Williams nodded toward the town house. "I also knew Captain Hamill."

The lieutenant's expression sobered at once. "I'm sorry, sir. Did you also know Major Lewis?"

"I did not."

"I had the privilege of meeting her once. A very impressive woman."

"I've been told," Williams replied. He glanced around the front of the building. There was a high picket fence, as much to block the sounds of traffic on the first floor as to afford protection. He saw a Stroud Safe at Home shield just beyond. He presumed that would have had to be disabled before the killer entered by any door or window. How? Wires cut and the circuit rerouted, or sensors somehow severed—though he presumed they had battery backups. Everything he knew about home security, which was not much, was based on his apartment at the Watergate.

The admiral did not see any obvious sign of jimmying at the front door or street-facing windows. Perhaps on the roof? He saw and heard signs of activity inside, though no one was visible through the windows on this side.

"You've been here since first call," Williams said to Trayne.

"How can you tell, sir?"

"You dressed for middle-of-the-night cold. And your companion just checked his cell phone, suggesting that relief is overdue?"

She smiled again. "That's impressive, sir."

"It's nearly four decades of observing navy and sentry behavior." He smiled. "Tell me—do you know if the alarm was active last night?"

The woman's smiled straightened. "Admiral, sir, I've been instructed not to discuss anything relating to the incident. I'm sorry."

"Of course. There's no need to apologize."

She leaned toward him slightly. "But I can tell you what is public knowledge. When one of the investigators went in this morning, the security system was off, and he turned it on to see if it worked. The siren shrieked like an incoming mortar. There were a lot of cross faces in windows up and down the street. After that, and with the city coroner being turned away, what happened here was an open secret."

Williams did not want to consider the irony that it was a major U.S. intelligence operation conducting what should have been a clandestine operation.

"What about Captain Mann? Has she been here?"

"I do not know that officer, sir."

"Naval Support Activity commander."

"I have not seen any captains, sir, but I really—"

"I know, I'm sorry. I believe she was Captain Hamill's replacement when he retired. I thought if she were coming, I'd wait."

"I can find out, sir."

"That's all right. I'll see her at the base."

Williams was surprised. Breen had looked up the command structure at Naval Support Activity. That kind of visit by the CO to personnel stationed at this kind of crime scene would have been obligatory, showing that the ranking officer took a personal interest in her predecessor. That meant the Naval Support Activity had been locked out along with non-navy law enforcement.

Vice Admiral Nathan must not want anyone but ONI personnel inside, Williams thought. Not until every fiber, fingerprint, and stray hair had been collected.

Williams had more questions about who had been here and what Trayne might have overheard, but her companion on the other side of the door was beginning to throw curious looks in their direction. Williams did not want to get the master-at-arms in trouble.

"Well, master-at-arms, it has been a pleasure meeting you. Thanks for the chat."

"I assure you, sir, the pleasure *and* honor were mine," she said, saluting.

Williams returned the salute and took a final look along the façade. He noticed someone looking down from inside, probably having heard them talking. The person withdrew quickly, and Williams walked back to the van.

"MA seemed chatty," Rivette observed.

"She recognized me." He got behind the wheel. "Captain Mann has not been here, looks like ONI are still looking for clues, and there's a stop I want to make before we go to the NSA. Stroud Safe at Home. I want to find out how someone was able to get inside without tripping alarms."

"Maybe it wasn't on," Rivette said.

"Atlas was working undercover. He was more cautious than that."

"If the system is networked or monitored, it could have been hacked," Breen said.

"That's something we should find out."

"They have offices on Seventeenth and John F. Kennedy Boulevard," Grace said, looking at her phone. "Around the corner from the Comcast Tower."

Williams put the number in his phone and doubled back the way they had come.

"Do they have a business profile?" Breen asked.

"Been in business since 2005. The website says, 'Number One in the Commonwealth.'"

"Of course it does," Breen said. "CEO?"

"Burton Stroud Jr."

While Breen looked up the name Williams headed northwest, following the GPS directions. The admiral had been to the City of Brotherly Love many times during his career. It looked busier than he'd remembered. Probably young people moving in, supplanting the Main Line gentry. For better or worse, that was something else upsetting the traditional order that had been in place for most of his life.

The storefront of Stroud Safe at Home was only one story high and occupied a small footprint on the corner, but it reminded

Williams of every Apple outlet he'd ever visited. The exterior walls were all glass with a white SSAH logo on the door, along with the slogan, "You Can Trust in Stroud." There were white walls and young people in matching black polo shirts working behind a long, black plastic counter.

"The world of Stroud is black and white," Rivette observed.

"And crowded," Grace observed.

"Murder in their backyard, people panic."

"Or perhaps several systems 'went down' and people are complaining," she suggested. She used air quotes, supporting Breen's idea that the shutoff could have been intentional.

Williams pulled to the curb down the block, out of view from inside.

"I think you should go in," he told Breen. "You're the only one in civvies."

"The civilian play won't work. That kind of crowd, my JAG credentials may be useful."

"Makes sense. Whoever you talk to, you'll have to hit them hard. We may not have time for a second turn at bat."

"Planning on it," Breen said as he opened the door.

"Hey, Major?" Rivette said. "My hood, an alarm guy shows up, half the time he's rigging the system so he can go back and steal something."

Breen stopped and looked back. "Nice, Lance Corporal. That may actually be the answer we're looking for."

Rivette beamed a little as Breen walked off.

The major eyed the shop as he approached. He held the door for another man who had arrived simultaneously. Not visible from the street were clear glass shelves holding an assortment of alarms, sensors, panic buttons, locks, and keypads. There were several customers here and others gathered at the sales counter. A man emerged from a pocket door that opened into a back room.

"Good day, Mr. Stroud," a young woman behind the counter said.

"Good day, Ilene."

Breen edged through the crowd and approached the man who had already turned to a customer. The major reached into his shirt pocket and turned on his phone's audio recorder.

"Excuse me, Mr. Stroud, a quick word?"

Stroud turned, a smile half formed on his lips. The movement of his mouth seemed slightly limited by a prominent burn scar on his right cheek.

"If it's quick," Stroud replied with a hint of impatience. He indicated the other customer, who made a disapproving face.

"It will be, I promise. I'm Major Hamilton Breen."

"What can I do for you, *army* Major Breen?"

That surprised the major.

"I'm a former Ranger," Stroud said, making a point of touching the scar. "You acquire an eye, don't you?"

"Apparently some do." Breen smiled. He removed his wallet, showed his identification.

Stroud glanced at it, then looked back at Breen. "Is JAG's interest in my business commercial, Major Breen?"

"Absolutely. We're concerned about security for personnel living off-base at Letterkenny, New Cumberland, and Tobyhanna. I was in the area and thought I would stop by to look into a unified system of security."

"That's a big question, and I have little time, as you can see—"

"Of course. I'll come back later, but I've two quick questions, if you don't mind."

"If they're quick."

"First, how secure are your networks?"

"Have your best JAG IT person try to get into any of my systems. Succeed, and I will write you a check for the cost of the system so you can buy it elsewhere. The second question?"

"Current downgrade detection."

Stroud regarded the man for a long moment. "That's rather specific."

"It happened to my father with his system," Breen said. "Someone detoured the signal with an ancillary line—panel read all's well, but someone created an opening he could slip through."

"That's not possible with a Safe at Home system. When there is a momentary dip in power, as brief as twenty milliseconds, alarms sound at our monitoring desk."

"Which is where?"

"In the basement, staffed 24-7, far from curious eyes."

"Thank you," Breen said. "I'll see you about three?"

"Not much later. I have a call at four."

"I'll be here."

Stroud returned to his impatient customer. The major turned

to go, took a business card from the counter, and stopped. His prosecutorial instinct would not let him leave—not yet.

"One more thing, Mr. Stroud. Didn't you protect that house on Spruce Street? The one that was entered."

Stroud's curious smile returned, but the eyes went cold. "A subscriber must turn the system on for it to be effective. That house was turned off last night."

"I see. Sad."

"And careless."

Breen left, and Stroud looked after him, his smile struggling, his slightly bloodshot eyes lingering until the man was out of sight.

The major returned to the van, pausing only to forward the voice recording to Matt Berry. He handed Williams the card as the others looked on.

"Stroud says the security system is unhackable and confirmed that the Hamill house wasn't turned on. He seemed pretty annoyed about that."

"Gee, that's nice of him," Grace said.

"I don't mean it like that. The man's a former Ranger. There's some pride tied up in this."

"And his livelihood," Grace said. She held up her phone. "His name's on the lawn of a man who was savagely murdered. That's going to take some damage control."

"I'm betting half those people in there want refunds," Rivette said.

"That's not all Stroud has on his mind," Williams said.

"Matt texted to say the ONI plans to see him as soon as their investigation at the house is done and they can question Mrs. Hamill about the alarm—sometime tonight, he guesses."

"I'm not going to wait that long," Breen said.

"What's got you going?"

"Stroud has his monitoring system on-site, in the basement. I want to try and find out more about it, see who has access to it. I told him I'll come back before four."

Williams checked his watch. "That's two hours. It'll be tight, but let's give it a shot." He started the van, then regarded Breen. "You're snagged on something."

Breen nodded. "What you said before. Leaving the alarm off seems like an unforced error on Captain Hamill's part."

Williams headed toward the Lawncrest section of northeastern Philadelphia. As he drove he thought once again about General Diane Karl and a time when the work of protecting the nation did not revolve around the seat of a team's pants . . .

CHAPTER NINE

Atlanta, Georgia
January 16, 1:34 p.m.

After the videoconference, Mark Philpotts felt as if he were made of high-carbon stainless steel. It was a spiritual as well as a physical feeling, as if the strongest of the earth elements had been poured from his hands up his arms and into his body.

With exactly one hour and eight minutes until he and Honda struck, Philpotts was having a late breakfast in the outdoor café at the Piedmont 22 Hotel. He had already bought an old, used Cutlass Supreme, paying cash, and left it in the Publix grocery store parking lot on Piedmont Avenue NE. He had selected a spot far from surveillance; in any case, in the immediate aftermath of the attacks, there would be no reason to look for those two men or that car. Returning, he had done his hour workout at the hotel gym, running and then lifting the fifty-pound free weights. It was a daily regimen the six-foot-four-inch man had begun before enlisting in the Marines and had continued now for four decades.

After that, it was a brisk walk in the damp, misty wintertime Georgia morning. It was a magical time to be out, when there were fragrant hints of the parks and flower beds that defined this region a century and a half before. It was not a time the Black man could think of with anything but revulsion. But that was the point. It had taken a civil war to force change on a self-interested populace. It was time to do so again. Being here, on the very ground trod by slaves, only strengthened his resolve to overthrow what he had dubbed the Brittle Confederacy—a generation of souls who lacked inner strength and so demanded others to support them.

He had gone to check the van where it was parked. He checked to make sure no one had disturbed it, that the tires were full, that the gas cap had not been tampered with.

Following that, invigorated and sharp, Philpotts had returned to the room for the last mission-morning drill: he did his daily, exhausting sets of Silat knife-fighting drills. The Malaysian fighting style was one of many he had learned; he chose this one because it was also effective against large animals, and more and more police departments had K-9 corps. The workout was important this morning because his movements had to be precise. One mistake could tip public sentiment the wrong way.

Mass casualties was an awesome responsibility.

Alert and ready, Philpotts allowed himself to enjoy his leisurely meal.

Honda had remained in the bedroom, the living room providing the room and privacy Philpotts needed to focus on his moves. At fifty-nine years old, he was starting to feel stiffness around both thumbs, especially with the larger Bowie knife. The weapon was sixteen and a half inches long; the hilt required a tight grip, especially with a thumb-on-top forward thrust. He could not afford to lose a stroke. Especially because he would have the smaller, curved karambit blade in his other hand. He practiced with both blades simultaneously, arms pinwheeling asymmetrically, occasionally switching off so he was equally proficient with both blades using his left hand or right.

A five-inch elk skinner was the one Sarno had used to cut Hamill's throat; the karambit was more deeply curved, with finger holes in the grip that also served as a sheath. It was easily concealed in a pocket and perfect for the mission. He wore the Bowie knife up the sleeve of his black windbreaker in a drop-down scabbard. Turning the arm toward the ground caused the hilt to slide from just above the wrist into the palm. The blade was still hidden along his inner forearm, ready for use in a slashing, outward arc.

Between himself and Eiji Honda, this was going to be a historic day. It would not seem glorious from the outside, but the Black Order did not need accolades. What they required was compliance. Philpotts was devoted to Burton Stroud's political goals, of course. Everyone on the team was—with the possible exception of Jackson Poole, who was less of an ideologue than he was someone who seemed to care primarily about what he called Techvox, the multiple forms and layers of tech havocs he could cause *and* control. That was one reason Stroud had kept the electronics wizard close. He did not want the thirty-two-year-old getting bored with the enemy and turning on the Black Order for fun.

"Nation builders must deal with the population they have, or else eradicate them," Stroud had said more than once.

It's funny, Philpotts thought having finished his muesli, half melon, and now drinking his second cup of black coffee. *Stroud could end up killing hundreds, possibly thousands before this matter was concluded, yet you consider him entirely sane and grounded.* Philpotts dismissed these thoughts with a private little snicker. He had not joined the Marines, or then the Black Order, to indulge in abstract reasoning. He had signed up to combat those who saw American manifest destiny as a blight. It took five different fingers to hold a knife. Working separately, with their own self-interest, those five fingers were weak and damn near useless.

Philpotts rose, energized, fueled, and ready. He donned the simple disguise Sarno had made for them. That man was a repository of every post-traumatic tic and pothole a person could suffer, who had lived undercover for as long as that swarthy lunatic had. But among his other skills, he knew disguises. He had made Philpotts a mustache and goatee that were applied with a syrupy collodion-based mix.

"Ladies I knew in Istanbul used it for pasties," the man had explained.

That attested to the adhering policies of the paste. Philpotts had watched those superfast Zeybek dancers online.

There was not a lot of activity in the pool when he left. Most of the guests had gone on the tour of the film studio or were shopping at nearby Piedmont 22. Their ignorance was the nest of his own particular power trip: they did not know it, but many of them were destined to rendezvous with himself and Honda, and a select few of those with destiny.

He did not go through the café door but walked around the rising, curving walk to the front door. The delicate smell of morning had been replaced by the stronger odor of the freshly watered greenery. It filled his nostrils, and the sun warmed him.

He smiled broadly.

Lord God, what a day!

Eiji Honda checked out of the room online.

He had remained in the suite since the videoconference, ordered room service, double-checked his wig and goatee, and was now in the restroom outside the ballroom, in a stall, readying his armory for the mission. He had chosen the lavatory because there were no cameras here. There had been some discussion about holding the room another day, even though it would be unoccupied, but there were families staying on either side. Sometimes things went wrong with explosives.

His part of it would begin when the inevitable shelter-in-place order was announced at this venue.

To all the world, Honda had presented himself and Philpotts as the proprietors of the Supple-Mint Company, manufacturers of mint-based herbal vitamins and cures. Natural cures were a hobby of Honda's, a family practice dating back centuries, and he could talk articulately about saw palmetto and ubiquinol and every type of mint from spearmint to pennyroyal.

Not only were the samples above suspicion, the screw caps made perfect detonators. He had tested them on the Pennsylvania farm. Push down, twist, and the heating element or concussion bolt became active five seconds later, his desired setting. Honda had rigged it so the process could be activated wirelessly from his smartwatch.

He had been sure to promote his wares in the two days they were here, giving away samples and endearing himself to hotel staff and guests with charm and tips. Pleasant and open, he was the last person anyone would expect to be carrying explosives in most of his sample jars. He had been very specific about which compound Taikinys was to deliver to the drop-off point. He wanted only the extremely stable explosive TATB—triaminotrinitrobenzene. The chemicals could not degrade in the changing temperatures and altitudes of a cross-country drive; the explosives could not be so sensitive that rutted roads might jostle them enough to detonate.

Honda and Philpotts had driven a white van they had bought off Craigslist in Philadelphia, for cash. In the back were ladders, brushes, cans of paint, and turpentine, which hid the jars of TATB and grenades. They had business cards that said *Sachem Head Paint* if anyone had asked. If anyone had asked too much, they would have been killed and added to the cargo.

But no one asked, and nothing had gone wrong. The men had not even been stopped for a traffic violation. In a way, the social justice warriors they opposed had done the Asian and the Black man a service. Law enforcement was overly solicitous whenever they passed through construction sites or even a road that had been detoured due to a landslide in the mountains. The two men had even joked about registering as newlyweds, but decided that would be too cynical.

And later, he thought, when forensics finds molecules of plastic and collodion and law enforcement goes looking for Inshiro Tsuburaya and Adam Nicks, they would find no one. The images on the security cameras would show men who wore false mustaches, wigs, beards, and sunglasses—just enough to confuse facial recognition software, according to Jackson Poole.

The checkout was completed ahead of time. The plan was for Honda to take his two suitcases full of samples downstairs and sit in the lobby, waiting for the keynote speech to begin. He had known, from his new best friends at the reception desk, that Ric Samuels had arrived the night before to deliver that address. The fast-rising TV star was not only a passionate advocate of herbal supplements but had also joined with Planned Parenthood to advocate organic, natural abortions to replace surgical procedures.

"It's much safer for the woman," he had said to the *Atlanta Journal-Constitution* just that morning, while carefully avoiding the term "mother" or how obviously *un*safe any abortion was to the fetus.

The man—a brainwashed boy, really—the interview, and the fawning interviewer had been the equivalent of a moral supplement to Honda.

If life is that disposable, then no attendee who survives should have a problem with what Philpotts and I are going to do.

But, of course, the hypocrites would respond with shrill,

tearful hatred. Which is why Stroud had conceived of ways to expose them in the most emphatic way possible.

Before leaving the room, Honda had checked his suitcases full of samples, had a luggage cart brought up, and reviewed in his mind the escape route. He had barely acknowledged Philpotts when his partner came back to the room to change from workout clothes to slacks and a sport jacket, the better to hide his weapons until they were needed.

With a silent nod to Honda and veins flowing with adrenaline, Philpotts left the room for the short walk to his destination to wait for a rendezvous with history.

CHAPTER TEN

The White House, Washington, D.C.
January 16, 1:37 p.m.

"The reality, Mr. President, is that we are tracking an evolving situation," Vice Admiral George Nathan said. "It's highly fluid."

"Excuse me, but what you really mean is you're trying to catch up to and *then* track an evolving situation," the president clarified. "I want to hear reasons, good ones, why we should not bring the FBI, Homeland Security, and the Philadelphia police into this."

Matt Berry was glad Midkiff asked that question, and also called out the ONI director for his painful bureaucratese. Nathan had been summoned to the Oval Office—summoned "with urgency," meaning he was to drop what he was doing and go. Unfortunately, as his summary statement had revealed, the vice admiral had little to offer.

With the noteworthy exception of Chase Williams and Op-Center, the military and intelligence communities routinely tried to sell major screwups as something less. *Misestimation* and *undervaluation* were current buzzwords for unpreparedness. Blaming the entrenched system established by a previous administration was also big. But with the "evolving situation," Nathan had crafted a new level of cover-your-ass. His phrase implied ongoing, systemic vigilance, like his ONI was the vigilant supreme. In fact, on this matter, the ONI had been completely blindsided.

In addition to obfuscating, the director of naval intelligence was defiant, not humbled. He sat on the sofa with Trevor Harward on his left and Matt Berry across from the officer. Nathan was leaning forward, both feet planted solidly on the floor, his hands on his knees as if at any moment he intended to get up and do something more important. But there were tells, just as with Chase Williams. They told a different story. The officer's long face seemed drawn even longer, and his eyes were bloodshot, for two good reasons. First, for over a dozen hours, the "evolving situation" had been putting more and more distance between itself and his investigators. Second, this meeting was going to be less an update than a trip to the woodshed for the man who had not known what was going on in his own organization.

Berry had no desire to watch. He was here, ostensibly as an advisor, but in fact as an observer for Op-Center. He was on his tablet, waiting for intelligence updates from the NYPD. So far, they were few and not worth passing along to Williams. For one thing, as Breen had expected, the pursuit of Leopold Kramer had turned up nothing. And with their secure systems clearly vulnerable, New York law enforcement would not be trusting anything sensitive to the internet.

Sitting beside Berry was Angie Brunner. Even though Wright and the outgoing president held opposing views on most policies, the president-elect felt it would directly undermine Midkiff if he were to take an active hand in this matter. Angie's role was to represent Wright's views as needed.

Even before the election, Berry had been impressed by the woman's instant grasp of issues and politics, if not her fiery liberal views, her sense of entitlement, or her Hollywood-bred inability to accept excuses . . . just results. She was accustomed to hit films, and when the numbers came in low, she demanded answers and heads. By invoking Wright's name, she got them. Berry knew that that would not last, however. The first misstep Wright made—and he would make one—Angie and his staff would be used as cushions.

Angie was the next to speak, having leaned forward in the way she did and gotten an approving nod from the president.

"Admiral, I understand that the Black Order is elusive by design," she said. "What I do not understand, and want to be able to explain to Governor Wright, is how there is no record of the ongoing investigation of this group."

This was part of Nathan's punishment. The person with no seniority got first crack at him.

"We have over seven thousand active investigations at any given time, in over one hundred countries," the silver-haired officer replied. "We contribute to and watch another fifteen hundred with other intelligence branches. All of them are graded from one to ten in terms of priority, ten being the lowest. This was 10M—on the A-to-Z subset—an *extremely* low-burn matter.

The group was a rumor. The group had done nothing that the agent in charge was apparently aware of—"

"Other than to spy on your entire organization."

"I said 'apparently aware of,'" Nathan answered sternly. "That, as you must recognize, is the definition of 'spy.' Major Lewis's investigation did not even have a name for billing. Invoices were folded in with 'miscellany.' There was no obvious need for anyone else to be in the loop. They were busy watching known, active dangers to our nation."

"Which is why all of us are struggling now," Harward jumped in. "In fact, the only reason you were able to contain this is because Captain Hamill had had the foresight to give Major Lewis's number to his wife."

"You're saying that one of our assets actually did the right thing?" Nathan remarked. "Do you also agree that the deep budget cuts to all departments promised by the president-elect are on the money?"

"Trevor, let's fix the system later," President Midkiff said, turning to Nathan, "and it clearly requires fixing. I'm more concerned by what one of the nation's cornerstone intelligence departments still does not know."

"Mr. President," Nathan said, "what we're dealing with here is standard operating procedure for Contact Only Assets who are part of an *unofficial* investigation. It's been that way since 1995, and sensibly, I might add. If you put something in a file, you have to add personnel who have access to that file, others who update the file, others who cross-pollinate the file, others who might leak the file. For a 10M, that is an unrealistic burden."

There went the time-tested ace of spades, Berry thought. *The blame-the-system card.*

"Isn't 'cross-pollination' exactly what the intelligence community is *supposed* to be doing?" Angie asked.

"You're living in 9/11, not today, Ms. Brunner. A veneer of cooperation—and it was just that, a coating—lasted a decade, until Edward Snowden at the CIA leaked classified information from the NSA. Who can blame anyone—especially someone like Major Lewis, who is responsible for the life and security of her operative? Now every scrap of information is quarantined. It has to be. And here's something else to sop up all that indignation. NYPD and DC Met Police share with other agencies. Because the Office of Naval Intelligence is part of that system, and we were compromised, surveillance around the major's building went dark, and so did Lower Manhattan. Because we shared, because we were linked, the perpetrators knew they could get away. What you propose actually emboldened the action."

Well played, Berry thought. In this case, the vice admiral was not wrong.

"So there's another system that needs fixing when this is done," Midkiff said.

"Which one?" Angie asked. "Linked technology or deflecting pertinent questions by magnifying one chink in the system?"

"The lady is referring to a chasm, not a chink," Nathan replied.

Angie smarted more from the designation "lady" than the rebuke itself.

"You want to know our biggest problem?" Berry cut in. "Arguing about match safety while the house burns."

The remark sent everyone to their corners for a moment. Their critical looks at each other, then at him, made Berry glad he did not have a government job to lose. He went back to typing notes for Chase Williams.

"All right," Midkiff said, "if we're done with that, where do we go from here, Admiral Nathan? What is that status of Mrs. Hamill?"

"Her physical and mental states are basically unchanged. We spoke with her. She had no idea where her husband hunted. The last few times he did not bring home any game—but he didn't seem disappointed. He said—she thinks—he hiked looking for bear . . . but she may be confused. He never called or texted from the woods. We checked her phone for photographs her husband may have sent from the field—there weren't any. Captain Hamill understood how things worked."

"What help can we get from law enforcement and the other intelligence services?"

"Mr. President, there is another reason I've embargoed the sharing of information. Electronically, the point of entry for the dark web hack was a satellite uplink to our Irregular Warfare–centric intelligence center. NSA has ties to that information through component supply lines. Because Captain Hamill had been compromised, we assume that someone Major Lewis knew or someone at NSA Philadelphia learned of his activities. That's why we brought in personnel from NSA Mechanicsburg."

"Why assume that?" Berry asked. "The dark web overlay

could just as easily have been created in North Korea, Russia—anywhere."

"That's right. But it's unlikely the captain would have been investigating them."

"The gunrunner, Taikinys, mentioned cartels," Angie said.

"Also possible, though the ONI has no interest in or jurisdiction over Drug Enforcement Administration operations."

"Wisely," Berry said. "The DEA won't even let the FBI know who their undercover people are. Friendly fire is a real risk."

"I mention them because Taikinys may not be your only problem. We've heard they traffic deadlier materials to and from former Soviet republics, through Venezuela and Cuba."

"Not traffic," Harward said. "They use them to extort concessions from other cartels and the government. Risky sneaking toxins across the border in secondhand hazmat containers. A trail of death would lead right back to the point of origin."

Berry made a note to pass that information along to Williams. Harward was right, but a slow-leak canister might be just the kind of delivery system a terrorist might want.

"Back on topic, please," Midkiff said with growing impatience. "Do we know who at the NSA Captain Hamill remained in contact with after his retirement?"

"His replacement, Captain Ann Ellen Mann, for one. We're checking her contacts and movements for the last few months. We're looking to see if there were others."

"Are we still concerned that the bad guys are watching what we do?" Angie asked.

"No. They self-blinded when they shut their system down. That's another reason for keeping this internal and nonelectronic. We have a covert unit from Counter Proliferation ready to go in as soon as we have something actionable. We don't want to tip our hand."

"Go in where?" Harward asked.

"At a site of interest," Nathan answered.

Berry caught Angie's short, probing look in his direction. She obviously had the same thought he did: Midkiff would have to okay any Counter Proliferation mission, but those troops would not be informed about Black Wasp. If there were tactical convergence, Williams's people might be mistaken for hostiles. Berry would have to let him know if such a move were imminent.

"All right," Midkiff said. "If we let ONI continue to handle this on their own, how soon do we see results?"

"Mr. President, we are still—"

"*Ballpark,*" the president demanded.

"This evening sometime. I'm sorry I can't be more precise than that. Every resource we have is on it. What we cannot afford, in the meantime, is to have other agencies, through territorial haste or unfamiliarity, getting in there and destroying the enemy's footprints."

Harward shook his head. "This is nuts. First ONI misses this thing entirely, now you're arguing for an extension."

"Mr. Harward, *everyone* missed it," Nathan replied. "Homeland Security has an entire division monitoring the dark web. They missed it. The FBI watches for domestic terrorism. They missed it. The National Reconnaissance Office was watching the movements of the arms dealer who provided the initial intel to Major Lewis. The major should have—*would* have—informed her superiors if she thought the investigation itself had triggered something of immediate significance."

"Two assassinations and a homicide," Harward said. "A self-declared war. I would say that's 'immediate significance.'"

"Hindsight is proving to be your chief skill set," Nathan snapped.

Berry quietly cheered that one. Nathan had crossed the line, but so had Harward.

The president once again called off both dogs with a look that was now more exhausted than stern. It was an expression that Berry interpreted as, *I've done this for too long.*

"All right, we were caught flat-footed," Midkiff said. "None of us is happy about that. Matt, you had some questions for our timeline."

The punt had been prearranged. Op-Center needed as much information as possible, and Berry was the one to get it. Both Nathan and Harward seemed mildly perplexed.

"Angie's in this too," Berry said inclusively. "There are a few gaps we'd like filled about last night."

"If I can."

"Walk us through Major Lewis's night, if you can."

"I'll have to work from memory—as I said, there's nothing electronic."

"I'm sure that's fine."

"At 11:24, Major Lewis received the call from Sophia Hamill's cell phone—"

"Let's back up. Do we know what the major's actions were before the call?"

"She went to dinner with a friend. We know that from a reservation she made at Beppo's. It was with a woman. We talked to the maître d'. The major seemed relaxed, laughing, but that's all he could tell us."

"Surveillance of the other woman?" Harward asked. "Or did the Black Order knock it out?"

"They did not. The major was out of uniform, and the image we have of her companion is a woman in a floppy felt hat and a scarf, a generic shoulder bag—"

"So the evening was personal."

"As far as we know. The major did not sign a PDP. We have just secured a court order to access her private email and social media accounts."

Personal Data Permission allowed certain government employers to access an employee's private email accounts. Berry was not surprised Major Lewis had not granted that permission. The military frowned on outside activism, and Major Lewis's personal file came to a hard stop at the Lucinda Project.

"The major was off duty?" Berry asked.

"Yes, and in civilian attire, which tells us that the Black Order and Captain Hamill's mission were not on her radar. The major was still out when Mrs. Hamill called, had just phoned for an Uber. After she got in the car—alone, according to the driver—she phoned an aide, Lieutenant Catherine Sabal. She said she was going home."

"Why was Lieutenant Sabal still on duty?"

"The lieutenant's shift is from six p.m. to four a.m., I think it was. The major told the woman to wait for instructions, said she wanted to get to her tablet and would be in touch. The lieutenant was not in the loop on this project. Still isn't. She never heard from Major Lewis."

"The tablet?"

"Melted in the fire. But the major issued one general alert to her superior, Colonel Jared Chipkin, saying only that a COA had apparently been murdered, that the 10M was upgraded to 1B—it went to 1A after confirmation of the death was received—and that any information should be locked down."

"Because she feared spies or leaks?"

Nathan nodded.

"Was there anyone she might have confided in who wasn't navy?" Angie asked. "A friend? A colleague at another agency?"

"There is nothing on her work devices. We are in the process of talking to family members—who are cooperating but distracted, as you can imagine. We have located a few college friends, but they haven't given us anything relevant. Neighbors in the building say Major Lewis was personable but kept to herself."

"Where do we stand interviewing Mrs. Hamill?" Berry asked.

"She's still under the effects of the initial treatment."

"Do you know what was administered?"

Nathan thought for a moment. "Halo something."

"Haloperidol?" Angie asked.

"That's it."

"Very high on the sedation scale," Angie said. "Who made that call?"

"The attending naval physician in the ambulance, and I agree. We've spoken with him and the other EMTs. Mrs. Hamill was barely coherent, she was screaming, and what information she provided was unreliable. She was talking about a dark face, a whisper, pain—there was a cut in her side, presumably from a knifepoint. She said something about her husband hunting bear or couldn't bear something—none of it was clear."

"There are twenty thousand bears in the state," Berry said, reading from his tablet. "Would ONI have had any interest in them?"

"Is that a joke?"

"It isn't, Admiral. The Soviets had a plan to infect California bear with rabies, make it unsafe to timber there."

"To my knowledge, Mr. Berry, that was not on anyone's radar."

Berry forwarded the results of the interview to Williams.

Nathan went on. "A more immediate concern was the panic Mrs. Hamill might have caused being removed from the house in that state."

"Security was not yet in place," Berry said. "The Philadelphia police might have gotten there first."

"That's right, Mr. Berry. I okayed that decision." Nathan regarded the president. "Sir, we have a large and active investigation ongoing. I'd like to get back to Suitland."

He was referring to the Suitland Federal Center, home of the Nimitz Operational Intelligence Center, the heart of the ONI.

"If that's all there is?" Midkiff looked at Berry, who was typing. "One more question," Berry said. "Have you determined anything about how the killer gained access to the Hamill home?"

"The home operates by a keypad access, four digits linked to the alarm system, which appears to have been turned off."

"So the door was unlocked."

"That appears to be the case," Nathan agreed.

"Does that make sense for a man who was doing intelligence work, who lives in Philadelphia, and—I checked—whose front door is seven feet from a SEPTA bus stop?"

"Are you married, Mr. Berry?"

"What does that have to do with anything?"

"Are you?" Nathan pressed.

"Not anymore. Why?"

"My wife and I assume that the other does things, like taking out the trash or turning off the garage light. That may have been the case here."

"I see," Berry said. "Point taken."

"Sorry." Trevor raised a finger. "Before you go, Admiral: the press hasn't linked the three attacks. Mr. President, who's going to take point when they do?"

"Governor Wright asked the same question," Angie said.

"So did my press secretary," Midkiff said. It had clearly not been a top priority.

"We should keep the announcement as small as possible," Harward said. "If we open in the East Room, there's nowhere else to go."

"Announcing here would also give the war legitimacy," Midkiff said. "If we let Navy Public Affairs handle it, at least for now, it will seem smaller."

"I'm not so sure about that," Berry said, looking up from his tablet. "How will the terrorists react to the demotion?"

"My concern as well," Angie said. "If the message is too small, they'll dress the set with dead bodies."

Berry had to look away. The Hollywood reference was trivial and incongruous.

"I don't think it will change a thing," said Nathan, who had gone halfway to the door but turned. "They've played the media. The uninformed but graphic images from Philadelphia and Washington made the morning news. The New York attack was on the East Coast news at noon. I believe the plan is set, whatever it is."

"I'm sure Governor Wright will agree, though I want to request that no form of the word 'terror' be used."

The men froze.

"Why not?" Berry asked, gladly taking the bullet and hoping his disgust showed.

"Because we do not know the identity or interests of the perpetrators. This will turn people against the traditional suspects."

"The Irish Republican Army? Japan's Aum Shinrikyo?"

"Don't be insulting, Mr. Berry," Angie said. "You know exactly what I mean."

"I agree with Angie," the president said, "but not because of racial sensitivity. We should keep the panic at as low a boil as possible, at least until we have more information. That word will raise fears. Having the navy announce may also force the perpetrators to speak a little louder. Now that we're watching, we may pick up a trail."

Berry shrugged. Angie sat tight-lipped and said nothing.

"I'll inform Public Affairs," Nathan said, then left.

"That was a stupid answer," Angie said.

"At least it was honest," Berry remarked.

The woman's frustration was understandably the highest in the room; at this pace, the problem would not only belong to Wright, it would taint the inauguration.

Trevor rose and regarded the president. "I'll let the press secretary know to drop-kick inquiries to ONI for now."

"Thank you," the president said.

Harward followed the vice admiral out. The door shut behind him with a heavy click.

The president smiled mirthlessly. "That is one of my favorite and least favorite sounds. It shuts out the career bureaucrats and pass-the-buck officials, but it also locks the problems they cause in."

Angie did not seem in the mood for reflection. The president turned to his deputy chief of staff. "Please tell me that Op-Center is further along than Nathan and his people."

Berry finished sending Williams the last of his notes, then regarded the other two. He was grinning.

"The team went to the Hamill house where Chase did the recon personally. They are on their way to the NSA. He wants to talk to Captain Mann. But none of that is the headline." He leaned forward. "They're looking into the possible involvement of Stroud Safe at Home, the firm that provided the security system to the Hamill home."

"What would their interest be?" Midkiff asked.

"Chase doesn't know."

"Then I don't understand—"

"Sir, I just checked them out and notified Chase. Stroud Safe at Home not only handled the Hamill home, they have a contract to provide security to the NSA and other military assets and residences throughout Pennsylvania and New Jersey."

Midkiff did not seem impressed. "Then it makes sense that Atlas would have used them."

"Getting a good deal is not where I'm going," Berry said. "You heard what Nathan said. The Irregular Warfare–centric intelligence center was the point of entry for dark web access—"

"And he said it's linked to NSA Philadelphia," Angie said with rising enthusiasm. "We should let ONI—"

"No!" the president said. "We tell no one."

"Not even the Philadelphia PD?" Angie said. "They know the city."

"We don't know *them.* The buck isn't the only thing that stops at this desk. Highly sensitive information does too. It must. Don't let Governor Wright learn that lesson when he's got special ops on the ground in some foreign hellhole."

Angie sat back with a look that was part disgust, part resignation.

And that, Berry thought, *is why the system will never change.*

CHAPTER ELEVEN

Naval Support Activity, Philadelphia, Pennsylvania
January 16, 2:30 p.m.

Built in 1942 and known as the Navy Aviation Supply Depot during World War II, the Naval Support Activity Philadelphia covers 134 acres, most of that by warehouse and office facilities supporting local navy units. Presently, the primary occupants of the base are the Defense Logistics Agency and Naval Supply Systems Command. Other forces have a presence in the U.S. Air Force Clothing & Textile and the U.S. Army Recruiting Battalion, Mid-Atlantic.

The news about Stroud's navy contract reached Black Wasp as they approached the base.

"Can't say I'm surprised," Breen said. "The military buys everything in bulk."

"Guess that means we have to watch what we say in there," Rivette said. "Big Brother may be listening."

"That should apply to everywhere," Grace said.

"It didn't in Yemen."

"We were being chased, and no one spoke English," she reminded him.

"A rule is a rule, yeah?"

Grace let it drop.

The news about the CP operation did not bother either Williams or Breen. The navy would not be dropping a team into Philadelphia, and there were no other targets on the radar. Not yet.

If and when there is, we'd damn well better be the first ones in, Williams thought. His team beating the others to an objective would be a personal coup.

Breen closed his tablet as they neared the gate. "The health clinic seems the logical place to have taken her."

"Most likely, but I want to see Captain Mann first."

"Really? Do you know her?"

"Not even by reputation. But I'm hoping she's heard of me and is feeling a little bit marginalized. It'll make our job easier."

"You mean just still gathering information," Rivette said. The young man was not accustomed to the sidelines and was clearly getting restless.

"That's right."

"Are you going to tell her about Black Wasp?" Grace asked.

"I am not." He looked in the rearview mirror and grinned. "Navy bonds are one thing. Trusting someone with our lives and mission is something else."

"Just checking," the woman said.

"You were right to," Williams said. He knew the two

warriors had to feel diminished. On Black Wasp's previous two outings, he and Breen had not taken the lead.

The van reached the squat, brick guardhouse at the front gate. The flag was at half-staff in honor of Atlas Hamill. Beside it, a concrete security barrier funneled traffic into a single lane. The barricade was relatively new; it had not yet had time to acquire the droppings of the harbor birds that circled above. A two-inch-diameter metal bar stretched yard-high across the road. There was a tire deflation system just beyond that.

There were no other vehicles on the access road, and Williams felt a sense of homecoming as he pulled up. The uniforms, the style and colors of the signage, the faint smell of the sea as he rolled down the window; it was all a big welcome sign from the United States Navy. How could so many years gone by—six, seven—since he had felt that?

The guard came around to the driver's side and saluted smartly.

"Admiral, sir. Welcome to NSA Philadelphia."

Williams returned the salute and read the man's name tag. "Thank you, Warrant Officer Edwards. Somber day."

"Yes, sir, it is. How may I help you?"

"Admiral Chase Williams and party to see Captain Mann."

"Is the captain expecting you?"

"No. We did not expect to be stopping here on this tour."

A look of consternation settled on the man's beefy features. He peered in at the rest of the team, then stepped back. "I'll phone the captain's office, sir. See what I can do."

"Again, thanks."

The warrant officer made his way back to where a second guard had been watching.

"If I tried that, they'd send a squad of MPs or MAs or whatever they've got here," Rivette remarked, peering ahead. "Or the director of psychological health."

"There doesn't seem to be added security," Breen said, looking around.

"When you don't know who the enemy is, who would watch the watchers?" Williams asked.

"The watchers are on the roof, aimed right at us," Rivette said. He was pointing at the two-story building to the northeast. "Remote-controlled .50 caliber, looks like hundred-round belt. Can punch through nineteen-millimeter steel armor at forty-five hundred feet. Someone tries to get past the guard, they get dead-slapped."

"Nice get," Williams said. "They're portable?"

"Packs down to the size of a car seat. Hasn't been there too long, either. Remote operator is making little movements—see the sun glinting, changing? They're still calibrating."

"Why not just have someone like Jaz up there, the way they do at the White House?" Grace asked.

"Because bad guys got snipers too. This close to the gate, they could take a sharpshooter and the guards out before rolling in. Or if they're buying smuggled arms, Turkey's got a machine gun drone—eight blades, two hundred rounds, armored against return fire."

"Combat by proxy," Grace said. "A new *Art of War.*"

Williams was less concerned about the future than about

the present, and he was glad someone at ONI was on the ball. He was also proud of the lance corporal. Again and again he was reminded that whatever his thoughts about a generational gap between himself and the world, he admired professionals.

The guard returned with a proud bounce in his step . . . and a bar code pass for the window. Williams was surprised to see his own face on it.

"This will raise the bar, sir. Directions to HQ will be transmitted directly to your GPS."

"What if I take a detour?" he asked. "It's been a while since I've been here."

"Seven years, eight months," the guard said. "We'll get a ping when you go off path. But given your rank and clearance, sir, we can overlook that."

"Much appreciated," the admiral said.

The noncom returned to the guardhouse, and Williams edged the car forward.

"Wait for the bar to elevate," the car system informed him.

"Everything by proxy," Breen noted.

"How many years before we're all obsolete?" Williams wondered.

"The fact that we're here where ELINT failed answers that, I think," Breen replied.

After a moment, the bar lifted, the spikes in the road rolled down, and Williams eased the van in. He pressed a well-worn button as the van drove past the gate.

The narrow streets were more than just empty, they seemed deserted.

"Nobody coming or going anywhere," Rivette said.

Williams drove past the first row of buildings, Defense Logistics Agency Troop Support, on his way to the Department of the Navy offices. He detoured here to swing past the parking areas.

"Spaces are full," the admiral noted.

"Why wouldn't they be?" Breen asked.

"I don't know about JAG, but half-staff is time for navy personnel to mourn. Civilians are typically invited to stay home."

"In case the investigation turned up leads, I'm guessing ONI wanted everyone who should be here *to* be here," Breen said.

"Substance over form," Williams said. He stopped in the parking spot indicated by the automated system. Base HQ was directly ahead.

"What are you going to tell Captain Mann, and what can we do in the meantime?" Breen asked.

"I'm going to stick as close to the truth as possible. I'll say the president asked me to look into the death of my old friend."

"If she asks about the rest of us?"

"I'll say you're here for legal counsel if needed, Jaz and Grace for security."

"But you're not expecting any of that to happen," Rivette said.

"Correct."

The lance corporal slumped back.

"I have a lot of questions for the captain, things only she might know. In the meantime, here's what I need from the rest of you." Williams pointed to the map on the GPS. "If Mrs. Hamill is in the Naval Health Clinic here, we need to know. Go look it over."

"I doubt we'll get permission to see her," Breen said.

"How bad do we want permission?" Rivette asked with rising enthusiasm.

"We can't afford to be held here," Williams said. "Keep that in mind."

"We'll do a drive-by, see what makes sense," Breen said. "Text me when you need a pickup."

"Sounds good," Williams said and left the van. Breen came around to the driver's side.

"Doesn't sound good to me," Rivette said. "Five minutes inside could save us five hours of getting nowhere."

"You may not be wrong," Breen said. He nodded toward the guns. "Then again, you may not get out."

The lance corporal slipped lower in the seat, and Breen eased the van forward.

The admiral stood in the comparatively warm sunlight as he took a moment to unfold legs and fingers and look at the base website on his phone. He read the short biography of Captain Ann Ellen Mann. She was a Miami native who, like himself, attended the U.S. Naval Academy. Unlike himself, she made Superintendent's List Honors every semester at Annapolis. She spoke Pashto and had served as an interpreter in Afghanistan, taking part in a clandestine August 2011 effort to find and destroy the Taliban fighters who shot down a Chinook. The attack on the helicopter had resulted in the death of thirty U.S. soldiers, including seventeen SEALs who were part of the Naval Special Warfare Development Group. The special forces' objective was achieved, though then lieutenant Mann—moving impulsively to protect a bomb maker handcuffed to a desk where he was providing key intelligence—took a bullet in the hip that put her in the Landstuhl Regional Medical Center in Germany for five months. The Secretary of the Navy Vector 7 Education for Seapower report cited her as being among the top five percentile of "experience-rich" officers.

Williams wondered what a translator and combatant was doing here, running a supply line. He also wondered how the security downgrade sat with her. On the Taliban mission, interrogating locals for sensitive information, she would have been at mid-level clearance: "secret." Here, she probably held the bottom-level "confidential": what arms and systems were being dispatched where.

Which meant she probably did not know anything about the Black Order. She had most likely agreed to see Williams for what she might learn. He had no intention of being "first light," revealing that top secret information.

The Op-Center director continued toward the HQ. He entered, returned the salute of the guard, and was directed to the captain's office. He walked slowly, giving his eyes time to adjust to the lower light. He passed photographs of past commanders on the wall. Someone had hung black crepe on the picture of Atlas Hamill.

An adjutant stood, saluted, and bid the admiral to enter.

The room was small and sunny. The captain stood with some small effort and saluted when Williams entered. She was tall, just under six feet, and solemn looking. He had no idea whether her expression was due to lack of sleep, sadness over Captain Hamill, or something deeper. Possibly all three. Officers were forced to keep a lot of garbage buttoned up under the tight uniform.

"Thank you for seeing me," Williams said as he returned the salute.

"I'm honored by your visit, sir. And that's not flattery. Please sit."

Williams smiled and eased into a leather armchair. It was creased enough to have been here since early in Atlas's tenure. The admiral had a flash of something bittersweet.

The captain sat with some effort. "Is your visit personal or official?"

"Both. I knew Captain Hamill. He was well liked. The president asked me to assess morale."

"Mine or the base?"

"Both."

Mann smiled appreciatively. "You have a reputation for honesty and clarity."

"I also demand it. Blown sunshine doesn't do anyone any good."

"In my experience, sir, neither does complaining."

"If you answer my questions about yourself and the base truthfully, I can handle the rest."

"All right," she said, settling in her seat. "Since I've been in my office all day under orders, I will address my morale first."

"Who issued those orders, Captain?"

"Vice Admiral González, U.S. Fleet Cyber Command."

The information confirmed what the president had said at the outset. USCYBERCOM was a Unified Combatant Command under that larger umbrella. Vice Admiral Nathan had obviously hot-lined the urgent need to secure NSA Philadelphia.

"You were saying," Williams urged. "About morale?"

"It's low, sir. Part of that is the loss of Captain Hamill. I liked him. Everyone did, so there's that. And I'm not afraid that someone's killing captains, despite the . . . I'm sure you've read what was said to Mrs. Hamill. It's in the medical report."

"Yes."

"The warning about people dying has made its way around the base. Personnel are wondering if we're going to be ground zero for this war."

"I have no information about that, Captain. The automated guns—?"

"I sat down with my next in command, Commander Hall, and consulted the plan our security advisors drew up—"

"Was the Stroud organization part of the team?"

"Not directly, but this part of the system was part of the original white paper they prepared for us. So the turrets and keeping the streets clear were precautions I was able to recommend to USCYBERCOM. And your being here tells me something."

"What is that?"

"Why I had to get approval for what should have been my

call. The president reached outside of channels to bring you in. Vice Admiral González sent over Mechanicsburg masters-at-arms. Makes me wonder: Is the navy leaking?"

"There is that assumption." Williams did not want to say too much, but he had to be careful not to insult the captain's intelligence.

"Am I a suspect, Admiral?"

"Until the threat is neutralized, that would be my assumption."

She smiled thinly. "Well, as I said—honesty." She put her hands flat on the desk, looked at them. "Sir, you have the ear of which president? The current one?"

"Yes."

"Good. He'll be too busy to retire me for saying this." She looked at him. "I want to express my disappointment in the navy. If you are of a mind, tell the commander in chief that I've helped pull corpses, friends' corpses, from the desert sand. I had to brush blackened flesh to get that sand off so I could read the dog tags. I have walked in places women, let alone Christian women, should not have gone. Yet I was informed this morning that I could not set foot in the place where my predecessor was killed. That, sir, and putting it bluntly, is why my morale stinks."

"You are right to be disappointed. I would be too."

"Thank you. If you'll pardon a judgment, sir?"

"Speak your mind."

"If the navy has its fears about security, they should have gotten their asses over here and asked me about the fourteen tenant commands and their officers. They're untouchable. Instead, they've locked us down, refused to share information, and outsourced security. Tell the president our morale is what the navy has made it."

"Your morale is what makes the navy, Captain."

"Yes, sir. There is that. I requested a contingent from the Chaplain Corps. The navy has not yet responded."

Williams suspected she was serious, and he smiled for the first time. The mood in the room was suddenly more relaxed.

"Captain, how close were you and Captain Hamill?" Williams asked. "Daily contact? Weekly?"

"Nothing like that," she said. "I saw him when he came by. There was nothing social, except the annual Christmas party."

"Did he ever talk about what he was doing?"

"He said he went hunting a lot. He seemed happy."

"Did he say where he hunted?"

She thought for a moment. "Western part of the state. I don't know that he ever mentioned a spot, specifically."

"He never showed you photographs?"

"Twice, I think. He didn't take the usual posing-with-your-kill pictures. They were of deer being off-loaded with members of the Veterans Advisory Commission for an organization he founded to feed needy veterans." Captain Mann allowed herself a critical look. "Was Captain Hamill under suspicion of wrongdoing? Is that what this is about?"

"It is not." The statement was short and final, designed to keep the man's name clean. Williams was prepared to stake his reputation—and more than that, the safety of the nation—on that belief.

"Do you know if he went hunting with anyone?" Williams asked.

"If he did, he never mentioned it. When I saw him, he mostly asked how things were going with me, if I needed advice, if I wanted him to set anybody straight about anything. I think—I *suspect*—he knew I was not entirely happy here, desk-bound and landlocked, so he made an extra effort."

"Did he ever mention any concerns, fears, anything about being in personal danger?"

"No," she said, then shook her head and stopped. "Well, maybe. I made some comment about him going hunting. He said the game was different and he was looking forward to it. I let it pass. I thought he meant, I don't know, wild turkey instead of deer. But I thought about it later. He had a strange look, like he wasn't swapping one animal for another. It had a different kind of focus to it."

"Captain Hamill's old computer files here," Williams said. "Were they locked?"

"Welded," Mann replied.

"I'm sorry?"

"That's what my IT man calls it when your own code is overwritten by an outside agency. I had Captain Hamill's password. As soon as I heard what had happened, I went to secure the files, assuming that might be what someone was after. The code had already been changed, the files sealed."

"On whose authority?"

"The order was signed by ONI assistant director Greg Wetzel, Intelligence Group. My files were also locked. I had to call

NSA Mechanicsburg to find out why his personnel were entering my base."

"Who runs the NSA there?"

"Captain Walter York. He was the one who called me, trying to find out what was going on. We are both deeply in the dark. That was before the ONI followed up with a D2."

"All personnel?"

"Everyone."

D2 was a "Don't Discuss" order that applied both inter- and intra-base. It meant that if anyone at NSA Philadelphia had suspicions of wrongdoing, they were not to discuss them, even with Captain Mann. The same was true about Mann and York. Someone might know or suspect or even stumble on the truth, tell the wrong person, and end up like Atlas Hamill. The order meant that all personnel were to wait for an ONI debrief, and there was no one on base with the rank to countermand that directive. That was one reason no one was about except on essential base business. Sailors liked to talk, and talk could deliver you to a court-martial.

Mann sat back. "There's also a curfew order, of sorts. I'm here till six. Commander Dick Brandon is here for the next twelve. We're to be local and available at *all* times."

"I see."

Once again, Williams wished he could say more. But the dark web investigation was top secret, and he was not at liberty to reveal what had happened.

"A personal question, if I may?" Williams said.

"By all means."

"Did you ever file a transfer request with Naval Personnel?"

"Every six months, after each previous one was turned down. Unfortunately, I'm a valuable PR pawn."

Mann had already said that she had no fondness for complaint. She stopped there. Nonetheless, Williams opened his hands, encouraging her to continue.

She sat still, but then it came out.

"A woman, wounded in combat, in charge of a base. I'm the go-to poster person of the *Navy Times*. To them, I've overcome adversity. To me, I'm a victim of it. When Captain Hamill was here, he was one of the human faces of the navy for the reasons stated. I'd rather be that."

"The navy is jealous of its assets."

"That's one way of putting a positive spin on things, sir."

"Here's another. I'm not sure how long my assignment will keep me in Philadelphia. If I call, will you be available?"

"If Vice Admiral González would agree, I would agree."

"I can make that happen."

"Then absolutely." She gave him her card, and he entered the number on his phone. "May I ask for what?"

"Can't tell you that, but before my assignment here is through, I may need people I can trust."

There was new life in her eyes, along with gratitude in her smile. She wrote the number of her personal cell phone on a Post-it and handed it across the desk.

"Whatever you need, sir, just ask. And please tell the president something."

"What's that?"

"My morale is definitely on the upswing."

Williams rose, and Mann did likewise. The captain was smiling now.

"Thank *you* for your assistance," the admiral said.

"Thank *you* for involving me, and even more for your trust."

Williams had looked into the eyes of countless sailors and officers over the decades. In them, he had seen countless grades of elation and pride, psychological hurt and physical pain, loss and disappointment; sometimes combinations that came in waves.

Mann's eyes showed none of the frustrations she had expressed. Even in pain, in disappointment, she was as steadfast as every officer on every bridge he had ever visited. Hurting though she might be, she held tight to the luster of the Annapolis undergraduate she had once been.

Her eyes, like the woman herself, were unbowed navy.

CHAPTER TWELVE

Naval Support Activity, Philadelphia, Pennsylvania
January 16, 2:32 p.m.

Major Breen pulled up to the curb facing the health center. He put the van in park but left it running and looked across the street.

Two stories tall, the health center was an austere brick building with two thin gray columns supporting a flat gray canopy. Beyond it were two sliding doors. Like the rest of the administrative buildings, it was designed to be functional rather than evocative of the city's historic past. The history buff in him felt it a missed opportunity.

Breen paid careful attention to the MAs who stood on either side of the double door. The sun was behind the building, the guards' features in shadow. If they had pulled a twelve-hour-plus shift, they still seemed alert.

Or maybe they had frozen there once the sun passed over.

Grace and Rivette were once again leaning between the front seats.

"The admiral wanted us to reconnoiter," Rivette said. "I don't think he meant sitting here like this."

"What are those sentries holding?"

"The firearms? M4A1 assault rifles," Rivette said. "Why?"

"Used by the SEALs."

"Right. And?"

"They aren't for show."

"Right. *So?*"

"I just want to be clear about your mission objective," Breen said.

"Reconnoiter," Rivette said and looked out. "Do you really think they'd shoot fellow soldiers?"

"We don't know who is on our side . . . and neither do they. We don't want to find out by provoking them."

"We can still walk around," Grace told Rivette. "We have a base pass."

"I thought we *came* here to talk to Mrs. Hamill."

"Missions change," Breen said.

Grace had had enough talk. She zipped her wool-lined bomber jacket, rolled her arms to flex the sleeves and get blood flowing, and popped the door. "Let's go."

Rivette had to stifle the urge to reach for his bag. The empty holster on his hip had been bothering him.

"We've done this drill," Breen said. "Deconstruct the camp of an adversary from one turn around the perimeter. If—*if*—we have to come back for Mrs. Hamill, we need to know if there are other automated systems on rooftops and what the arc of fire is. How many masters-at-arms are there? What does the rear gate look like?"

"Yeah, I got it," Rivette said. He stepped from the van and joined Grace in the back. "Southern California, I miss you," he said as he wrapped a scarf under his chin.

Breen watched as the two walked off. He still was not entirely certain they would stick to the plan. There were times when the cockiness of Rivette and the lone-wolf cool of Grace grated his team sensibilities. But the military was partly responsible for nurturing those traits. Armed and martial confrontation were in their blood. This was not a courtroom trial with recesses and built-in delays. This was high-stakes surveillance with two kinds of danger: the one they had discussed and the ones they did not know.

As Breen watched them go, he was concerned that there was likely to be more of the latter than the former. And in spite of what the two Black Wasps had been sent to do, he was not entirely convinced they would—or could—stick to that plan. It would be a coup to leave with Mrs. Hamill, and those two were big on overperforming.

Which was why he had left the van running.

Grace and Rivette were walking down a street that ran perpendicular to Route 232. The road they were on was the equivalent of a six-lane highway with parking in the center two lanes.

"You could have a helluva street race here," Rivette said, puffs of white breath coming from over his scarf.

Grace ignored him. She knew, from drilling, that she

would be doing the actual reconnoitering and Rivette would be providing color.

A short orbit of the health center revealed that the back of the building was almost a replica of the front, but without the canopy. There was a double door, two guards, and rows of big windows above. There were very few naval personnel about. Part of that was the cold, but most of it was probably the lockdown.

"This place reminds me of Naval Support Activity Bahrain," Rivette said. "I went there to compete once. It was a long ride away but a lot warmer. Didn't mind that."

"The military is like McDonald's," Grace said. "Stamp out the patties and dress them the same. Only the size is different."

Rivette laughed. "You come up with some good ones sometimes." He was looking ahead. "They got more automated systems ahead."

"On the Navy Exchange building, I saw."

"Back there?" he said, cocking a thumb toward the van. "I didn't really need my guns. The sentries have some. I can use those."

"Yes, but no."

"What do you mean?"

"You're not taking them."

"Back up. You saying we're not going for the lady? I thought that's why we're here!"

"You thought that because you tuned out for most of the ride. Drill lesson, about four months ago. Remember the difference between a 'wish list' and a 'to-do' list?"

"That stuff the major talks about? It's mostly theory. This is real. The war is real. We are *here*. Hell, we *live* on a base. This'd be like breaking into our own house."

"That makes no sense."

"Neither does two elite soldiers, who do nothing but train for situations like this, whose job this exactly is, walking around with their hands in their pockets doing nothing but fighting with their eyeballs."

Jaz was not wrong: he had just quoted, in part, their transfer papers to Fort Belvoir. But Grace saw the other side too.

"Jaz, the admiral is right. We can't afford to be detained."

"We won't be—"

"Be quiet and *think* for a second. If we make the call to go in, we are *all in*. That means taking out the guards and anyone who tries to stop us."

"That's what war is, yeah?"

"That means those machine guns firing down on us—"

"That won't happen. Arc of fire has to be high; otherwise, they'd shoot out their own windows and the people behind them. We stay low, we're good."

"Except for the sentries and their weapons."

"Two grunts against two Wasps? That's got you *worried*? On the ride? I *was* listening. You know what word I heard over and over? 'War.' Have you considered that the lady in the ward may know something to prevent the rest of this shit from happening?"

"Or she could still be sedated, and we make things worse by kidnapping her, fighting the Black Order *and* the navy."

"Okay, so we don't grab her. We get in, slap her awake, ask

questions, leave. Get the hell off the base on foot, hide somewhere, and text the major where to find us."

"Jaz, please be quiet."

The lance corporal shivered, as much from frustration as from the cold. "Am I the only one who understands that what we're doing right now is playing defense, and that is not what Black Wasp does for a living?"

Grace did not respond.

"We have just, for the first time, walked past a target," Rivette said. "I'm ashamed of us."

Again, Grace did not entirely disagree. But NSA Philadelphia was a koi pond with gun turrets and piranha. An attack *would* be repulsed unless they were willing to kill. And she was not.

Then again, she thought, *reconnoitering does not just mean looking.*

The options might be more nuanced than in the past. That was one reason Williams had taken the lead; it was not necessary to mow enemies down to reach the target. There were other tactics they could employ.

They reached the far side of the building and turned left toward where the van was parked. It was still idling. Grace considered the situation a moment longer, then turned back toward the rear entrance of the health facility. She studied the guards.

"What?" Rivette asked.

"Let's talk to them," she said.

"Talk about what? They probably never even saw Mrs. Hamill."

"People talk on the way to their cars. Maybe they heard some ONI investigator say something."

Rivette was looking past her. "Hold up."

"After all that? What's—?"

"Let's keep going the way we were going, like we're heading back to the van. I may be looking at our war."

Grace turned and looked around casually. To their right, down a road perpendicular to the one they were on, parallel to the road where Breen was waiting—but not visible from the van—was an office building. In one of the parking spots out front was a yellow van with red lettering on its side: STROUD SAFE AT HOME. There was no one in either seat. The doors in the back were shut. The engine was running.

"I listened real good when Matt Berry told us Stroud's got a navy contract," Rivette said.

"Okay. Where's the jump to this van being part of a war?"

"Look behind the seats. The back of the van is closed off. They got a small gun on the side."

"I don't see that—"

"Nah, I'm talking about the antenna, the amplified antenna. The one that's shaped like a QCW-05 submachine gun."

Grace saw the device, painted white and nearly lost against the *d* of Stroud. "They receive signals from their security devices, probably to test them."

"Lieutenant, that's a *broadcast* antenna, not a receiving antenna. He's probably sending hi-def surveillance video. Cops in LA had the same thing. I'll bet he's got a dish on the other side to receive and scramble incoming."

"That proves nothing. Surveillance of the health facility could be going to the ONI."

"Man, you are dug in!"

"Me?"

"Look, let's get a closer look at the van, see if the dish is there."

"That still won't prove anything."

He started walking. "Sure it will. Would you let someone snoop around *your* spy-cart?"

Rivette had her there. "All right, Jaz. Just hold off a minute."

He turned back. "Why?"

"Just wait here till I get back. I'll be a minute, tops."

Rivette stopped walking, and Grace headed toward the van. The likely result of the lance corporal's plan was—guilty or innocent—whoever was in the van belonged here, they did not, and MAs would be summoned. She needed something to try and blunt that.

Breen lowered the window as she approached—at a walk, in case anyone in the van was watching.

"There's a Stroud van next block," she said. "I'll brief you later."

"What do you want to do?"

"Knock on the door, see who and what's inside. You have that business card from Stroud?"

"Sure."

As Breen reached for it, she looked back—and swore.

"What?"

"Jaz is going over."

Grace snatched the card and hurried away.

"Dammit," Breen muttered. There was nothing he could do other than prepare to get off base and regroup if Grace and Rivette were stopped and detained.

Just then, Williams texted that he was finished with his interview. Breen revved the engine slightly so Grace would hear, then pulled away. The woman acknowledged with a wave as she cut briskly across the lawn of the office complex, once again rolling her shoulders back, getting used to movement under the thick leather garment.

The absence of the van brought a slight psychological shift. Grace knew, felt, that she and her partner had no backup now.

The lieutenant caught up to Rivette as he neared the Stroud van.

"Lance Corporal, what are you doing?"

"We are being watched."

"How do you know?"

"The mirror on the driver's side? It followed you when you left. See the way the glass is turned?"

She looked over. The mirror was angled forty-five degrees from the rearview.

"He may be feeding that to the front gate, Jaz."

"Or not. Cops in LA used to watch my cousins the same way. Mobile unit truck was facing one way, like they were looking at a beach and digging the view. Inside, John and Judy Law looked another way. This dude probably has a camera behind the glass, nice fish-eye lens to watch the whole block. Probably got facial recog, communications, a whole setup."

"Please wait."

Rivette was about to turn from the front of the vehicle to the passenger's side. He stopped, saw the dish, nodded.

"Right there is incoming. Think about it. If he were here for ONI, he'd use a secure phone to give and get. He'd be their remote eyes and ears. They wouldn't have a major digital dump for him. This van needs that dish for heavy-duty bandwidth—just like the cops had multiple, linked vans to track people."

"Other Stroud vans."

"Or the store. Or multiple locations."

"If you're right, then they aren't watching Mrs. Hamill—"

"She's bait. They had to figure more than ONI would be looking into this. Maybe that's why they let her live. Otherwise, Black Order could've phoned their message in."

"Let's go around to the other side," Grace said, nodding toward the small satellite dish. "The guards won't see us there."

Rivette smiled. "Roger that."

Grace did not believe that the masters-at-arms were complicit in whatever was going on in the van. If they were, one of the four would have questioned their own presence here. The gate had to have informed them—

By radio, she thought, *which means that the van knows too.*

"Let me do the talking," she said.

"Why? I know how to ask goddamn questions."

"Your right hand is a fist. What's your rule about being tense? You telegraph your intent?"

"Says the woman who fights with her fists. You're suddenly Ambassador Lee?"

"At the moment, I am. Let me handle this."

Rivette knew she was right. He missed his Colt and reluctantly deferred.

When they reached the rear of the van, the lance corporal stopped under the dish. Grace went ahead. There were two thick panes of darkly smoked glass on the back doors. She knocked quietly.

"Hello in there!"

They heard movement. Rivette's face became as tight as his fist. Grace stepped back. If someone came out and they were attacked, she wanted room to move.

"Who is it?" a deep voice sounded from inside.

No echo, Grace thought. *A lot of hardware.*

"We were at your store asking about security for navy personnel. Mr. Stroud told us we could see some of your work here."

"Who are you?"

"We're with the air force contingent on the base, clothing and textile."

"Do you have security clearance to view our installations?"

"We do."

"Show me, please. Hold your ID to the glass."

"I left my wallet in my quarters. Didn't think I would need it."

"You need to be credentialed or this conversation is over."

"I have Mr. Stroud's business card."

There was no response.

"All right," Grace said. "I'll get it and bring it around."

She put the card and her right glove into her jacket pocket

and went back to the driver's side. Rivette was openly confused when she motioned for him to follow her.

"Stay on my right side," she said.

He walked to where she had indicated, leaned close. "What are you doing?"

"I need you to block the mirror."

"From moving or seeing?"

"Seeing."

Still perplexed, Rivette did as she had instructed. As the mirror began to turn, Grace slipped her phone from her coat pocket. She took a picture of the van's base pass as she went past, then kept walking.

Rivette scooted ahead to catch up. "Okay, smooth. What does that get us?"

"If you were right about this van being part of the war, we may have our biggest lead yet." She held up her phone as they walked toward the captain's headquarters, showed Rivette the man's base pass.

"If he's involved, the name'll be fake," Rivette said.

"But not the photo," she said. "A fake name would pretty much seal the deal."

CHAPTER THIRTEEN

Naval Support Activity, Philadelphia, Pennsylvania
January 16, 2:58 p.m.

Jackson Poole would have punched the back door, but was afraid the two interlopers would hear. Instead, he pushed a fist into an open palm until his biceps cramped.

Why did people have to *bother* him? Especially when he was helping put the country on course to realize its full potential.

In Poole's world, potential was more than just the energy of a charge at a particular point in an electric circuit relative to another point in the circuit. It had to do with what a person could accomplish in a chosen field of science. Since he was a boy of five and built the Visible V-8 Engine model kit on his own, everything he did, everything he thought, was in terms of electronics. The human body was fired by electric impulses. Energy itself could be as small as a subatomic particle or as vast as the cosmos. That was a different kind of potential, but there the word was again.

The Pooles lived in Garden Apartments on Flower Road in Valley Stream, Long Island, and there was no money for advanced education. Even if there were, the boy did not have the grades for it. He likely would never have made it out of South High if his science teacher, Mr. Harrison, had not argued for matriculation on the teenager's behalf. Poole heard the discussion through a self-made microphone he had hidden in the teachers' conference room. It was concealed in an ashtray he had sculpted in ceramics class, the electronics insulated with asbestos to survive the kiln.

"He built an electronic calculator from radio parts he took from shop class," Harrison had said.

"Stole," the shop teacher, Mr. Bredice, had replied. "He *stole* those components from shop class."

Making no headway there, Harrison took the case to the principal, Mary St. Mary. The teenager did not hear that conversation—a second ashtray had exploded during firing due to air bubbles—but the woman called his father, Tony. The Vietnam vet, who worked as a deliveryman for Dugan's Bakery, reached a compromise with the school. A certificate of graduation in exchange for enlistment in the armed forces.

The adults—educators and parents who were supposed to care—seemed relieved to punt the boy's future to the military. Fortunately, thanks to a powerfully worded letter from Mr. Harrison, Poole had been able to maneuver himself into the army's division of Electronic Warfare Support. He had taken a calculated risk to achieve that; he used an Apple III, literally spliced into the recruitment office electronics storage system, to read several official white papers on the subject. He memorized one passage, which astounded Major Bob Trolley and his father.

"Major Trolley," he had said, "I would like to be assigned to Electronic Warfare Support, the division of electronic warfare involving actions tasked by, or under direct control of, an operational commander to search for, intercept, identify, and locate or localize sources of intentional and unintentional electronic energy for the purpose of immediate threat recognition, targeting, planning and conduct of future operations (JP 3-13.1)." He went on, "For additional information about what I seek, I refer you to paragraph A-11."

The major was not just dumbfounded. He was eager to have this boy in a uniform, with his own name attached to the placement.

Like high school, the army proved woefully restrictive to the young man. He served out his tour, then wangled a consultancy with the military. He was happy enough with that, though it pained him when his hero Steve Jobs was booted from Apple and that one-trick pony Bill Gates ascended to stardom, and the brightest of them all, Jackson Poole, languished in Cherry Hill, New Jersey.

That was when Burton Stroud found him looking for a job as an electronics tutor to students at the Office of Adult Education. The sun had smiled on him, and the world had opened up. And now, on the morning that was supposed to inaugurate his long-awaited ascension, when he would lift the Black Order to a place of supreme influence, when electrical engineering rather than social engineering would fire up the old American can-do spirit, everything was suddenly in jeopardy.

From the moment the first of the two liars had rapped on

his van door, Jackson Poole was on edge. He had suddenly felt there was—like the latent charge in an electric circuit—the *potential* for exposure. Not in reality, not yet. But imminent, unless he acted swiftly. They had not fooled him with their obvious maneuver. They had blocked his view so they could access his pass.

That's exactly what he would have done.

The back of the van was lined with monitors and a variety of carefully stored and organized consoles, amplifiers, spare parts, jamming devices, and cameras—including infrared—to suit any mobile requirement. There was something more: the Gull. It was the size and configuration of a computer mouse, stored in a small recessed storage unit set in the roof of the van. When the Gull was spring-propelled skyward, the rotor came on and the gull wings of the drone unfolded. The device was virtually silent with a matte coating that absorbed sunlight for partial stealth flight. Possessing twenty minutes of battery-powered flying time, the foot-wide drone fed sound and images directly to the van.

It had another capability, one of which Poole was especially proud.

The security specialist waited until the two visitors had rounded the corner before popping the hatch with the whisper of its rubber latches. The drone sailed off, guided by a touch screen. Poole watched as the supposed USAF personnel headed toward where a van had been parked a minute before. He focused the drone camera on the woman. She apparently thought she was being clever when she took her picture. She had taken care to have her companion block the side mirror but had not realized the capabilities of the rearview mirror front and center. It was static but concealed a wide-angle lens with a 260-degree fish-eye range. He had witnessed everything.

The phone was in the woman's hand. When the drone's camera eye was locked on it, Poole pressed an anthropoid see-no-evil icon.

The drone was equipped with a Targeted Pulsed Electromagnetic Field Generator. The instrument was flat and mounted to the underbelly of the drone. Developed over three decades by medical researchers in Eastern Europe, it had been designed for therapeutic applications such as arthritis and joint deterioration; Poole had simply turned the beam outward where it had a radiant range of four yards. That was too little for most military applications, and at this distance, it was useless against tendonitis. But the enhanced microcurrent was enough to corrupt a smartphone. The woman would not realize that, of course, until she tried to use it.

Bundled against the cold, the young man and woman had stopped, were busy looking for the van. The Gull saw it. Soaring forward and circling around, it took video on all sides. Then it turned back. As soon as he had guided the drone back to its crib, Poole ran the high-definition video against his database of footage from the feeds outside the Germantown house and the Stroud Safe at Home offices. He also ran the plate of the Ford Transit through the Pennsylvania Department of Motor Vehicles.

Then, for dessert—saving the easy get for last—he accessed

the computer at the front gate. There was nothing. No base pass, no photograph.

"What the hell?"

He was momentarily surprised but not confused. Something in the van had generated an IFSC—an intermediate-form source code. As soon as the pass was printed, the push of a button sent a signal from a "jigsaw verifier" that shattered the information into "obfuscation bits," a useless jumble of information.

Who are these people? he wondered.

Poole texted a *7 to Stroud, indicating a high level of urgency. The boss would be at the store now and would get back to him as soon as he could.

In the meantime, Poole sat in his cushioned swivel chair, fighting a surge of anxiety. Despite having been able to cover his being here for the moment, he knew it was only a short-term fix. He did not like being exposed, or even suspected. That was why he had chosen the name Canadian Hemlock for his dark web file. The plants thrived in the shade.

Stroud phoned within two minutes. It was audio only; the authorities had intercept capabilities as well, even of heavily guarded communications. The Ford might be like the Stroud van, a TOW truck—Tech on Wheels—and there was no reason to give them additional help from images.

"What's the problem?" Stroud asked.

"We are being investigated by at least three people driving a white Ford Transit with unregistered plates," Poole told him.

"They had your business card, said they had been to the store. I had to shut down a cell phone after they snuck a picture of my base pass."

"Was their vehicle outside the shop earlier?"

"Down the street, around one thirty."

"I knew it. Did they try to see the widow while they were there?"

"Two of them walked around the center but did not approach the guards. After that, they came directly to me, said they were air force and wanted to know about security systems."

"Did they visit Captain Mann?"

"Someone did," Poole said. "I saw the van pick up a man in uniform outside her HQ. Looked like an admiral. I couldn't get the destination listed on their pass code; they had tech to erase it."

Stroud was silent for a moment.

"They're supposed to come back here," Stroud said. "It will be easy to find out what they know. Send Sarno a text, star ten. I want him here in fifteen minutes."

"Will do. Smack these people down."

Stroud ended the call even as Poole was sending the text and resuming his surveillance of the health center.

The equation, Stroud thought, *is not quite even.*

Stroud was standing behind the closed door of his Stroud Safe at Home office, the only location in the store that had sound silencing and opaque walls. Stroud pitched his company to institutional clients as lean and strong, and the décor reflected that.

The desk and fixtures were chrome and glass. The art on the wall were gelatin silver photographs of old Philadelphia.

The people in the van did not try, likely did not have permission, to see Mrs. Hamill. That would put them outside the ONI. They also suspected, but did not know, that Stroud Safe at Home was involved. They also had no idea what was coming, or when. Conversely, Stroud knew they were coming and had time to plan.

Not much has changed, not really, he told himself. He had always expected that others would be coming for them. The trick was to make sure they played catch-up, that they responded to what the Black Order did rather than anticipating what they were about to do.

Unfortunately, he did not know who these new people were. He had not tried to identify the JAG officer—even if he were one, his records would have been sealed or destroyed—and he was not sure there was anything to be gained by that. The man said he would be returning. Either he could give him nothing while trying to learn what he was about—or he could get rid of him as soon as possible.

He opted for the latter. All he had to do was stonewall them for another forty-five minutes or so.

It would take the van about twenty minutes to get from the NSA.

This was one of those exceptions Stroud would have to allow to his oft-stated aversion to improvisation. Since he would be running things, he could steady Sarno, keep him from ranging too far from what he would be asked to do.

While Poole contacted Sarno, Stroud accessed the store surveillance camera on his phone. He grabbed an image from the man's visit and sent Sarno a text.

White van, 3 possibly 4 occupants. Undercover ops. Wait for this individual to emerge. Escalate a shoulder bump. Call as much attention to the encounter as possible.

CHAPTER FOURTEEN

Philadelphia, Pennsylvania

January 16, 3:17 p.m.

"What the hell?" Jaz Rivette shouted.

Grace was grimly silent, but Rivette was openly puzzled by the fact that her smartphone had gone dark and would not turn on.

It was only moments since the van had left the base. Breen had swung back to pick them up after collecting the admiral. The lieutenant had just described the encounter with the Stroud Safe at Home observer, rolling over Rivette's interjections, and was leaning forward to show Breen the image so he could check the name and, more importantly, the image.

"I'm not even getting a turn-on response," she said.

"The battery?" Breen asked.

Grace was already fishing for the power cord plugged into an outlet in the rear armrest. She plugged it in; nothing happened.

"This phone is dead," she said.

Rivette fished his device from the inside pocket of his jacket. It, too, refused to come on.

"What the damn hell? Something fried them."

"Someone on the base pulsed you, probably the man in the van," Williams said.

"They can do that?" Rivette asked.

"The National Security Agency was close to having a working localized pulse a year ago," the admiral said. "The problem was making it directional so it didn't self-short."

"It appears somebody licked that," Breen said.

"Maybe that's how they cut off Captain Hamill's system," Rivette said.

"Not if it reset, which it appears to have done," Williams pointed out.

Grace was busy personalizing one of the spare phones they kept in the back, but Williams knew she was listening. The woman was constantly alert, which added to the annoyance she had to feel having her phone shut down without her being aware of it.

"Should we contact Captain Mann, get a copy of the pass?" Breen asked the admiral.

"I doubt if it's there," he said. "Black Order's plan has gone operational. I'm betting this same van has removed every identifying or nonessential scrap of information about this man from NSA computers."

"Good point," Breen said.

"You're going to have to use every skill you picked up in court to get something out of Stroud," Williams said.

"Maybe he won't even talk to you," Rivette said.

"I think he will," Breen replied. "He'll get a report from the man in the van. He has to have questions too."

"The question is, what are they planning next?" Williams said. "We know there are at least five people on the team. We know that three of them are or were in Philadelphia, one in New York, one in D.C. How many others are there, and *where* are they?"

As they spoke, a text arrived from Matt Berry. Williams read it aloud.

"Burton Stroud service record exemplary. SSAH is a privately held company, initially financed by a loan from father, Bo Stroud, now deceased. No debt, no late rent. Stroud personally owns a town house in Germantown, leases a Tesla, no other registered holdings. No club memberships, no hunting or gun organizations, not even a gym. One item: has donated time to the Free Library of Philadelphia Office of Adult Education. Has excellent placement record."

"When you have something bad to conceal, do charity work," Breen said.

Williams considered the man's clean—too clean—background.

"How many of us lead such an exemplary life?"

"Not just exemplary but almost antisocial," Breen said. "There's not even the Lion's Club, Rotary International, or Little League sponsorship. You'd expect something like that from a local business."

"What do you make of the Adult Education thing?"

"If I were being cynical? Great place to find people who needed money or a job or both."

"Maybe he needs workers for his business," Rivette said.

"Possible," Breen admitted.

"There's also a chance he's not involved," Grace said. "For all we know, that man in the van might be running this right under Stroud's nose."

"We'll find that out soon enough," Breen said. "I'm going there to talk, but if Stroud is aware and in charge, he can't afford to play defense. He may take preemptive action."

"You talking about another EMP?" Rivette said. "A bug? Or something else."

"I'm thinking casualty of war," Williams said. "They probably saw the van, found no record of our tags. That will cement the fact that we're spooks."

"So something down and dirty like an accident," Rivette said.

"Warfare," Williams said.

The lance corporal took his Colt from the bag and rested it in his lap. "I think you should let us out a couple of blocks away. We can watch—"

"They saw us at the base," Grace reminded him.

"Exactly. They see us again, they may hold off. Or they may come at us, which will be a mistake. Either way, it leaves us ahead of where we are now or sitting on our four hands."

Williams felt there was a certain streetwise logic to that.

"I'll go along with that," Williams said.

"Can't hurt," Breen agreed. He added, only half joking, "Just remember, Lance Corporal. Philadelphia is not an open-carry city."

"Neither is San Pedro. I learned from the masters," Rivette said with a smirk.

Before Williams was able to maneuver to an open spot on the curb, the young officer had already removed his holster and stored it in his grip. He was not only meticulous about keeping his guns clean but also about the location of everything in the bag. Their training had included sessions at night, in fiery smoke-filled vans, in simulated crash landings. It was necessary to be able to perform the three *R*s by touch: Recover, Repair, Rearm. Even in complete darkness, he could target an enemy by sound—anxious breathing, halting footsteps. Or in most cases, an adversary would be bringing their own light.

Rivette slipped the loaded weapon into the deep inside pocket of his black canvas winter coat. The rigid fabric concealed the outline of the Colt. Rivette slipped on sunglasses, his eyes and attention already on the street.

"Give me a block-and-a-half lead," Breen said.

Grace acknowledged, and the two left the van.

Williams did not immediately pull away. Breen turned toward him.

"That talk about them hitting us?"

"It's got me concerned, yeah," Williams said. "How hard are you going to push?"

"There's no point pretending. If he knows we're coming, he also knows why. We've got to stick the landing and stay." He looked three blocks ahead, toward the bright glass frontage. "Street's crowded, probably the store too. I don't think he'll do anything reckless. That would invite the Philadelphia PD in."

Williams looked ahead. Grace and Rivette were window-shopping at a bakery, lingering over the wedding cakes. Rivette was on the right so that when he looked at her he looked down the street.

Practicing being casual. Good man.

Satisfied that there was nothing else they could anticipate, Williams pulled ahead while Breen slipped on a left-ear wireless bud with a built-in microphone. It would look like any other smartphone hookup. Williams put his phone on speaker and tapped the Record button.

"The time is twenty minutes past three," Breen said.

"It's good," Williams said as he looked for a space to pull over. He found one two stores ahead, right by the Comcast Tower.

Williams gave Breen a thumbs-up, and the major got out. He was all business, working—as he had so often—to put a guilty person behind bars.

The admiral watched in the rearview mirror. Breen had walked less than a car length toward the shop when it became evident that things were not going to go as planned.

CHAPTER FIFTEEN

Atlanta, Georgia
January 16, 3:54 p.m.

The Ur-Burger Shack—simply UB to the acolytes—was a local sensation. Since opening the spot two years before, the owners had elected not to expand, not to franchise. Their sole interest was to become a tourist destination and take care of the ever-lengthening queue of lunchtime visitors. Their business model was simple: buy the best foods from Mexico and South America, support across-the-border neighbors to inspire prosperity in much-needed regions.

It was located in an unassuming A-frame structure toward the center of Piedmont 22, the commercial Shangri-la carved from a small lot that was once the outlying perimeter of Renaissance Park. The Urban Design Commission had forbidden any entity from touching most of the prime real estate, but the forward-looking Piedmont 22 managed to find a spot along with its own local loyalists and out-of-town visitors. Many of the latter were tourists who had already spent their day at the studio, on trams, and did not want to pay for another day of shopping. Piedmont 22 had history-themed shops to satisfy the UDC and attractions that gave the long, festive strip the illusion of being part of the past.

By his posture and stride, as well as his nondescript black clothes and black baseball cap—which bore an Atlanta Police Department logo and had been purchased from a souvenir shop at the hotel—Mark Philpotts looked as if he were there to protect the citizenry. He had taken a long, slow walk through the area, noting the location of the real guards—private security all—mostly out of shape or older. He saw no mustered-out soldiers among them, erect, attentive younger men and women. He saw no one paying particular attention to their job. They checked cell phones, stared vacantly from behind sunglasses, were not asked to pose for tourist photos like bona fide law enforcement. They did not carry firearms, just walkie-talkies.

As he walked, Philpotts used an app to make a prepayment; there would not be time later. The charge went through successfully. He replaced the phone and looked around.

The morning mist that covered the higher elevations to the north and south of the city had dissipated. The sun was warming, the air dry, and it was too early for the blustery winds that sometimes whipped in the afternoon. Sprinklers raised pleasant odors from the flowers that had accompanied his walk. They surrounded the hotel, lined the sloping sidewalk, brought him to the entrance to Piedmont 22. He had passed nothing but groundskeepers, custodial workers, and street cleaners. He marveled that a state so aggressively devoted to equality was so devoid of that policy in practice. That hypocrisy strengthened his resolve. Innocent blood would be spilled on the festive pastel tiles outside Ur-Burger. As Gray Kirby had done, Philpotts intended to try and minimize fatal wounds. Most victims would assume a defensive posture, or flee, allowing him to inflict injuries on arms or backs that were not life-threatening. Once someone went down, all they had to do was stay there. Burton Stroud wanted numbers, bloody optics, not death. But there were always would-be heroes . . .

As he neared his destination, Philpotts uncrossed his arms. The Bowie knife slid into his right hand. His left hand slipped into a pants pocket. He withdrew and palmed the karambit knife and then checked his watch. Ahead, dozens of people already stood in a line that wrapped—and conveniently trapped those within—through a series of side-by-side orange-striped black ropes, the colors of the eatery.

Stroud had selected this target, at this time, because after the first hour of lunch, every day the owners did not charge undocumented refugees for meals.

The banner over the eatery read—in Castellano, Farsi, Cantonese, Malay, and finally English for virtue-signaling: "To eat for free, just sing to our owners, Bob and Jay, in your native tongue as they move down the line."

People who sang in English were charged the regular price.

As Bob and Jay emerged from a side door, smiling and waving to the cheers of the lunch line, a sense of power rose in Philpotts's chest. It did not come from the ability to destroy but from the knowledge of what was to happen. These people, laughing or waving, some holding purchases and some each other, a few already singing, had no idea that their lives and world were about to tilt dramatically.

Philpotts knew that, and though it did not quicken his step, it helped raise his heartbeat as he took his place in the back of the line, savored the moment, then prepared to strike.

The grand ballroom and pre-function area of the Piedmont 22 Hotel were jammed with vendors and entrepreneurs from all nations. The tables they would use to display their goods were already set up in the terrace meeting rooms, their holistic goods and supplements neatly arranged, signage erected, hotel workers scurrying to find extension cords for unanticipated electronic displays. The trade-only show would kick off as soon as the address by Ric Samuels was over and the gymnasium seats had emptied.

There were paparazzi as well. They were not there for cures but for Samuels. With the exception of a crew from MSNBC, most of them did not even deserve to be called paparazzi, Honda thought. They were shooting video on cell phones. Still, he was happy to see them. The vloggers could not know it, but they would soon have the story of their pathetic careers.

Honda snaked through the crowd inside the grand ballroom. He held his backpack under his arms, careful that his special samples did not get jostled as he maneuvered through the pockets of people.

He stopped near Vivian Tomar, the head of venue security, and waited. Honda had made a point of meeting him the day before, asking whether the silver leaf embossing on his capsules would set off the metal detectors. Tomar gave him a printed pamphlet of items that would trigger security alarms. Vark—the silver leaf—was not on it.

Ironically, Honda's plastic and 3-D modeled detonators, and the wireless microchip charge inducer, also were not on the list. Neither was Semtex. He had ten pounds of the explosives stuffed into the backpack. Honda did not bother to remove the distinctive detection taggant; the venue had no odor sensors and, to the untrained nose, the smell would seem like his holistic goods. He had chosen plastique because each 1.25-pound brick was enough to destroy a bus. And that was just the initial blast. A second wave of devastation resulted from the low pressure caused by the blast. Like a tsunami, the outflow of gases left a void in the center. When the air rushed back, it pulled objects along toward ground zero.

Before finalizing his plans the previous night, Honda had seen how seats were being arranged and then had selected the precise site he would use. There would be random, incidental projectiles—parts of chairs, phones, water bottles, and other fragments—but no shrapnel. The point of the attack was to destroy, create panic, set the venue ablaze along one of its four perimeters: the main door. If there were deaths, it would be caused by the mob in flight, the holistic, organic health purveyors clawing over their colleagues to reach safety.

Checking his watch, Honda made his way unhurriedly to the staging area. He held the backpack in such a way that his wristwatch was visible. It had been set precisely to match the one worn by Philpotts. The attack on Piedmont 22 would come first, while the illegals were still in line. Samuels was expected to be on time; MSNBC was airing his speech live.

Tomar lifted his index finger and made a circling motion, signaling team members around the room. Samuels was on the way.

The attendees took their seats, clutching illustrated programs in the hope of securing an autograph after the address. He overheard a few people remark that they had no idea who the actor was, but they had daughters and younger sisters who did.

For Honda, Samuels was not the target, just the draw. The man slipped a Bluetooth into his ear. He checked his smartwatch. It was exactly 4:00 p.m. He feigned a phone call and plopped his program there to "save" his aisle seat, smiling at the woman beside him as he left the auditorium. He smiled again, at a young usher beside the door, and left. He had not planned on that and was sorry for the young woman.

Though the call was a sham, Honda was in fact on his phone. Hotel security had an internal communications system, and Poole had plugged the frequency into Honda's phone. The chatter was all about Samuels's journey. He would be entering through the back of the room to reach the stage unhindered.

The double doors closed after Honda. He was alone in the carpeted hallway. He heard the thunder of applause and cheers from the hall.

The untrained voice of the actor bleated from the podium, through the speakers, causing Honda to briefly lament the tics, jargon, and undistinguished delivery that were the hallmarks of a modern gen X celebrity and gen Z influencer.

And then, over the security channel, he heard the urgent alert he had been waiting for.

An apparent terror attack was under way at Piedmont 22.

Bob and Jay had been close enough so that Philpotts could smell the product in their hair.

Young, curly topped, smiling, the twin brothers had been handing free food cards to everyone who sang in a foreign tongue. It was a Tower of Babel, encouraged by a pair of ignorant nimrods.

Two people had gotten into line behind Philpotts, a young man and woman holding little Mexican flags and speaking Spanish.

The man standing directly in front of Philpotts was heavyset, wearing a bright blue polo shirt, and looking at a graphic novel he'd bought. It was a Farsi edition of the French hero Asterix.

The two owners and those three customers: those five would be the first victims. If Philpotts could reach more before the customers panicked, before the ropes fell, there were two men in Peruvian soccer shirts in front of the Asterix reader. They might just be tourists, but they had sung, they got cards, they would pay in blood. He knew he could probably get them before people had successfully jumped the ropes. After that, it would depend on who remained standing and who had tripped and fallen to populate his stabbing gallery.

Philpotts checked his watch. It was thirty seconds to H-hour. The man with the comic book sang, and then Bob and Jay moved past the American, the combat veteran, the patriot. He had to fight the urge to shout at them, *I'm wearing something from my native land, you stinking, treasonous worms.* Bleeding hearts? They did not know the true meaning of the phrase.

It was five, four, three seconds to zero.

The Spanish-speaking couple were smiling and singing, Bob and Jay applauding heartily, as the curved blade snapped from its handle and locked in place. The steel was projecting several inches from the bottom of his fist as he turned and slashed backward, laterally, chest high, severing the right and left subclavian arteries. Bob, in his orange-and-black T-shirt, wearing an unassuming name tag like any ordinary employee, stopped applauding. His hands hovered in mid-clap; he seemed surprised when the horizontal cut spewed blood over his ten fingers and several of the people in line. The surprise evaporated as he fell to the ground in a lazy spiral, the spray trailing like Fourth of July fireworks.

The two Mexicans were in the way of him getting to Jay. To Philpotts, he was the only one not moving in slow motion. The couple saw him swing sideways with two blades. Each felt a slight sting and a small push backward. They did not immediately feel the cuts that ruined their matching Falcons T-shirts. By the time the razor sting of the slashes reached their brains and generated a scream, they were already bleeding heavily into their shirts, clutching their chests, and falling to their knees. These were superficial cuts; with quick medical attention, the couple would not die.

Philpotts did not see them fall against the people who

had lined up behind them. The assassin's gaze was fixed on Jay, whose eyes had dropped with his brother. The killer flipped his Bowie knife over so he could jab rather than slash. He pushed it into the belly of the remaining owner, slicing up. The man fell backward and landed on the ground, on his back, white fat blossoming through the skin.

By the time the expanding line found its shrill voice, Philpotts had already pushed the Bowie blade through the right side of the man in front of him, He pierced a kidney and part of the man's intestines. The tip of the blade emerged from the man's lower back, and Philpotts slashed outward to free it. The tourist staggered to his left and fell, blood staining his pants leg and then the ground.

The screams were now an ocean roar of horror that filled the killer's soul. He laughed as he moved toward a young American couple in front of that man. The mob moving past the rope kept them from getting over. They looked back, eyes filled with terror.

Philpotts used his left shoulder to push them over, tripping several people rushing past them. No one helped anyone to get up; the feet of those behind them rushed over and around them in an endless cascade. Philpotts charged the men in the soccer shirts. They turned when they heard the man cry out and drop over. Both received defensive wounds across their palms and fingers as they saw the curved blade sweep toward them. The man on the left screamed from deep inside as the top of his index and middle finger flew to the side, landing beside the bleeding man.

Philpotts used his left shoulder to charge between the

men, stabbing a young mother who was also speaking Spanish and holding her small daughter's hand. The woman lurched and grunted under wide eyes as the blade went into and through her shoulder, just above the heart. She, too, would survive. She plunged to her knees, pulling the five-year-old with her. Philpotts stepped around the screaming child.

By now, the ropes swung empty, the escape routes briefly clogged as the streets filled with people emerging from the shops. Philpotts's options narrowed to those who were nearest. He attacked the fallen whose cries were in foreign tongues, avoiding young children as he inflicted slices and stab wounds in limbs or sides. There was blood loss but no major cuts. That changed when the first hero emerged from the chaos to try to stop him. The young man was a brawny six-two, fighting his way against the tide and, with a final lunge, throwing beefy arms around Philpotts.

The Bowie blade went deep into the man's belly, penetrating his tensed abdominal muscles. The wound did not stop the hero's forward momentum, resulting in the steel severing his spinal cord. Still holding Philpotts, the man slumped like beef being fed into a grinder, the knife cutting upward, pouring blood onto the asphalt. Philpotts wrenched from his weakening hold. Dripping blood, he looked around at two men who had thought to help him and froze. They became the next victims, with deep, diagonal incisions across the back or stab wounds in the sides.

The killer's own heart was beating louder than anything

around him. As the screams retreated, Philpotts could hear the wheezing from punctured lungs, the moan from ruined stomachs or bladders, agony rising from every move he made, every step he took.

The first security guard arrived then, shouting into his radio. Philpotts leapt over several potential victims to inflict dual wounds on the man, a cut from side to navel with the karambit that caused white tissue to bulge from the large wound, and a stab under the armpit with the long knife. Like Bob, like several others, the man was frozen by the sudden and unexpected attack, making the cuts easy. The victim drifted down like a deflating parade balloon.

Philpotts looked back. He was breathing heavily, partly from exertion, partly from exhilaration. There were over fifteen persons down and no one nearby. Grabbing and quickly unhooking one of the queue ropes, he turned south toward the parking lot. There, he headed toward the van, pausing only to slash the back passenger's-side tire of the security sedan parked there.

People who were just emerging from their cars, who saw the man unevenly bathed with blood, running with the two knives, jumped back inside. People who were outside his line of retreat stood protectively behind their vehicles, watching or using their cell phones. Some may have noticed the man's gory hands and bloodstained clothes. Philpotts hoped so. It was an inducement to stand far back.

Philpotts made his way between parked cars, ducking and

weaving, his face turned down, his cap drawn low. He got into the white van, dropped the knives and Ur-Burger rope between the seats, and stuffed his hat and bloody shirt into a canvas laundry bag. The wig came off with it, and he threw his false mustache into the sack. He used baby wipes to clean his face and hands. Then he slashed his own left arm across the biceps, wide but not deep. He let it bleed. In case he was stopped:

"*I was* there, *Officer! It was insanity!*"

Which was true, as far as it went.

Philpotts covered everything with paint-covered rags, mostly red with flecks of green and blue. Underneath the shirt, he was wearing a vintage Los Angeles Rams T-shirt, quarterback Roman Gabriel era—*his* era, when Rosey Grier and Deacon Jones of the Fearsome Foursome represented diversity, were exemplars of talent over charity.

Thirty seconds after climbing in, and unzipping the bag with new clothes—which he would don as soon as he collected Honda—Philpotts was headed toward the exit. He looked back, saw guards arriving cautiously, following the trail of dripped blood. He heard sirens in the distance. Seven or eight vehicles in the parking lot were leaving; he would get away in that wave. Other new arrivals had not yet moved from cover. He would be gone before anyone could place the attacker in this van; it would be a burning husk before it could be located.

Besides, he thought, *the police will have other things to concern them. Two attacks—will there be a third, a fourth?*

The parking system was automated, and he had prepaid the maximum fee using the app. When it was his turn in line, he held up his phone and the bar rose. Within moments he was on Ralph McGill Boulevard doubling back toward the hotel.

"Guests in the private and public areas of the hotel, attention!"

The male voice rolled from the loudspeakers in the ballroom, managing to exude both calm and urgency at the same time. Presumably, telephones in every room were also carrying the message.

"There is a situation off-premises that does not affect the hotel or guests but has triggered our Automatic Safeguard Process," the voice continued. "The ASP has been designed to assure the well-being of all guests and visitors. Law enforcement is currently handling the incident, and we ask that everyone shelter in place until we have been notified of a successful resolution. I repeat: shelter in place."

Honda heard but did not listen to the announcement. He set the backpack where the double doors met, then walked briskly toward the staircase that led to the lobby. He was not yet visible from above when he paused, turned, and twisted the knob on his watch. A red light on the watch face turned green.

He had five seconds and hurried up the curving stairs toward the front door. A security guard passed, hurrying down. Honda grabbed the man's arm.

"Sir," Honda asked urgently, "what's going on, do you know?"

The guard wrested free. "I need you to wait in the lobby!" he said as he resumed his rapid descent.

With luck, Honda had just saved the man's life. The guard

would have been right on top of the blast when it went off. But Honda had cost himself several seconds and took the stairs two at a time.

Even a flight up and some five yards from the top step, Honda was tossed against the back of a sofa by the ferocity of the explosion. The floor rose under him and cracked audibly in several spots before settling haphazardly, the carpet sunken or bulging. The thunder of the detonation rolled through the lobby, shattering glass that overlooked the front courtyard.

Honda quickly pushed off the sofa and continued toward the door. Smoke plumed thickly from the staircase, and there were muffled screams coming from all directions, piercing even the aftermath of the explosion. The cottony silence was further disrupted by the ominous sounds of cracking wood and plaster. Those snapping sounds were followed by further shifts in the floor.

"Everyone leave the building *now*!" someone shouted from behind the registration desk.

Guests tried, without having to be told. They leapt over lumps and depressions, a few making it out before the sitting area over the pre-function area vanished, dropping almost whole to the lower floor. The fresh fuel fed the fire caused by the blast, red light and rising flame dancing from below.

Honda was far enough away to make it outside. Many of those who did not fell backward on the now badly listing floor, vanishing first in the smoke and then into the flames below.

Honda was not happy—though he felt perversely vindicated. He had wondered if the newly adopted Urban Ecology

Framework with more environmentally friendly building materials might undermine the brawnier construction safety codes.

The hole coughed up white powder from burning Sheetrock and dried wallpaper paste. Outside, save for a few cracks near the door, the pavement was intact. The palm trees stood tall and oblivious to the destruction.

As Honda emerged in the sunlight, his phone pinged with a text from Philpotts:

ETA 2 Min

Honda considered whether to invest one of those minutes going back to help—and also to catalog the damage. The lobby seemed to have settled into something passing for stability, but he decided not to risk going back. He could not only see what he had wrought, he could smell it. The foul odor of burning plastic and flesh were faintly present, and his clearing ears heard that the screams had been replaced by moans and tears.

That was enough. It was not that he was faint of heart; he had seen far worse in war. Honda simply did not need to know anything more right now. There would be video enough before the day was done.

Arching his back, which had been hurt when he hit the sofa, Honda crossed over the shadow of the high-flying American flag and ran from the semicircular drop-off zone to the main road. Other guests who had gotten out before he had were now walking, now hesitating, unsure where to go or what to do.

Some looked back at the building, as though assessing the integrity of the structure, watching to see if it was coming down.

Honda had no further investment in the site or the outcome. He continued past the small parking area, where attendants were clustering, unsure what to do. He reached Central Park Place NE just as the van was pulling up. Jumping into the passenger's seat, Honda removed his tie and sports jacket and tore off the wig and goatee, and the two headed toward the Publix.

As soon as Honda was settled, he turned to Philpotts. He saw the blood on the man's hand, the paint on his face.

"How did it go?" Honda asked.

"As planned. You? I see a lot of smoke."

"The hotel took it harder than expected. But we got the result."

Philpotts gave his arm a squeeze before pulling away. "You can't answer for the target, only for yourself."

While Philpotts drove, Honda opened the glove compartment to prepare the next phase of their action, one that was less dramatic than the first but necessary. They would not contact Stroud until they were safely away, lest they and the phone be taken.

With the number of news media, firefighters, and other first responders speeding toward the hotel, Stroud would hear of the success soon enough.

The men reached the Publix grocery store. Philpotts went to the Cutlass to start it. The men had no luggage; they would be driving to Hartsfield-Jackson Atlanta International Airport for a chartered 5:00 p.m. flight to Altoona–Blair County Airport.

They would be on the ground at seven and at the Homestead less than an hour later.

Honda briefly stayed behind to rig the three incendiary devices he had placed in the glove compartment. One minute after the timers were set, the thermite weapons would ignite paint cans filled with gelled oil that the men had brought from the Homestead. The van would be a blackened ruin within minutes.

Honda joined Philpotts, and they headed toward the airport. While law enforcement was still racing to the nearby kill sites, the men heard the blast at the grocery store. The heavy Oldsmobile vibrated a little from the explosion. Its interior was coated briefly with a faint orange light as the van, along with any trace of the men, their belongings, or their deeds, was obliterated.

CHAPTER SIXTEEN

Philadelphia, Pennsylvania
January 16, 4:00 p.m.

Breen missed the danger because his eyes were studying the target ahead. He wanted to see how many people were inside, if Stroud was still inside, if there was a Stroud van on the street. The function he was performing now was the same he played when Black Wasp drilled: making sure the target zone for Jaz and Grace was clear.

As a result, Breen missed the incoming on his own position.

The man who walked into Major Breen did so with such force that both men bounced back a little. Watching from the driver's-side mirror, it appeared to Williams that the other man had tucked his shoulder in slightly before making contact, ensuring that the impact was not just a brush.

"Sorry," Breen stammered after the hit. From the man's fierce expression, he already knew that it was too late.

"Watch where you're friggin' going, asshole!" the man shouted.

"I said I'm sorry, very sorry," Breen said and attempted to move around the man.

But the man moved with him.

"Sorry doesn't get it done!" the man shouted. "Look at all the people around you. You think you own the goddamn sidewalk?"

Breen stepped back a few paces. Pedestrians bundled against the cold, starting to step wide around the confrontation, quickened their pace to get past.

He felt a unique sensation of helplessness. A lawyer's tools, logic and words, were not going to work here. The man had been dispatched to do this. Breen was unarmed, would not have used a weapon in any case, and there was nothing he could do to dissuade him.

"I asked you a question, *jerk*!" the man said.

The attacker did not give Breen time to answer. He drew both arms back, bent at the elbows, intending to push Breen again.

A small woman in a leather jacket eased between the men, her back nearly pressed against Breen's chest. She raised her hands waist high, palms out, fingers relaxed and nonthreatening.

"What's going on here?" the newcomer said through the thick scarf that covered the lower half of her face.

The attacker checked his move, stared. "What the hell?"

"Yeah, what the hell!" the small woman said. "I saw you come right at this man. You were just standing there, by that store, then walked right at him. My friend has the video."

The man turned, saw Rivette standing apart from them near a fire hydrant. His left hand was gloved and wiggling a cell phone tauntingly. His right hand was bare and in his coat pocket.

The man scowled and looked back at the woman, then at his target.

"Video this," he hissed and reached out again, intent on grabbing Breen. He moved forward a half step and walked into the woman's flaccid hands, intent on plowing her under.

He was unable to take another step.

The woman's fingers had stiffened, thumb at a right angle to the others, and twin Tiger Mouth battering rams went into his belly. Christopher Sarno doubled over, his arms dropping to the woman's shoulders. When his long arms came unwillingly to rest, Grace Lee's palms turned up under his stiffened elbows. His rigid right arm went up, while her other palm slid snakelike over his arm to the crook of the elbow. That arm went down. At the same time, she lowered her center of gravity by bending at her knees and turning to her left. The woman's windmill movement caused the attacker to pinwheel to his right, his left leg leaving the ground as he went sideways.

Grace did not let him drop to the pavement. He might have a weapon, judging from the thickness of his own coat; backing off, he could draw it. Instead, she used the momentum of her move to continue along the Cheng Style Bagua Zhang, walking the circle to keep the man off balance. His arms flailing, his feet firmly planted on air, she propelled his head into the wall of the building beside them. The concussion was not hard, but it was enough so that his arms went slack, his thighs wobbled, and he plunged to his knees.

More shocked than stunned, the man put a palm against the wall, intent on getting up.

Rivette ran up beside Grace. Breen had stepped back to give them room.

"Stay, Fido!" Rivette said, looking down at the man.

"You're going to die!" Sarno growled.

"Not without company," Rivette threatened, his eyes locked on his target.

"Don't threaten me, punk!" Sarno said and started to push off the pavement.

"It's okay," Grace said to Rivette and stepped back. It was not a retreat; she was making room.

By this time, pedestrians had stopped moving around them but had formed a wide circle on two sides. Several were recording the encounter, a few muttering at how the tiny woman had tossed the "mugger" into a wall.

Their comments seemed to inflame Sarno, who had his right hand on the wall and was rising slowly. With a snarl, he shot out his left hand to grab Grace's coat at the waist. It never arrived. The woman's right foot shot out, toe pointed. With arrow-sharp precision, she drove her instep under his chin and snapped his head back into the wall. To the oohs and aahs of the crowd, the man dropped a second time.

"Who got punk'd?" Rivette muttered.

Grace clearly had control, and the lance corporal took a moment to glance toward the street. Williams was still inside the van.

Smart, Rivette thought. They had all been seen now, but the admiral had remained hidden.

There was a commotion as a man pushed his way through

the crowd. Rivette turned as Burton Stroud emerged in the sidewalk arena. He looked at Breen.

"Major, are you all right?" Stroud asked, showing concern.

"Untouched. This man was the only one hurt."

"Thank God."

"Do you know him?"

Stroud's eyes swiveled like little machines as Sarno rose. "He works—*worked*—for me from time to time, making deliveries and pickups. I told him I didn't have anything for him today. I won't have anything for him going forward, either."

"What's your name?" Breen asked the attacker.

Sarno was fiercely quiet.

"His name is Kelly. Are you going to press charges?" Stroud asked.

Breen said with a calculated smirk, "No need. As I said, he never touched me."

The major's flip tone caused Sarno to fill with hate. Stroud squeezed the man's arm.

"Come back to the store, Kelly. I'll pay you what you're owed, and then you're done."

Grace had joined Rivette at the curb. Sarno's narrowed, angry eyes went from the major to the woman standing a few steps away. Sarno had rage enough to act but enough presence of mind to control it.

Stroud walked the taller man back to the store. The crowd was dissipating, but someone had called the police; Stroud clearly wanted to be somewhere else when they arrived.

Breen looked over at Grace and Rivette and gave them a silent nod of thanks. He considered following Stroud. He wanted to ask, *What did you hope to gain by this?* Was it just about roughing him up, threatening possible investigators with injury or worse? That seemed a stupid tack to use against someone who might be representing the United States Army.

A toot from the horn in the van drew Breen's attention. The major made a point of looking at Grace and Rivette and cocking his head in that direction, letting them know there would be no pursuit.

As the two Black Wasps got back in the van, Breen glanced back along the street. Stroud had made a point of pausing at the door and watching without expression as the three left. He obviously knew, from his spy at the NSA, that these two were with him, that they had come to the store with a plan of offense and defense.

Suddenly, unexpectedly, Stroud grinned. It was a chilling look, the kind Breen recognized from convicted killers.

The major got in the van. Williams pulled away even before the doors were shut. His dark expression and urgency took all three by surprise.

"What's up?" Breen asked.

"There's been another attack. In Atlanta this time, simultaneous knife attack outside of a Ur-Burger with sixteen injured, one fatality, and at a vitamin convention at a local hotel. The venue took a massive explosion, dozens hurt, partial collapse of the lobby. Deaths not yet known."

"Did the perps get away?" Breen asked.

"More or less clean. Surveillance did not go down, but Berry had not yet heard anything from the police. The escape was apparently coordinated using the shield of chaos."

"Stroud knew this was coming," Breen said, thinking back at the smile. "He did this to see what kind of force was closing in. From his spy at the van, he knew there were at least me, Grace, and Jaz. This thing told him we had at least one more."

"But we know where he is," Rivette said.

"Was," Breen said. "That store cannot have been his operational headquarters. He has to figure it will be raided very soon."

"A burner HQ," Rivette said.

Breen understood that the analytical response was not unfeeling. In his case, it was a way of deflecting the horror of what they had heard from Williams. They could grieve for the nation and its wounded some other time. Right now, there was a war to fight.

"Unfortunately, we will not be the ones closing in," Williams said. "There's more news. The president has recalled Black Wasp."

That hit hard.

"The ONI?" Breen asked.

"Matt says it's partly jurisdictional. This is no longer in the lap of the ONI, and the president doesn't want us caught up in a confluence of agencies, have them fighting one another instead of the enemy."

"But the bad guys are here; we just met them," Rivette said.

"The bad guys are also in D.C., New York, and now Atlanta," Williams said. "At least seven, and we have no idea how many more. Neither does the president. But his sense is—and I agree—that after the double hit in Georgia against two socially progressive targets, there will be more foot soldiers and copycat crimes."

"Support is not far behind condemnation and horror on Twitter and Instagram," Grace said, looking at her tablet.

"Fringe nutjobs," Breen said.

"No, Major. TRAC analytics have this expanded beyond the usual white supremacist, Nazi, fascist hashtags."

"Administration policy is going by social media now?" Breen said.

"Wait till Wright is sworn in," Grace said. "They are going to live by data like this."

"Every politician is tried hourly by their peers." Breen shook his head. "Admiral, do we know if ONI has eyes on Stroud?"

"I didn't get to ask. Everyone was still processing the latest hit."

"Then I suggest that until we know, we don't just fold our tent here."

"I raise you one. I say we go back and take Stroud apart," Rivette said.

"And risk retribution from the Black Order?" Williams said. "That very discussion is going on right now in the Oval Office. Do you accept casualties to finish this—possibly greater than we've seen—or do you talk this out?"

"Talk, shit," Rivette said. "We do nothing while they keep making war—that sounds a lot like surrender."

"Expect more of *that* when Wright is sworn in," Grace said.

The van traveled a few blocks farther along John F. Kennedy Boulevard when Williams pulled to the curb and regarded the others. He broke the heavy silence.

"I happen to agree with everything you've said, and we're not folding anything," Williams told them. "I'm staying here to see what these sons of bitches do. They haven't seen me, so I should be all right."

"They took your picture, got your name at the base," Breen said.

"Shit, right," Rivette echoed.

"That's a negative," Williams said with a trim smile. "I've learned something over my years at Op-Center." He pointed to a button on the dashboard. "It triggers a signal that erases our tracks, a holdover from our plans to revive a Paul Hood–era plan, the Regional Op-Center—Mobile ROC we called it."

Breen shook his head slowly. "Stroud is a former Ranger. He knows soldiers, and he clearly knows tactics. He used that guy to smoke out our spotters, probably matched them to the NSA encounter, knows our strength."

"He's also had a free ride till now. The Black Order has the resources of the nation bearing down on him. He had us on his tail. He'll have to watch his perimeter three-sixty, but he may not be expecting a lone wolf."

"In uniform?" Grace said. "That will stand out."

"The military authority may help open doors. I've got the overcoat in back, if you'll pass it up."

Grace handed over the knee-length, navy-blue overcoat. Williams threw it over his arm.

"Let us stay here and shadow you," Rivette said.

"No. The president is right to recall Black Wasp. I don't think the move has anything to do with stepping on the toes of the FBI, ONI, or anyone else. I'd stake my pension on the fact that Matt and Midkiff figured out the same thing we did, that this isn't about Philadelphia but wherever the weapons were dropped for pickup. He wants Black Wasp ready to move as soon as he gets a whiff of what's next."

"You packing?" Rivette asked, offering a handgun.

"Just my instincts. City's got too many metal detectors."

"Risky."

"Comes with the uniform, soldier."

"Uh-huh. So did my M11."

"Where are you going to stay?" Breen asked. "What are you going to *do*?"

"Right now, reconnoiter." He regarded Rivette and Grace. "Check all the maps you can of Western Pennsylvania hunting, hiking, and timberland. I have a feeling we'll be needing those."

"Won't the ONI be doing that?" Grace asked.

"Certainly. And then they'll use the tactics of an amphibious landing to take the place. They go in like that, who knows what countermeasures they'll unleash. No—we have to get there first."

With that, Williams checked for oncoming traffic, opened the door, and stepped out. Breen asked Grace to take the admiral's place behind the wheel, and the team drove off.

Williams was sorry to see them go, since this was the only theater of operation they had and he had just sent away the only defense they had.

CHAPTER SEVENTEEN

Philadelphia, Pennsylvania
January 16, 4:22 p.m.

"'They now commingle with the coward angels, the company of those who were not rebels nor faithful to their God, but stood apart . . .'"

Stroud let Sarno recite his poetry. They were standing in the parking garage under the store, and the man needed something familiar and comforting. Besides, there was not a lot of time for caregiving; Stroud had more immediate concerns at the moment. The enemy—the one he had just met—had been defined as a small mobile force with tactics and spotters. They had done an exceptional job of pouring through cracks in his defenses and tracking him. They had to be dealt with. At the same time, their hot breath on the back of his neck energized him.

Offensively, events were moving as quickly as Stroud had planned.

After going back to the office, where the staff seemed confused by whatever had happened but too busy to dwell on it,

Stroud had emailed Gray to make sure he was in position. He was. Then he sent Poole a message to make sure he was ready.

The answer came back affirmative. Stroud erased the hard drive, grabbed his shoulder bag, and walked Sarno to his car. The man had been muttering Dante the entire time. Not like a lunatic on a street corner but as an apostle uttering a Bible verse. It had taken until this moment for Stroud to realize that Dante was more than just a touchstone for Sarno. Lucifer, the rebel, thrown from heaven—the saga was both a tether to his previous life and a road map through the present.

How else do you survive years of fomenting in-country espionage, except with a zealot's fervor and a dark angel's independence?

Stroud believed that the man was all right. His pride was injured—"It goeth before destruction," Sarno remarked—but his core, his courage seemed undamaged. Now it was time to test that belief.

"I want you to go to the Homestead and wait there," Stroud told him.

"The Homestead? Out to pasture?"

"You know better," Stroud said.

"What I know is that we have to go after these clowns. They know who we are."

"At five thirty, that won't matter," Stroud said.

That stopped Sarno short. "What's happening at five thirty?"

"We turn up the heat."

"All the more reason to go after them now. Whichever option you've called, they will come back with reinforcements—"

"Chris, you're letting this thing get to you, the girl—"

"That bitch."

"Capable, though, so use your head. You know the game plan. We don't waste time and effort with defense. We counterattack. That was *always* the plan."

The man calmed. "Sure. But the Homestead? What if you need more backup?"

"I shouldn't need more than Gray for cleanup, and there's a lot Poole can do." He moved closer, put a hand behind Sarno's neck. "Besides, if we need to go to DEFCON 1, whose hand do I want on the throttle?"

Sarno relaxed further. "Thank you."

"Now go there and rest. You're tired."

He became alert. "Gray—what about Germantown?"

"You know we're ready for that too." Stroud grinned. "The house is protected by Stroud Safe at Home."

"What if it doesn't work?"

"For God's sake, Christopher, it was Poole's senior class project!"

"Mice in a dollhouse."

Stroud shrugged. "If it reaches that point, and if it doesn't work, we are far from helpless. You can trust in Stroud."

Sarno was not in the mood for humor. He was trying to process all of this. The foot soldier did not know—no team member knew—everything that Stroud had prepared. He knew there was a dead man's switch, but only Stroud knew how to trigger it. One signal from him would signal death on a scale unprecedented on this continent.

"All right," Sarno said. "Thanks, and I'm sorry. I feel like I let you down back there—"

"You did not. You confirmed what I suspected. We'll launch our harshest attack so far just as soon as I do my part."

"You'll stay at the library?"

"For now. I'll be safe unless they're stupid enough to put my name on the news—but I don't think they will. They still have only supposition, not fact. As for you, Chris, you're good. You did fine."

Sarno seemed to accept that. Stroud waited until the man had gotten into his car and driven off. He got into his own car and headed to the Free Library.

The attack in Atlanta had been a success. Word had just begun to circulate before he came down with Sarno. Philpotts and Honda had gotten away, he knew that too. Both men had texted A-OKs once the van had been torched.

As he drove through the thickening late-afternoon traffic, Stroud could not help but wonder about the three who had stopped Sarno. They were military for certain. An army major. A hand-to-hand combat instructor—*Probably an officer too, someone who was shuffled upward through affirmative action.* And a kid whose thug attitude dishonored the military tradition that once recruited patriots.

Plus the man in the car, Stroud thought. He was smart enough to trick the base ID system so the question remained: Who was he and who else was he working with?

Stroud parked at an outdoor lot and went to the Adult Education office. Chuck Boyd was at a meeting and would be going home directly. The only people present in the office were two other volunteers: fine artist Andrea Pace and retired Philadelphia mayor Tom Albert. Both were on the phone.

Stroud took his tablet from his bag, plugged in the earbuds, and streamed the news.

"TV star Ric Samuels was injured in the Piedmont 22 bombing and is about to undergo surgery at Emory University Hospital," the newscaster said. "His condition is listed as critical, though he is expected to survive. So far, ten bodies have been pulled from the rubble of the convention hall."

The death toll is unfortunate, Stroud thought, though he did not blame Eiji Honda. No one had anticipated the partial collapse of the hotel lobby.

On nearby Piedmont 22, there had only been one casualty, a man who tried to take down the assailant. But the coverage had more onlookers, more tears from witnesses, more horror.

A third headline said that investigators "suspected" the attacks were tied to a van fire in a Publix parking lot.

Stroud shut the feed. The devastation would increase pressure on authorities to do something. The right choice would bring an end to hostilities. The wrong choice would incur more blood and fire. Stroud would give them that opportunity to choose after they paid the price for the team that had challenged them.

It was nearly five thirty when the other two volunteers got up to go. Andrea left and the squat, jowly mayor finished up a call before turning to Stroud. Stroud looked directly into the eyes of the other man. Albert's policies had helped to turn Philadelphia from a good and growing city into a stagnant metropolis with rising crime, gang violence, and the flight of businesses and the upper class. With an eye on a congressional run, the unrepentant liberal tried to rehabilitate his image by coming to work here every afternoon.

"It's been a helluva damn day," the mayor said. "This is your business. What do you make of these attacks? Soft targets? Cowards?"

"I make of it, Mr. Mayor, that someone is very, very angry."

The mayor seemed surprised. "You call carnage like this *angry*? Angry at what?"

Stroud smiled. "Not at *what,* Mr. Mayor. At *whom.* They are angry at you and others like you who turned the American dream into an American nightmare."

The mayor seemed surprised by the other man's candor. His bushy brow knit. "That's a big jump, Mr. Stroud."

"Actually, the jump from Rachel Reid to Ric Samuels is very, very small."

"You're blaming the victims?"

"I thought I was answering your question," Stroud replied.

"What about the hotel guests, the patrons at Ur-Burger?"

"Don't defend a food stand that rewards unlawful immigrants for their crime."

"All these months of working here, I never thought . . . You call it a crime to want a better life?"

"You know better than that," Stroud said. "It's the method, not the goal that I disapprove of. And obviously I'm not alone. As for the innocent victims—no one wants to see that, of course."

"I'm glad to hear that, Burton," Albert said, though Stroud

was not sure the man had actually heard anything. "In *my* line of work, when people don't like what we do, they vote us out. They don't murder."

"What was it that Malcolm X said of civil rights? 'By any means necessary'?"

"That was about civil rights—"

"What is this, then? Aren't the rights of a good majority of Americans being crushed by tank-tread progressivism?"

"My God," Albert said. "You do approve of this."

Stroud was silent. The former official went and got his hat and coat from the rack. He turned before leaving.

"I'm going to speak to Chuck Boyd about this," Albert said. "A man who holds such views is not suited to work in a place like this."

Albert left, leaving Stroud in a place of exquisite self-satisfaction. For there, in a phrase, was the dogmatic arrogance that had birthed the Black Order.

The elevator was a few paces beyond the door. As soon as Stroud heard the doors open and close, he removed a burner phone from his shoulder bag.

Of all the moments since just before midnight, this was the most important. It would tell him just how long the war would last and how far he would have to go.

Stroud inputted a number and waited. A human voice answered. He knew the call would be recorded.

"The White House, how may I direct your call?"

"The president's office, and please do not put me into the automated system."

"I'm sorry, sir, but—"

"Tell Natalie Cannon to inform the president that the Black Order is calling. She will know the name."

He looked at his watch. The call was put through in fourteen seconds.

"This is Trevor Harward, the president's national security advisor. With whom am I speaking?"

"In approximately two minutes, Mr. Harward, there will be another incident. I will call back after that. Please see that the president answers."

"Wait! What—"

Stroud disconnected the call, removed the battery, and returned the phone to his shoulder bag. He selected a second phone, set his tablet before him, and waited with a sense of expectation and rising exhilaration.

Just one more action remained to establish the irrevocable tide of this war.

Tom Albert was pissed as he walked to his car.

The politician had eschewed the staff parking in favor of a lot on Callowhill Street, a two-minute walk. It cost him a few bucks not to use the staff lot, but the owner had been an early supporter, one of the first to hang an ALBERT FOR PHILLY banner, and promised to do so again when the mayor decided on his next political move. Parking in a public facility, where he was seen coming and going, also reinforced his status as a man of the people. He would need those people to give him a job.

At the moment, treading heavily in the dark, cold night,

Albert wished he could announce for Congress *today,* wipe the smell of that man's hate from his nostrils.

"That attitude reinforces *everything* I've said about these wealthy autocrats who want to support the discriminatory status quo," he muttered. It was noxious, toxic, and if he were not wearing gloves he would stop and text Chuck Boyd *now* to get rid of Burton Stroud. But it was too cold for that. Maybe when he got to his car. He could linger a minute, still get to his home in Chestnut Hill before the heavy traffic.

Half a block away, Albert saw a pair of young men and a man in an overcoat and a black Russian Cossack hat walking toward him. The former mayor made it a policy never to hide his face or look away. He did not want to seem aloof to potential voters, and he could take whatever critical word or two someone might dish out in passing.

The man in the overcoat stopped to light a cigarette—Albert would still have to be nice to him—and the young men passed first, huddled against the wind and not recognizing him. The mayor walked on, toward the man in the overcoat who looked at him, smiled, then cut to his right and stepped in front of the mayor, drew a Maxim 9 handgun with a built-in suppressor, and shoved it into the politician's belly.

Gray Kirby angled the gun up, putting three bullets into the man, one atop the other. They ripped through his intestines, stomach, and heart and dropped him to the pavement like a trash bag.

Pedestrians across the street saw the mayor fall, and someone shouted that a man needed help. One man started to run across Callowhill, and the two men stopped and turned. Gray pocketed the gun and ran back the way he had come. He had arrived hours before and waited for a parking spot to open on Carlton Street. Stroud had provided him with Albert's schedule. He had determined that the target was there by posing as a man who wanted to turn his life around. If the former mayor had left early, Kirby would have seen him coming.

Stroud was insistent that the hit be done as close as possible to five thirty. He had not said why—in case of capture, only Stroud knew the entirety of the plan. All Kirby knew was that the credibility of the Black Order depended on that.

Kirby raced to his car, shoving the compact gun in his inside coat pocket. He got into the Jeep Wrangler before anyone thought to give chase and took a moment to text the word "Done" to Stroud. Until the first of the young men reached the body, saw the blood pooling thickly under the body, no one even realized there had been a shooting, only that a man had fallen.

Without haste now, Kirby replaced the magazine, put the gun inside his coat, and pulled from his spot headed toward Vine. His only immediate goal was to put distance between himself and the crime scene. Poole had not had time to access the security cameras in the area, nor would there be a need. He was to head for the Homestead, where Sarno and Dee Dee were also headed, as were Philpotts and Honda. There, they would await Poole and Stroud. Together, the team would contact the members of social media who were with them, begin to assemble the army that would ensure the rights and liberty of all Americans.

Kirby made his way through rush hour traffic as sirens converged in the distance. He did not use the car GPS in case he was stopped. He had memorized the route from the city to the Homestead and set out at a leisurely pace. He would conference in at six from a rest stop somewhere along the way. He was finally able to relax and savor the successful completion of his second mission of the day. He ate the chicken salad sandwich he had bought earlier. It had stayed cold and fresh on the seat.

Though he was tired, he was invigorated by the modest meal . . . and by a twilight filled with the promise of tomorrow. All he had to do was hide in plain sight and, when instructed, head to Drexel University to collect his teammate. Then he would head west, to dark, frozen roads that would do two things. First, they would make travel exciting—except for his chronically white-knuckle passenger. And second, they would make any pursuit slow and difficult by ground, and shielded by bare but thick, intertwined branches from the air.

The worst is over, he thought. And if the enemy were foolish enough to press on, they would do so under a single thread with the sword of Damocles hanging over them.

After the rest of Black Wasp had departed, Chase Williams doubled back and went to Stroud Safe at Home. Though the shop was still crowded, Williams did not see the owner and asked about his whereabouts.

"He's left for the day," a salesperson informed him, obviously wishing she could do likewise.

Stroud could not have gone far. Williams took a chance and

headed toward the parking garage just beyond the shop. He put on his overcoat, in case Stroud was still there and the uniform caught his eye.

The fluorescent lights kept the garage safely lit. Williams descended slowly and saw both Stroud and the other man. Williams ducked into the garage office to inquire about monthly rates. He turned in time to see Stroud depart, then texted Stroud's license number to Berry. Williams requested permits, tickets, and anything else tied to the vehicle.

The phone chimed as Williams walked back to the street.

"Why do you want all this?" Berry asked. He was whispering; that meant the president was nearby.

"If Burton Stroud isn't behind the Black Order, he's one of the people running the show," Williams said.

"That isn't what I mean. Haven't you left for D.C.?"

"The others went, I didn't."

There was a loud exhale. "Chase, the president is not going to like this."

"You're probably right. Don't tell him."

"Really helpful, thanks."

"Matt, at some point, whether it's the ONI, the PPD, or us, someone's going to have to take this lunatic down. That means knowing where he is. Also, his service record. See what's there."

"Right. Yeah. Okay. One thing: the ONI found custom code in Captain Hamill's security system that matches something in the burned dark web overlay. I don't understand a word of it. Anyway, Nathan has undercover people out there. Just make sure your paths don't cross and they mistake you for one of the bad guys."

"There was a time when we'd be watching one another's backs."

"That time isn't now, Chase."

"I'll watch myself, thanks."

Berry had promised to get Williams the information he requested.

Williams went to a coffee shop and searched for any information about Stroud Safe at Home, an employee of the month or year, hiring history, anything that might point him in the direction of the other man. There was nothing. It was as if Stroud had kept everything but the advertising and his slogan—"You Can Trust in Stroud"—invisible.

On purpose, preparing for this, Williams surmised.

While Williams sat there, Stroud's service record arrived.

Eleven minutes, Williams marveled. The email chain went directly from the secretary of the navy to the president to Berry. The speed suggested two things: respect for Midkiff, which would be an uphill climb for Wright; and concern about possible dark web overlays in other parts of the system. The fewer stops the file made, the securer.

The dossier was thick with honors. Stroud served with distinction in the Seventy-Fifth Ranger Regiment. There were citations, a medal, and a great many dates and places of engagements with hostile forces. The file was exemplary—and ultimately unhelpful.

Why does a man like this go rogue? Williams asked himself.

To which he replied, *Why does a man like you put a bullet in the brain of an unarmed terrorist? Who was it who said the truth is more important than the facts?*

It was just over ten minutes before the next item came up, the only one pertaining to the Tesla. It was a parking permit for the Free Library of Philadelphia. There was also a note that Williams did not understand: the PPD was already watching for the Tesla, though why and for whom Berry did not know.

Williams focused on the library. *Why there?* It suggested a lot of off-line research—which left no footprints—accompanied by a hefty financial donation. Or else Stroud was on a board of some kind. There was also a third possibility, tied to one or both of the others. A good tactician would have planned for the resources of the United States government to find the workplace and home of a leader of the Black Order. He would have given himself a safe house. One with multiple exits. The library might be such a refuge. It was certainly not a place any force would enter with guns drawn.

Rather than wasting time having Berry check library documents, Williams had decided to Uber over. While he waited for the car, he received a screaming text from Berry.

B.O. CONTACTED . . . AWAITING NEW STRIKE

The world around him suddenly seemed very frail, impermanent. That feeling also emboldened Williams. It was his sworn duty to protect these shores. There was no time to dance around Stroud; if he was behind this, Williams had to know.

Arriving at the magnificent edifice, Williams approached an elderly man seated behind an information desk. The gentleman's cobalt-blue uniform sat loose on his frame like the binding of a wise, old book Williams expected to find here.

"Good afternoon," Williams said. "Can you tell me if Mr. Burton Stroud is here?"

"Is he expecting you—General?" the man asked.

So Stroud *was* there. The admiral had not bothered to correct the guard's error. Wrong information and misdirection was valuable too.

Williams smiled and glanced at the man's name tag. "I don't have an appointment, Mr. Fitzpatrick. I tried to see him at his store but was told he'd come here. Is there a board meeting?"

"Board? No, Mr. Stroud isn't on the board. He volunteers in the Office of Adult Education. But—and I mean no disrespect, sir—if you want to see him, I still have to call up."

The man reached for the phone on his desk. Williams shook his head.

"You know what? Don't bother him; it isn't that important. I'll stop by tomorrow."

"You sure? Everything that's going on in the world—who knows if there'll be a tomorrow."

"You are not wrong, sir," Williams answered. "But I'll wait."

Thanking the man, Williams walked from the library and kept walking to stay warm. He decided to wait for Berry's update before deciding on his next course of action.

That was when Williams heard the muffled pops, knew

the general direction from which they had come, and ran toward them. A figure was sprawled on the sidewalk, and another man was running away. The apparent assailant had a substantial head start on anyone who might consider giving chase. Williams decided to try by going around the block, paralleling his flight. The gunman was not in any of the parked cars he passed on Carlton Street. Williams continued onto North Sixteenth Street, did not see the shooter on foot.

Too clean a getaway to be random. Too close to the library to be coincidence?

Williams went back to the crime scene. Several people had gathered around the man on the pavement. Blood was pooling, and the man's back was not rising and falling.

"It's Mayor Albert!" someone said, bending close.

There were murmurings of disbelief, motorists were rubbernecking, and sirens announced the approach of police. One of the pedestrians went into the street to wave cars ahead so the PPD could get through.

Williams turned away. He stepped into the doorway of an apartment building and called Matt.

"The former mayor of Philadelphia was just gunned down a few blocks from me."

"Tom Albert?"

"The same."

"So that's the war. Another liberal mouthpiece. I'll let the others know."

"Matt, Burton Stroud is at the Free Library."

"Now?"

"Yes. That's just a few blocks from the hit. We have to question him. The local police or FBI can make the collar—but I need to see him first."

"Why would he talk to you?"

"He'll want to know who's been playing tag with his team."

"I've got to think about this."

"Why? We need information."

"What we don't need now are loose cannons. I was about to call you. We're supposed to get another call from the Black Order. My guess is this one's going to be an ultimatum."

CHAPTER EIGHTEEN

The White House, Washington, D.C.
January 16, 5:43 p.m.

Matt Berry had taken the call from Williams in the president's private antechamber. Returning to the Oval Office, he leaned over and quietly briefed the president.

Midkiff nodded. His expression, which had not been hopeful, darkened when he learned that Williams had stayed behind.

"We can't afford loose cannons," the president said firmly.

"No, sir," Berry replied.

"You will relay that?"

"My very words."

The others in the room were stoic as Berry returned to his seat. But there was hostility in the air, a close second to fear. Trevor Harward looked at Berry as though he wanted to choke the man, not just for this but for years of consistent cross-purposes. Angie Brunner just looked at Berry with disapproval. She had assumed the call was from Chase Williams and had expected to be part of a private briefing.

The only other person in the room was Vice Admiral Nathan. He was openly annoyed to have been pulled from the investigation—especially since, as he had informed the president just before Berry left, they were close to moving against a person of interest. He sat impatiently, his cell phone in his hand.

On speakerphone were President-Elect Wright, Homeland Security Secretary Hewlett, and FBI Deputy Director Kim. One other person was listening in on the president's smartphone: Victoria Bowman, director of the White House Operational Technology Office adjacent to the situation room, which was located two stories below. The call from the Black Order, like all calls to the Oval Office, would actually be coming through her RA system—recording and analysis—before reaching the president's desk. The last call from the Black Order had been too brief to secure anything useful. Among her duties now was to monitor the call for any words, phrases, accents, or inflections that might be in the extensive print and audio database. The library consisted of surveillance from counterterrorism operatives. Though the president, Berry, and Angie knew about Stroud, there was a chance that he was not the leader, not the caller. If so, the caller might have been exposed or identified in some context other than the Black Order. A vocal stress analysis program was also linked to her connection.

The mood in the Oval Office was like nothing Berry had previously experienced. Meetings about terrorism and war were typically held in the Situation Room, but the president wanted everyone ready—not in transit—when the call came in.

He was certain it would; the caller had sounded too sure, had set too short a fuse, to be bluffing. The call from Williams suggested that it was imminent.

The only conversation after the first call was about media criticism of the ONI press conference. There had been no follow-up since the initial statement by Vice Admiral Nathan, and he had taken few questions. With the exception of Wright, who had condemned the attacks and had been informed that all intelligence services were fully engaged—his first big lie as president-elect, Berry reflected—every person in the room was happy to be out of the spotlight on this.

The call from the Black Order came a half minute after Berry's return. It was put directly through to the president.

"Hello, Mr. President, Mr. Harward, and anyone else who is listening. Tom Albert, former mayor of Philadelphia, has just been assassinated. Do you require further proof of my identity?"

"No," Midkiff replied.

"Good. That was a limited strike. At any point, including during this conversation, we can match that action or add to the body count considerably."

"To what end?" the president asked.

Everyone was sickened by the caller's cavalier tone. Though the president's voice was calm, he was visibly tense, both hands on his desk, pressing on the antique blotter.

"I think you know the answer," the caller said. "Rachel Reid, Ric Samuels, Tom Albert, the owners of Ur-Burger. All of these people have been scourges on the American body. The voices of tradition and patriotism have been stifled. The 'end' of the Black Order is to encourage those who share our views to stand up without fear of censure or harm—"

"The Constitution gives you that right," Midkiff said.

"—and to *fight* for what we believe in."

"'By any means necessary,'" Midkiff muttered.

"Mr. President, I am not here to debate the issues. Unless you wish to trigger further destruction, and on a scale that will truly earn the sobriquet 'World War III,' you will immediately do the following. First, do not interfere with myself or anyone who identifies with the Black Order online or in the streets. If violence issues from these people, I will put a stop to it. Second, do not attempt to block our message. Third, do not remove or deface our banners or image—which will replicate a bloody rope seized during the Ur-Burger operation. Inform those who do, law enforcement and civilians alike, that we will defend our property. It is our desire that going forward, we will require no further violence. We will achieve our ends through fearless, unhindered advocacy of our cause."

"You're asking us to legitimize lawlessness and anarchy, to overlook the crimes you've committed."

"Not asking, instructing," the caller said. "The pawns of reform have had free rein enough. No more statues will fall. No more supporters will be attacked."

"The public will demand action. They won't tolerate a reign of terror."

"They've tolerated it for years! We're simply reversing the polarity. The public wants safety and the untroubled continuation of their lives. What attacks or disasters move them, *truly* move them? Maybe they feel guilty enough to send food or water, maybe they send money. Then they go on with their lives. No, Mr. President. I will attack dissent that takes any form other than dialogue, and I will kill the guilty until the public has had enough killing. They will accept the Black Order if we call a cease-fire."

Midkiff shook his head. "You could have achieved your end within our system."

"By fielding candidates for change?" The caller laughed. "We did. We were met with violence, in the streets and on campuses. Our advocates have been banned, beaten, shouted down. No, Mr. President. The rules only apply to the anointed of the once-impartial fourth estate, the dishwater-deep intellects of Hollywood"—he paused to drive his sharpest stake—"your successor, Governor Wright, who teaches rights over responsibilities, forgetting that America was founded on both of these qualities. Are you listening, Mr. President-Elect? This war is on you."

Angie pressed her lips together to keep from answering. Wright elected not to.

"We once fought against taxation without representation," the caller went on. "Today, we do so again with retaliation that will be immediate and disproportionate."

"What if we need to contact you?" Midkiff asked. "We have to—"

"You don't. Good evening."

There was no click. The talking simply stopped. The president's hand moved slowly to end the call. He stared at the phone a long moment.

"He's military," Harward said. "The bastard called the fast-food massacre an 'operation.'"

That had been self-evident to most of the people on the call. No one commented. Berry was the only one not looking around. He was studying a map on his iPad.

The president was still holding his phone. He touched a button on the console. "Ms. Bowman?"

"Based on the recording, it is a ninety-seven percent certainty the caller was Burton Stroud," she said.

"What recording?" Harward asked. "Who the hell is Burton Stroud?"

Berry looked down. He had forwarded the recording Breen had made in Stroud Safe at Home. The president was tired; his timing was unfortunate.

"Later, Trevor. Go on, Ms. Bowman," the president said.

Harward made a disgusted sound and turned to his tablet.

"The man has been preparing for this call," she said. "He took his time to spell out his philosophy, justifying his deeds. He is no wild-eyed radical."

"He has spilled a great deal of innocent blood," Angie said.

"And he will shed more if we aren't smart," Midkiff said. "Please, Ms. Bowman, go on."

"In terms of amplitude, he made no distinction between threat and conversation. This suggests an equal commitment to thought and action. The delivery was natural whether he was talking to you or reciting dogma, which suggests he was not reading from a script."

"He believes what he said," Midkiff said.

"Deeply. Words like 'sobriquet' and 'censure' point to his being well read or well educated."

"Is there anything to suggest he was bluffing about World War III, Ms. Bowman?" Midkiff asked.

"Voice stress analysis uses algorithms drawn from a baseline of military radicals, terrorists, and psychotics. By every measure, this man fits none of those profiles. Further, based on words, modulation, hesitation, pace, even dry mouth, the reliability factor here—whether the speaker is telling the truth—is at eighty-nine percent. That ranks with Hitler at the Nuremberg Rallies as opposed to, say, Charles Manson."

"Thank you," Midkiff said. "Stay on the line, please."

"Mr. President, we obviously cannot accommodate those requests," Secretary Hewlett said.

"I'm open to suggestions."

"Call his bluff," Harward declared. "The Black Order may not possess the capabilities he described."

"And if they do?" Midkiff asked. "I grant you we need a better solution than all-out war or capitulation, but I won't gamble more lives to find out which of you is right."

"So, Burton Stroud," Harward said. "Owns a home security firm in Philadelphia. This is the guy who's threatening us? A Center City *businessman*?"

"Hitler was a paperhanger," Berry said.

"Not now, please," Midkiff warned the two. "And for now, people, the name Burton Stroud does not leave this room."

"Speaking of Philadelphia," Kim said, "we have no control over the Philly police and aren't likely to get it. That's sure to tick this guy off. The killing of Tom Albert has been confirmed, cops are on the scene, and there are witnesses. For that matter, the Atlanta Police Department are already coalescing resources around the target areas. How long before they learn about the Black Order and Stroud or whoever this is comes back with an ultimatum about both of those?"

The vice admiral leaned his big frame into the conversation. "I say we stop worrying about what the enemy thinks, or what he will do, and take him out where he lives. You can't hold America hostage."

"You know where to get him?" Harward asked.

Nathan nodded solemnly.

"I don't disagree," Midkiff said, "but I don't want to do anything that provokes a disproportionate response. Not yet anyway. Abe, anyone at HS have a sense about what kind of attacks we might be looking at?"

"Based on what we've seen, they appear to be hands-on, lone-wolf operations," Secretary Hewlett said.

"Hands-on?" Angie said.

"Guns, knives, grenades. With a guerilla group like we've seen him deploy—and mind you, we may only have seen a portion of it—his up-the-ante targets could be anything from the electronic grid to reservoirs or dams, possibly fuel supplies . . . maybe all of the above."

"How much pain are we prepared to absorb?" Allen Kim asked.

Angie was on a Bluetooth with Wright. "There's also the matter of explaining this to the American people, whatever you do," she said. "We believe they will want justice, but they won't accept an escalation of hostilities."

"The ONI has made a point of assuring the nation that this has only been ongoing for a few hours and that we have made progress—"

"We heard the press conference," Angie remarked. "'A few hours' is a year in Twitter time, and your progress has been behind the scenes. People have been dying in front of the cameras."

"You cut me off, Ms. Brunner. As you may have gathered, our investigation is turning up leads that we believe will be actionable early this evening. When we have our targets, and the president green-lights our plan of attack, we will hit the Black Order hard and fast. That's in both real time and Twitter time."

"Only if 'hard and fast' prevents escalation," Angie said.

"We are putting together a team from Naval Special Warfare Command. God help us—I can still say that, yes? God?—God help the United States of America if our shore unit cannot crush a band of lawless murderers."

There was an uncomfortable silence after the administrations briefly clashed. Berry seized it.

"Mr. President, may I see you in the anteroom?"

Every eye in the room turned toward the deputy chief of staff.

"Excuse me, Matt, but just this very morning, didn't Major

Lewis prove that it's a bad idea to segregate intelligence?" Harward asked.

"I thought the lesson here was if you put information out there, bad people can get it."

The president shot Berry a look and said, "Hold that objection, Trevor."

The president sat weighing the affront to the two men versus the need for Op-Center to operate in secret. He opted to retire briefly; Wright and Angie would understand.

"Excuse us for two minutes," Midkiff said to the open displeasure of Harward and Clark. Berry was not the only one who wanted a moment of privacy.

The men walked into the small, rectangular side office. There was a small hardwood writing desk, two chairs, a phone, and a laptop. The shades were pulled on the Rose Garden to help keep out the radiant cold.

Midkiff wondered what sin he had committed in his decades of service to have merited this crisis with eighty-odd hours left in his administration. It wasn't self-pity but a cumulative exhaustion that made it difficult to think clearly. Yet he had to.

Midkiff sat on the edge of the small desk. Berry stood with his arms folded.

"Who the hell wants this job?" the president asked no one in particular. Then he regarded Berry. "If Stroud is running this show, why wouldn't Major Lewis have made that connection?"

"All she had was a Pennsylvania arms drop and Stroud Safe at Home with a contract at NSA."

"Now ONI has it."

"You'll have to put a freeze on Nathan and his team, sir."

"That's not going to happen."

"Sorry? After what Stroud said?"

"ONI found this on their own through Hamill's alarm system. Everyone there has it. Nathan knows I won't shut down this chance for Counter Proliferation to prove its worth."

"Excuse me, but politics and budget—*now*?"

The president grew angry. "It's not that, dammit. There *is* no good next step. What happens if your own worst fear comes to pass, someone leaking information to the press—about Hamill, Stroud? It's better to take a good shot, if we have one."

"All right, assume that's the case. Let's give Op-Center a free hand for an hour or two, before Nathan rushes in."

"Don't sell the vice admiral or his people short, Matt—"

"I'm not. But he's got more invested in this than a low-profile takedown. Besides, Allen Kim is right. If you're not prepared to call off two municipal police departments, they're going to keep pawing at these attacks. You'll have internecine combat along with the bigger war. Hell, you may have to recall Breen to help argue this in court."

The president thought for a moment, then shook his head. "What is it, six, seven people in the Black Order holding us hostage?"

"Yes, but we've got four people on their tails. And who knows? Chase may find a way to get him."

"Where are they now? Chase is in Philly—"

"Black Wasp is somewhere in Delaware by now. Let me send them to Dover AFB to wait for instructions. Chase on Stroud, Black Wasp ready to go after the others."

The president was visibly uneasy with this approach. But then, Berry thought, he had not looked happy with any of his options back in the Oval Office.

"This plan worries me, Matt. By my soul, that man on the phone was the sanest-sounding madman this side of the Middle East. They're the most dangerous, rational till they blow. And it doesn't take much."

"If that is true, sir, then he will find a reason to lash out regardless."

Midkiff sighed. "All right. I don't think anyone on the call was an advocate of conciliation, and this seems like the best shot." The president checked his watch. "Stay in here and make the calls, monitor their progress. I want to know everything they're doing, and they must understand that abort power rests with me."

"Absolutely, sir."

"No, really."

"Yes, Mr. President."

"I'm going to clear the room. They can take their brawls to Twitter. I don't want to be distracted."

Midkiff left, and the weight of the office was suddenly on Berry as much as it was on Wyatt Midkiff. It was one thing to orbit power; it was another to suddenly feel like the center of the universe.

As Berry called Chase Williams, he wondered why any sane human *would* ever want this job.

George Nathan was fuming when he left the Oval Office. It was one thing to be shut down by a president he somewhat respected. It was another to be contradicted by the twin harvesters of every cause but America. Ever since the election, he had prayed, nightly, that the causes he had fought for during his career, that so many had died for, were not about to be kicked out the door along with proud tradition, God, and sanity.

And budgetary cuts to support more giveaway social programs. That is not going to keep America safe.

The vice admiral stalked down the corridors of the West Wing—perhaps for the last time, he knew—with his phone already pressed to his ear. Interns carrying boxes had to stop and weave. His exit was torpedo fast and straight.

Rear Admiral Cornel Gerst at Counter Proliferation was in charge of the Hamill investigation. Her team had started on the trail that found five minutes of "false time" on the Hamill security system's internal clock. It had shut down for five minutes, from 11:18 to 11:23, then rebooted. The reboot ran through the missing minutes to "catch up" using a separate program, not in real time. The investigators timed it out; it would have taken five minutes for an intruder to go upstairs, commit murder, deliver the message, and leave.

The off-line command was linked to an internal program that enabled an override from a wireless signal operating in the 5.8 GHz band. The same program was found embedded in the system at NSA Philadelphia. Threads were also located in the ONI system. Investigators had opted not to shut it down after finding twenty-two separate signals incoming from a series of rerouted sources. Cutting any of them at the end user would alert whoever was at the originating source.

That source had finally been located: a block in Germantown, Pennsylvania. It was the same block where Burton Stroud lived, the man whose name was on the company that provided the security systems. A team comprised of ONI military personnel had choppered from ONI Suitland and driven out to watch the area at the corner of Green Street and Walnut Lane.

A dog walker—Sergeant Abi Smith, dressed in work clothes—went in first to get eyes on the place and report to the unit. The place seemed dead.

The town house itself was empty, as far as electronic surveillance from the CP unit could determine. The call to the White House had not come from there. If Stroud himself did not return by mid-evening, the team would execute a search warrant they had obtained.

The course of action was clear to Cornel Gerst and to George Nathan, if not to President Midkiff. Burton Stroud was either involved or would know who was. His immediate interrogation was a matter of national security. And for more than just intelligence. Given everything Nathan had heard on the call from the Black Order, he was concerned that the NYPD, APD, and PPD—working with urgency, resentment, local political pressure, and media scrutiny—would soon reach similar conclusions and charge into Stroud with hobnailed tread, triggering precisely what President Midkiff was trying to avoid.

The ONI had to go in first, not just to question Stroud but to keep the others out and preserve the integrity of materials inside, the same as they had done with the Hamill house.

The unmarked cars surrounded the area, and the agents remained inside them. The target would be spotted, watched thermally, listened to electronically, and then the team would move in. Once the president gave the go order, the ONI could begin to dismantle the short, terrible reign of the Black Order.

Nathan got into his staff car. As his driver rolled away from the White House, Nathan called Lieutenant Commander Dave Richman, the officer in charge of Project Intercept.

"There is still no sign of Stroud at his office or here," he reported. "We're thinking he might have gone to dinner somewhere. We have his picture with TSA and Amtrak security, in case he is coming from out of town . . . or trying to leave."

"What about his vehicle?"

"DMV records show a company car, and the PPD said they'll watch for the car and tags. So far we haven't heard anything."

"Do they know to just watch for him, let us handle the intercept?"

"I told them. Remains to be seen whether they'll comply."

"Pricks," Nathan said.

"They were asking if we knew that the mayor was a target. They've got egg on their faces about that."

"Rest of the block quiet?" Nathan asked.

"Very. Except for short dog walks, people are staying where it's warm."

"Perfect. I'm heading back to Suitland. Call when he shows up, and I'll make sure Midkiff is on board."

Nathan hung up and sat back. Even if the president did not okay the mission, he would make sure they went in anyway. It wasn't just the future of America that was at stake, it was the honor and solvency of the ONI.

Growing a pair was a lesson John Wright had better learn, and this was a good place to start.

CHAPTER NINETEEN

Dover AFB, Delaware
January 16, 6:11 p.m.

Jaz Rivette was seated in a plastic chair in the Aero Club, legs stretched out under the top of the long table, his finger swiping across his smartphone. The room was full of base personnel who, Rivette imagined, were usually more raucous than they were tonight. He had seen this several times at Camp Pendleton. Whenever there was news about a possible terror-related strike at home or abroad, men and women in uniform went on internal alert. Any such attack could presage a larger event, another 9/11, leading to immediate deployment.

The finger stopped moving.

"Got it."

Grace and Breen were seated nearby looking at their own devices. Neither replied.

"It says here that 'cool your heels' first applied to horses back in the early 1600s. I guess that makes sense, since those shoes were iron and they must've gotten pretty hot from walking." He closed the page of idioms. "I'm guessing you all came up with nothing on wildlife."

"Nothing that helps," Breen replied.

The major was as frustrated as Rivette, though for a different reason.

Breen had asked Grace to drive so he could research Western Pennsylvania. He began his search by looking up PAVE and finding every article, every photograph he could about the charity food group. He had hoped the kinds of animals Hamill hunted would point him in a geographical direction.

The information was spotty and of no help.

He checked topographical maps. What hills could a man of a certain age climb, which woods were too steep? Again, the map was too grand for that.

They had arrived at Dover, their passes waiting, just minutes before. While Breen continued searching and Rivette tried to amuse himself, Grace suddenly came alert.

"Regulations," she said.

Breen looked up. "Whose?"

"Game Commission, Commonwealth of Pennsylvania," she answered, typing on her tablet.

"What will that tell us?" Rivette asked.

Breen wondered the same thing. He did not see how statewide ordinances could help to narrow the search.

"You don't work with katanas, bo staffs, nunchaku," she said, still typing.

"What does all that Bruce Lee stuff have to do with—"

Breen's confused expression changed. "Weapons," he said admiringly, and also began punching keys. "Sorry, I didn't mean to disparage them."

"It's okay," Grace said. "I'm used to that."

"I still don't follow," Rivette said.

"Washington, D.C., this morning," the major said as he also continued typing. "Major Lewis was killed by someone using a bow. Mrs. Hamill said her husband had come home without game after his last few visits—"

"Bow hunting," Rivette said. "No guns allowed. You're bad guys, you set up a wilderness HQ, you don't want people shooting all around you? Is that it?"

"Partly," Breen said.

"I'm back to being lost. Isn't that what we're gonna do?"

"Suppose law enforcement were to come in pretending to be hunters. You have cameras, sensors, something that picks up the trespassers. They're carrying guns—"

"Got it. They aren't hunters."

"You also want to feed your people locally," Grace said. "Fewer people coming and going, in trucks or vans. More challenging for any kind of surveillance to track them."

"So you hunt with a bow," Rivette said. "But didn't Taikinys deliver *guns*?"

"Yes. To defend a compound, if it came to that," Grace said. "I've used northern Fujian bamboo bows. For one-on-one, and stealth, they are superior to firearms."

"Maybe to you."

Grace let the proud remark slide. If Rivette's questions

bothered her or Breen, they did not show it. They were using the opportunity to think out loud, to question their own logic. There was no time to get this wrong.

Rivette sat up and joined in the search, Breen pausing only long enough to call Williams.

"Any news?" Breen asked.

"Waiting to hear from Berry," Williams said. "You have anything?"

Breen told him, then said they would likely need air transport to Western Pennsylvania and explained why.

"It's a good lead," Williams agreed thoughtfully.

"You don't sound like you believe that."

"I do, Hamilton. I also know that if you're right, you're heading into a situation where you don't know the enemy's strength or what kind of surveillance and trip wires they've got. They obviously saw Atlas Hamill coming."

"That's the job, Chase."

"I know."

"But there's something else," Breen said. "You're worried about retribution?"

"Everyone is, deeply. Stroud would not leave himself without a retreat or a counterstrike."

"Agreed. The alternative?"

"Well, there's the rub. There isn't one. That's what everyone's been wrestling with."

"We're going to have to bell the cat at some point. Or else surrender."

Hearing that, Rivette shook his head firmly.

"I know," Williams said, "though the sense I'm getting is that Midkiff wants to open a dialogue and at least tap the brakes."

"You think the president wants to run out the clock, have whatever happens happen on the next administration's watch?"

"If he can't shut the Black Order down for now, maybe. Vietnam playbook. Go to Paris, get the hell out of the jungle under the pretense of negotiations."

"I take it you're opposed to that? This isn't a three-hander, Chase. We need eyes on Stroud."

"I'll arrange the transportation for Black Wasp," he replied. "Let's shut them down."

After the call with Breen, Williams had determined that he had best become mobile, especially if Stroud was going to be on the move to who knew where.

Williams also needed to eat, something he had not done since the night before—which seemed like a month ago. That was the way with these missions. Minutes burdened by shifting dynamics and changing objectives had a way of flattening into hours. Ducking into a Thai restaurant with a view of the library-affiliated parking lot, Williams had ordered pho and called Captain Mann. She had seemed both surprised and glad to hear from him.

"What can I do for you now, sir?"

"If you were serious about giving me a hand, would you mind meeting me at Som Siam on"—he looked at the menu—"Nineteenth and Spring Garden?"

"I was serious, and I was just about to leave. I will be there as soon as traffic allows."

The woman thanked him for the call. The admiral did not want to tell her why he needed her. It was up to Stroud what he revealed to her at all. Given that the businessman would be on the phone, there was a little time to figure out what his next move would be. He would wait to hear from Matt Berry before deciding.

After the call from Major Breen, Williams contacted Sergeant Major Stewart at Fort Belvoir to arrange for Dover AFB to have a chopper standing by. Williams had the authority; now he had the responsibility. If he could not get through to Berry, he certainly would not be able to reach the president for his approval.

Williams was encouraged by Breen's discovery but also concerned: moving on the compound had apparently resulted in Atlas Hamill's death. Black Wasp was lethal, but so was the Black Order.

The admiral smiled at the woman who brought his tray. It was a small, human moment he very much needed.

Then he reviewed the news feeds while he ate, saw that there was nothing he did not know, and finished his soup while reading a history of Thailand on the placemat. He was just about done with both when Berry called.

"In an hour or two, Nathan closes in on Stroud's home," Berry said. "Thoughts?"

"Yeah. Don't do that. We don't want Stroud, we want to track Stroud and get the entire Black Order."

"The president's indicated he'll approve Nathan's plan. He has to do something, Chase."

"Correct. He has to *wait*."

"Give me an option. Please. What if you talk to Nathan, navy to navy?"

"Do you think he'd listen?"

"What if Midkiff rescinds your retirement?"

"To do what? Order him to stand down? The president can do that, Matt."

"But won't. Make the case for standing down, the way you just told me."

"That buys you, what, a half hour? The secretary of the navy will see through it and override. Look, you said I've still got time. Captain Mann is on her way to pick me up. If the Tesla goes mobile, I'll be able to follow. But, Matt? I'm betting it doesn't."

"Why?"

"Stroud was at the Free Library during the call. If that was his voice—"

"It was. Audio comparison matched."

"Then you just told me what he's doing there. According to the information desk, he works at the Office of Adult Education. He's hiding behind volunteer work. In fact, I wonder if Mayor Albert was doing the same."

"Easy to check—"

"Not important. Stroud won't risk going to his store or his home. He's probably got every safeguard there is. For now, he'll probably stay at the library until he's sure we won't dare lay hands on him."

"So what do you do?"

"What you just suggested about Vice Admiral Nathan."

It took Berry a moment to realize what Williams was suggesting. "You want to *talk* to Stroud? The man's a zealot. He won't listen."

"I don't expect him to, but what if he has a big-shot hostage? If nothing else, that might forestall future attacks and get Nathan to stand down."

"Or he may kill you and hang your body from a flagpole."

"You're talking as though Yemen and South Africa weren't dangerous." He snickered. "I guess there's a reason I can't resign myself to industry, think tanks, and academia."

Berry said nothing. There was no time to debate. He was still silent when Captain Mann arrived in a vintage Thunderbird.

"What do you say?" Williams asked.

"If I didn't trust you, we wouldn't be working together. It's your call."

"Thanks," Williams said as he put a five-dollar bill in the tip jar and went out into the night.

CHAPTER TWENTY

Philadelphia, Pennsylvania
January 16, 6:12 p.m.

To Stroud, the world always seemed very safe and protective in the early-onset dark of winter. It was especially so today as he sat back in his old, wooden chair at the OAE.

"It's done." He smiled. "We did it."

Their plans had been executed with barely a hitch. The ideas he had been nursing, contemplating, expanding for years had emerged fully formed and bulletproof. The most powerful people in America, in the world, had sat rapt and helpless as he spoke.

And now that the heavy lifting is over, the rebuilding begins.

Stroud rose, stretched, and packed his shoulder bag. He felt *good,* as if a stone had been lifted from his chest, allowing him to breathe. He walked toward the coatrack. At least, he hoped that was the case. He hoped that the entirety of the war had been fought over the past seven minutes. He hoped that the contingency wires were not tripped. If he was stalked or arrested, if any members of the team were watched or apprehended, there were attack plans in place for the others.

A gas attack at Temple University, a hotbed of radical thought. An arrow through the forehead of the Speaker of the House on his morning jog around the Mall. An explosion in the tower of Atlanta's iconic city hall courtesy of one of Jackson Poole's drones.

The destruction of an entire city.

The only reason actions like these had never been taken was a combination of the lack of know-how and the fear of getting caught. Stroud and his people had neither. They would rather die than live in the nation the United States was becoming.

But we will not die, Stroud thought as he took the marble steps to the lobby. *The masses and their leaders fear mere discomfort and inconvenience far more than we fear death.*

The war was the Black Order's to lose.

The clacking, shuffling heels of people leaving the building, their respectful murmurs, a few disrespectfully loud cell phone conversations filled the big, columned lobby as Stroud made his way to the exit. The security guard, Trace Fitzpatrick, was sitting behind his desk, waiting for the night officer to relieve him in ten minutes.

"Good evening, Mr. F," Stroud said as he walked by.

"Oh, Mr. Stroud, there was someone asking to see you before. He said he would call for you tomorrow."

Stroud stopped, turned, and approached the desk. "Did he give a name?"

"No, sir. He was about your age and a general."

"In uniform?"

"Yes, sir."

"Did he say what he wanted?"

"Just that he wanted to see you. He didn't want me to call up. A surprise visitor, I guess. You were in the army, yes?"

"That's right. Are there security pictures?"

Fitzpatrick was surprised. "I'm sure there are. The office is closed now. I can check in the morning."

Stroud smiled tightly. "That's all right. You say the man left? He's not waiting in the lobby?"

"He left."

The frozen smile lingered. "I think I know who it was. I'll see you in the morning."

"I'm off tomorrow, Mr. Stroud, so I'll see you . . ."

Stroud was not listening. The timing of this, of those operatives at the store, at NSA Philadelphia, was faster than he had anticipated the ONI acting. This had to be some outside player. He was burning inside. He hated not knowing, being at a disadvantage. The man had visited before the Oval Office call, so maybe it was all moot now. But Stroud knew Rangers, he knew special ops, he knew that they operated off the grid. Hadn't Captain Hamill?

Pulling on deerskin gloves and walking into the night, Stroud experienced a sense of vulnerability that was unfamiliar to him. He walked slowly to his car, wondering how anyone found him here. He participated in none of the OAE public affairs, appeared in no photographs—

He stopped at the edge of the parking lot on Fairmount Avenue, shivering as the cold air cut through his trench coat. He had not dressed for the chill. He intended to go from the library to his car to his home.

The car? Could someone have followed him, seen it in the parking garage? It could not have been . . . what was his name? Breen. Nor one of the two Poole had seen. Fitzpatrick might have described them, their quarry would be watching for them.

A person in uniform. They might be wearing a coat now, a different hat, *no* hat. Stroud's tactical mind went ferociously to work. What would a tail do? Attack? Call support? Continue to follow him? Might there be a dozen somebodies in and around the lot, waiting for him?

They know where I work. They certainly recorded my call. If they analyze it, they will learn nothing. I don't make public speeches—

The major. He may have recorded our conversation.

Stroud's mind raced through a litany of concerns. None of them should matter. The ultimatum he had delivered to the president stood: attack me or my people and the population suffers.

No. If this man is watching me now, the president needs a reminder, Stroud decided.

It was 6:17. He should have been on the way home right now, ready for the 9:00 p.m. videoconference. If not for the fear of being ambushed, he might continue into the open-air lot, to his car, and wait to be confronted by the man who was surely watching, somewhere. The man who was part of a military team that was going to learn a very harsh lesson.

Instead, Stroud went back upstairs and called Jackson Poole

on his LockLink phone. The LL7 sent its transmissions in alternate bursts through seven separate computers, with only the sender and receiver able to seamlessly receive and decode each burst.

The tech wizard had left the NSA after the woman and her companion had driven off. He had gone to Drexel University and parked there, using a scan of Stroud's old permit with the dates adjusted. That was his designated retreat in case things got too hot for the van elsewhere. Thanks to his uplinks, he was able to monitor the house and store from here.

"What's happening at the house?" Stroud asked when Poole answered.

"It's compromised. Woman walked her dog past the house three times. Doesn't show up on previous videos. Same four cars following a bunch of different traffic patterns at different times—usual scramble pattern."

"Plates?"

"From surveillance garage central, though whose I don't know. All different plates, different years, different makes."

"Idiots. I'm being watched here too." He looked at his watch. "I want you to immediately launch the Killshot Operation. Wait for my call before we go beyond that."

"Confirming Killshot Operation," Poole said. "You want me to give you time to change your mind? A minute? Two?"

"No."

"All right, then. I will signal when it's finished. What about the pickup?"

"I'll signal Gray to come and get you. Fry the tech while you wait for him."

"Confirming erasure of all van software."

"Confirmed," Stroud said and ended the call.

This was going to hurt him, being holed up in the OAE instead of in Germantown. He also could not leave for the Homestead—not when he had to focus on putting Midkiff and his people in their place.

Not when he had to be here, in this building.

They had been warned. There would be no more warnings, no more conversation. Only Black Order actions and the capitulation of two administrations.

The blood would be on their hands, not his.

"I mean, come on. It's been over fourteen hours. They're pulling people from all over—in and out of here, HQ. Why not relief for us?"

"Stop complaining, West. They're pulling people in because whatever they're doing, they don't have enough."

Masters-at-Arms Dylan West and Assad al-Maliki had flown in from NSA Mechanicsburg when it was still dark. Now it was dark again, and except for a fifteen-minute lunch break and two bathroom visits, the men had been on their feet, at the front door of the health center, for the duration.

For much of that time, West had been complaining. Al-Maliki was not so much listening to the man as ignoring him. Not that West was wrong; since the sun went down, al-Maliki had been struggling to keep his eyes open. The darkness and the cold had put him into a kind of torpor, in which the only one of his senses functioning at peak performance was hearing. He tried to listen past West, to the sounds of the base—they were preferable to the whining that had been increasing in frequency, duration, and volume as the day wore on. The only reason al-Maliki had not told his companion to pipe down was because it would not do any good. Over the past year, he had gotten to know the young New Yorker all too well. Even the navy could not drill or KP the mouthiness from the kid.

Because al-Maliki was silent, and because he was listening, the master-at-arms was the first to hear the unexpected sound. It was like a child walking a scooter on asphalt, both wheels turning but sounding a little different. He identified the sound as small gears moving, one set in front of him, one behind.

"Dylan, do you hear the—"

That was all Assad al-Maliki was able to say before the twin M2HB .50-caliber machine guns opened up on the street, the men, and the building behind them. West and al-Maliki were stitched across the lower chest in a straight, bloody line from right to left by the gun across from them, their lungs and stomachs perforated. The spitting of the gun and the clatter of empty shells were the last things either of them heard. Cut nearly in half, held together only by their spines, both men died within seconds.

The gun on the rooftop continued to slash from one side to the other, dim muzzle flashes flaring and dying as the twin weapons chewed up the door, shattered windows, and killed or gravely wounded anyone caught inside in the line of fire. Behind the building, on a low structure on an air force supply depot, a third gun blasted through the back side of the health center, peppering the wards, causing doctors and nurses to fall in awkward pirouettes, their legs shattered, abdomens torn open, hands and forearms ripped to useless stumps.

Rooftop spotlights flared on, and there were shouts from all corners of Naval Support Activity as service personnel thought, at first, that they were under attack, and then sought, in small clusters, to shut down the two machine guns. Firing at 850 rpm, the weapons had emptied their one-hundred round belts in seven seconds. Seventeen people were dead, twenty-nine wounded.

Shouts, moans, and the clatter of still-falling glass were all that was heard now, followed by a voice that announced the inexplicable glitches in the computers that remotely controlled the guns. Those voices were like lonely battle horns lost in the fading echo of combat and death.

CHAPTER TWENTY-ONE

Philadelphia, Pennsylvania
January 16, 6:20 p.m.

Getting into the Thunderbird reminded Williams of his early days in the navy, when getting back from shore leave depended on the kindness of motorists. The difference now was that the expression on the face of Captain Ann Ellen Mann was more welcoming.

"Good evening, sir!"

"Thank you for coming," Williams said as he climbed in.

"Not a problem," she said, continuing down the block. "This is near where Mayor Albert was killed—did you see it?"

"Heard it," he said. "Captain, if you wouldn't mind driving to the Free Library."

"Am I parking or waiting?"

"I'm not sure."

The way he said it, like an unfinished thought, caused her to give him a look. "If you want to bounce ideas off, I'm a good listener—translator, you know."

"And you're accustomed to risk," he said. It was more of a caution than an observation.

"Very much so."

Unless the captain dropped him off and left, which was not an option—he might need her—she was a part of this now. She deserved to know exactly what kind of situation she was in.

"Captain, what I'm going to tell you falls under the category of Controlled Unclassified Information. It's about the coordinated attacks that began with Captain Hamill—"

The phones of both Captain Mann and Chase Williams chimed almost at the same instant. Because Williams answered his phone, Mann answered hers. The captain's call was from Commander Dick Brandon, who had the evening shift at the base.

After the commander had spoken for just a few moments, Mann responded, "God—oh *God*!"

Williams had received the same message, but from Matt Berry, about the attack on NSA Philadelphia. He told Berry he'd call back.

"Captain—on speaker, please," Williams said.

Mann thumbed the button as she double-parked.

"—everyone who was on the top floor of each building took fire. We're still trying to organize people to assess the casualties and perform triage."

"Who's on the phone?" Williams asked Mann.

"Commander Dick Brandon."

"Commander, this is Admiral Chase Williams with Captain Mann. Do you know if there was a specific target?"

"Admiral Williams, the target was everything in the path of those automated guns. They fired without purpose, as far as I could tell. They just went back and forth."

"What about Mrs. Hamill?"

"We haven't gotten to her floor yet. There's a lot of confusion, and most of the lights were shot out, so it's dark in most of that area."

"Captain, go there," Williams said.

Mann did not need prodding. She told Brandon they were on the way, then tore into traffic. After her initial outburst, the captain had shown no emotion. Williams, on the other hand, felt sick. It was not just the act but the likely cause.

He called Berry back.

We triggered this. Stroud found out that I or the ONI or both were stalking him—maybe from the man at the library, he thought—*and decided to add to the body count.*

Berry did not pick up. Williams had a good idea why.

"Who was at the library?" Captain Mann asked, her voice hard as brick.

"The man I think is behind this. The man who installed the security at Captain Hamill's home, the base—"

"Stroud?"

"Yes. All of the attacks today, from Captain Hamill to D.C., New York, Atlanta, here—they're all his."

"And you're being cautious about taking him down because . . . ?"

"Because of what just happened. Shortly before I called you, he warned the president to keep everyone away."

"I see." Mann relaxed slightly. "I didn't mean to challenge your judgment just then. I'm trying to understand—"

"Believe me, I've been sitting here doing the same thing."

"You said 'everyone.' Who is in this besides you?"

"There are four of us in our strike group. After the attack in New York, we confronted Stroud in his store. The others were recalled after Atlanta and are waiting for instructions. Then there's ONI. They're watching Stroud's home."

Mann was silent for nearly a minute. Williams did not have to imagine the thoughts and emotions racing through her. Those same forces were playing havoc with his own efforts to think "next step." And then there was the guilt. One thing he had learned during his military career was that you could postmortem decisions that went wrong, but you could not second-guess yourself.

"What does Stroud want?" Mann finally asked.

"He's looking for some kind of rollback to the way things used to be in America. His approach seems to be to terrorize everyone to silence and inactivity."

"An Equalizer."

"Sorry?"

"I spend a lot of time at my desk, do a lot of reading. That's what activists call the new reactionaries. They're not supremacists exactly, not neo-Confederates, but the kind of individual I see at bars and officers' clubs. They say things after a few drinks like, 'Those SOBs pushed too hard, too fast,' referring to whichever group 'they' happen to be—immigrants, gay, transgender, other-abled. Equalizers are the pallbearers of the old ways, and they don't like it. What Stroud is doing is clever, in its monstrous way, and also predictable. Cancel culture, call-out culture, outrage culture—pushback was inevitable."

There was sadness but not bitterness in Mann's voice. Williams found himself moved.

"Do you know what kind of assets Stroud has?" Mann asked.

"We don't. That's what my team and I were trying to find out."

"If this new attack—" She choked, stopped. "If this is how Stroud responds to being spied on, what will he do if the ONI goes in?"

"I'm trying not to think about it," Williams admitted as he called Matt Berry again.

The decorum that had dominated the Oval Office for most of the day—tense though it was at times—was gone. The room was briefly in a state of open rebellion. Angie had gone to the transition team office in the West Wing to confer with Wright. Kim and Hewlett had left the conference call to turn the FBI and Homeland Security loose on the Black Order.

All had agreed not to mention the name. But all had said the terrorists must be stopped. Wyatt Midkiff did not disagree but felt that pressure from law enforcement would only ramp up the attacks.

"Sir, that may be," Abe Hewlett said before signing off. "But if we capitulate, we will have no status or standing in the world community from this day forward."

Kim said, "I am immediately advising the respective field offices to operate under title 18, subsection 2331, paragraph B, item 1: to investigate and dismantle acts that appear to be intended to intimidate or coerce a civilian population."

The president had remained silent in response to both of those pronouncements. Matt Berry had never seen him so disengaged from his team, if not from the crisis itself.

Berry was still in the antechamber, leaving Harward the only one left in the Oval Office.

"Mr. President," Harward said, "I believe it is essential that Nathan hit the Germantown residence while the ONI still has surprise on their side, and an uncrowded field."

"Stroud is not there. He will respond."

Midkiff was looking at the phone. He was dreading a call that he knew would come and was unsure how he would respond. His heart wanted to sue for a time-out. His spleen wanted to bury the man in a sea of gunfire.

"There may be files on premises that will give us the other members, the one who have been attacking the populace—a populace that is increasingly enraged and demanding action," Harward said.

It was a circular conversation; Midkiff had had enough of it. The more pressure they put on Stroud, the more carnage he would unleash.

Berry returned then. His expression was grave, and Midkiff expected to hear that Chase Williams had been at NSA Philadelphia and had perished in the attack.

"What have you got, Matt?"

"I wonder if I can have a minute alone, Mr. President."

Harward stood, scowling. "Sure, Matt! Why the hell not, Matt? The national security advisor doesn't need to know what's going on!"

"Trevor's right," the president said, then looked up at Berry. "I'd rather not lose any more advisors just now."

"I understand, sir," Berry said. "We, uh—we have a lead on the location of the Black Order's base of operations in Western Pennsylvania. A chopper has been requisitioned out of Dover AFB as soon as the target area can be narrowed."

"Timetable?" the president asked.

"Undetermined."

"Excuse me, but who are 'we'?" Harward asked. "Who's at Dover?"

Berry deferred to the president.

"Matt's referring to Chase Williams and a special ops unit," Midkiff told him.

Harward's expression locked, suspended somewhere between disbelief and disapproval. "You're serious, sir? The man who lost the Intrepid is leading a team?"

"He is, and that information stays in this room."

Harward's face twisted further toward disgust. "No worry, sir. I would not share that with anyone. I want to retain some measure of credibility." He shook his head. "Chase Williams blew it."

"Perhaps, but I needed the part of Op-Center that could still serve this nation," Midkiff said. "It was my call."

"I understand, Mr. President, and this is mine. You will have my resignation the instant this conflict is over."

Midkiff was too tired to respond. With a final, fully formed look of condemnation directed at Berry, Harward left the Oval

Office. Berry turned to the president after the door had clicked shut.

"I'm sorry, sir."

"Talk to me about Black Wasp. What are the chances they have something?"

"Breen is optimistic." Berry did not know what else to say. Everything Williams had told him was under the cloud of the base attack, short and incomplete.

"But there's no timetable?"

"No, Mr. President."

"I won't be able to hold Nathan's operation on Breen's optimism. I don't know if I should. Where is Chase?"

"He's headed to the NSA with Captain Mann. There was no word about Sophia Hamill."

It seemed to Midkiff both important and absurd to be worried about one life in the midst of the carnage. The president did not think any deeper than that when the phone rang. Natalie put the call through.

Stroud's voice was slightly more strident than before.

"Your people are following me," he said. "They are at my home. If they do not stand down immediately, the next strike will be overwhelming."

The call ended. Midkiff still held the receiver.

"Go to hell," he said under his breath as he put it down.

CHAPTER TWENTY-TWO

Dover, Delaware

January 16, 6:40 p.m.

"Rothrock State Forest."

Grace's pronouncement came after she had finished reading the statistics of the fifteen state game lands in the western half of Pennsylvania. Several forests had the criteria she was looking for, but one had them all. The woman felt vindicated by the discovery; her approach to the quest had been very different from what the ONI had seemingly taken. They were playing catch-up, trying to figure out where Stroud and his people were. Kung fu taught to get ahead of your opponent, be where they are going. Instead of following them, you forced them to try and anticipate you.

Breen and Rivette stopped their own research to listen.

"It's nearly ninety-seven thousand acres and has both working timber regions and natural gas drilling. In other words, there's legitimate traffic to cover whatever illegal activities might go on. It's also described as having 'rugged ridges'—the kind that make casual visits on adjoining sites unlikely. Bow hunting reserved for special regions where the mating and nesting habits of osprey and peregrine falcons might be disrupted by gunfire."

"I hear that," Rivette said.

"What about private ownership?" Breen asked.

"That narrows the search area," Grace said. "ClearWater Conservancy purchased 281 acres of Tussey Mountain several years ago, and existing structures were grandfathered in. Most of these are lodges, cabins, that sort of thing. No aboveground additions were permitted, but belowground improvements were allowed as long as they advanced the cause of sustainable practices. Meaning wells, solar and wind power, composting and recycling, drainage, and maintenance." She tapped the tablet. "As long as improvements didn't impact the land, the ridgeline, or wildlife, there's a lot of leeway here. And it adjoins an area reserved for bow hunting."

"I'll get some images," Breen said. Kathleen Hays, a former analyst at Op-Center, worked at the National Reconnaissance Office. Williams had obtained backdoor access to satellite files. The NRO would have photographs of the region for everything from erosion to bird migration. "But that's still a big area."

"Captain Hamill seems to have found it," Rivette noted.

"Over many months, apparently. Do we bet our one shot on luck?"

"More than luck," Grace said. "We helo in; that will not go unnoticed."

"Bring them to us," Rivette said excitedly.

Just then, word of the attack on NSA Philadelphia was announced by an officer at a table nearby. Everyone in the room turned to their phones, except for Major Breen. He turned to the others.

"We're going," he announced.

The platitudes were authentic.

Long ago, when greeting the families of fallen warriors, Chase Williams had learned that "Sorry for your loss" and "They won't be forgotten" delivered a welcome comfort however many times they were said. And he meant it, every one of the dozens of times he had been forced to use words like those.

So he did not dismiss, as a bromide, what Captain Mann said after a long spell of silence.

"You saved my life, Admiral. I had planned to visit Mrs. Hamill before I left. I would have been there—or more likely on the way—when the guns went active."

She could not have known what he was still thinking, still struggling with, that Stroud had done this as a result of being tracked by Black Wasp and possibly the ONI.

"I also want you to know that I know what you're going through. I missed . . . I don't even want to tell you how many warning signs. I've been going through them in my mind, starting with the background check I did not do on Sylvester Nielsen."

"Who is he?"

"The man who Captain Hamill had given security clearance to operate on our base. The man who was in the van. The man who was not vetted as thoroughly as he should have been. After you left, he left. After he left, I went back through the records of our civilian employees. His academic credentials at

Drexel matched exactly those of Burton Stroud's, including high school."

"Not because they were in the same classes, I'm guessing."

"No, sir. This Sylvester Nielsen was not in the yearbook, nowhere else on campus, including housing."

"He had manipulated the records online only as deep as he knew he had to."

"That he did. I called the university. They were still using physical documents then. There weren't any."

"Did you find out who Nielsen really is?"

"I did not. I planned to continue researching when I got home."

The silence resumed, though not as lonely as before. It was broken by a call from Breen.

"We may have them," the major said. "How soon can we be airborne?"

"Sergeant Major Stewart said to give them ninety minutes—that was about a half hour ago."

"It's about two hundred miles to get there, then we have about three hundred square miles to search by air—"

"I'll find out where you should go and get you airborne," Williams said. "Just be aware that we may see ONI move on Stroud's residence before that."

"Don't let them."

"Out of my hands. I mention this because Stroud will likely amp up the horror until we cry uncle—"

"I hear you. What we do will come after that, making his answer louder. We'll get them. I swear, Chase, we'll get them."

Williams hung up to call Sergeant Major Stewart at Belvoir.

Vice Admiral Nathan was behind his desk at ONI. Situated behind his conference room, the office was typically quiet enough. But with the news of the attack on NSA Philadelphia, everything outside was also still. He swiveled the chair toward the windows. Even the distant traffic seemed slower, respectful. This was an "industry" town, and everyone here was probably reading or listening to the news.

Immediately upon learning of the massacre—his smartphone came alive with updates—Nathan phoned the president.

"Sir, request go-ahead to immediately take and secure the Stroud residence."

The president did not immediately reply.

"We've already paid the price of admission."

"Your team hasn't."

"Our dog walker scanned for explosives, the windows do not appear to be wired, and every person here is willing to take the risk. This is where we start to take him down."

"Seems our best option. I'm going to address the nation at eight. Give me something affirmative to tell them."

"We will get you that, sir."

Nathan stowed his phone and picked up the secure landline to Lieutenant Commander Richman.

"We've heard," the field officer said. "Please tell me—"

"You're a go," Nathan said. "Bring me every scrap of that place that isn't nailed down."

"I will turn on the feed, sir. Thank you."

Nathan turned the chair back to the desk, to the computer. He entered the password to allow him access to the helmet camera of force leader Lieutenant Ciara Drye, to listen to all radio communications. Over the years the vice admiral had watched countless drills and classrooms, covert operations, and technology tests from his desk. This was the first time he felt that he was with the A-Team as they emerged from their vehicles, having shucked the guise of civilians for helmets, bulletproof vests, night vision goggles, and rubber-insulated gloves in the event of electrical booby traps. From her tour in Iraq, Drye knew that bomb makers often rigged their laboratories with electrified doorknobs and other traps to discourage intruders.

They converged on the home, each by a window or door. There were seven men and two women moving in; six members of B-Team were on the perimeter to keep civilians out and move in if necessary. Each member of the A-Team carried a little blue key, a baton, to break windows at their points of entry. The two operatives with Drye carried the big blue key—the battering ram that would open the front door.

Because the house was empty, none of them had weapons drawn. Their 9mm handguns, along with gas masks, knives, and radio communications were either worn or in rucksacks as they came at the residence from all four sides.

Drye asked as they neared the house, "Dogs, anyone?"

In turn, one through six voiced negative.

"Proceed," Drye said.

As she stepped to the front door, floodlights around the house came on.

"*Yow!*" Drye cried as the image on Nathan's computer twisted down and around in bright, natural light. "Remove your goggles—"

"Lieutenant, I hear water!" said a voice from around back.

"Sprinklers came on inside!" someone else said. "I can see them."

"Proximity trigger—he's trying to fry the electronics. Key entry, prepare to go but hold on threshold!"

The team discarded the goggles for flashlights. Within moments the sound of cracking wood and shattering glass rang through the still night, drawing neighbors to their windows. Drye stepped aside as the two men holding the battering ram came forward and broke in the big double doors. They swung inside, the right one scraping the tile floor on a wrecked hinge.

The team could both hear and see sparks through all the windows. "We're losing everything," Drye said. "Meyers, you got an incoming line? We can't set foot in there with active power strips."

The unit electrician replied, "Main cable is underground. I'll have to kill the master switch inside."

"You see any motion detectors?"

"Northeast corner, battery light on. Sprinklers must've triggered auxiliary power already."

"All right, we'll handle the responders. Go. You know the drill."

"Yes, sir. Entering through the kitchen. One sprinkler, over stove."

The drill was to avoid pooled water, even wet surfaces that could conduct electricity. The lieutenant and her team waited while Meyers entered through a back window and climbed onto a butcher block table to reconnoiter. They could see the reflected light sketching jagged lines in the air.

Nathan was proud of Lieutenant Drye's thorough efficiency. He saw the lights shift and grow dim.

"Oven will short when the water reaches it, but I can go around," Meyers informed her. "Coming up to the steps leading downstairs. They look dry—I see the electrical box. Making my way over."

There was a long silence, save for Drye's labored breathing. Nathan wondered whether that was concern for Meyers or rising adrenaline as she prepared to enter.

There was a chucking sound as the floodlights went off.

"Premises should be dead," Meyers said. "But I'm still seeing ambient light."

"That's probably us," Drye said. "Or some of the tech is on battery. Everyone in, get your bearings, then shut your lights to make sure we got it all."

The team moved in through doors and windows, stopped, looked around, then killed the flashlights. It was like pitch inside.

"Secure computers, drives, and devices first," Drye said. "Let's move."

As the team converged on Stroud's command center, no one noticed the motion detector that had been set away from any of the sprinklers. It registered the movement of the team. It had also been wired, based on an Iraqi design Stroud had dismantled, to generate spark through wires placed inside the gas line that fed the kitchen. As soon as all nine members of the team were deep inside the house, the line exploded.

Vice Admiral Nathan saw nothing but a momentary white flash, after which the picture died. A moment later so did the audio, but not before he heard the shrieks of Drye and her team.

Within moments, there was a call from Lieutenant Commander Richman.

"The entire complement is pulling back!" he shouted.

"What the hell happened?"

"The house is burning. B-Team is unable to approach."

"Where is A-Team?"

"Inside, sir," Richman answered. "Plumes of fire like they hit a gas line. No one's come out."

"Help evac surrounding residences. Tell the fire department whatever you can."

"Yes, sir."

Nathan ended the call. He felt hollow, dead—

No, not dead, the vice admiral thought. That description was reserved for the heroes who *had* died. His hand heavy, his heart heavier, Nathan picked up the cell phone to call the president. He did not feel like talking, only sitting and staring, but the news had to come from him.

As he called, Nathan could only reflect, in the most despondent and hopeless way possible, the degeneracy of the opponent they were facing. It made him ashamed to be a human being.

CHAPTER TWENTY-THREE

Philadelphia, Pennsylvania
January 16, 7:24 p.m.

There were few sites so mournful as one that had just suffered a major disaster. Even a funeral had closure. To Williams, the base reflected grief still searching for a bottom.

The occasional work lights added a pale angelic cast to spots as figures moved through it and around it like ghosts themselves. Captain Mann had been quiet, stoic in the car. She seemed numb as they maneuvered ahead and she saw the pocked, broken façade of the administration building and her headquarters. Triage had been set up in the lobby, and there were shrouded bodies in the office that belonged to the Naval Foundry and Propeller Center.

Outside medical help had begun to arrive from local hospitals and was still being waved in. As they waited in the line of vehicles, Mann asked, "Do you think any of them could be him?"

"I don't think so. He's done his dirty work."

"A devious man would return to hide in plain sight," Mann suggested.

"A coward would not. He'll move on to his next target."

The line moved quickly and, parking, Captain Mann asked one of her own MAs about Commander Brandon. The commander had seen her pull up and emerged from HQ. He was a barrel-chested man of average height. He wore a look of resolve and a uniform with a sharp, bloody tear across the sleeve.

"Dick, you should—"

"I'm fine, Captain." He nodded toward his arm. "One of the last bullets did this, grazed me, and then the gun stopped. Believe me, I'm fine."

"Of course."

Brandon turned slightly, tried to salute the admiral with his bad arm, made it partway. "Sorry, sir—no disrespect."

"As you were," Williams said. He realized that Brandon's expression was not determination but astonishment. The commander was frozen in that survivor's moment Williams had seen so often, the *Why me?* He did not even seem to feel the cold, a sign of hypovolemic shock.

Brandon half turned back to Mann. "We have a couple of outside EMTs setting up transfusions with donors," Brandon went on. "There's more power here than in any of the blown-out sick bays. If we had been able to kill the power in time—but we couldn't. I haven't been to see Mrs. Hamill. I'm told she's unhurt."

"Thank you, Dick. I'm going over with Admiral Williams."

"See to that arm," Williams said. "That's an order."

"Yes, sir."

Walking swiftly to the health facility, glass crunching underfoot, reminded Williams of bombed-out towns he had visited during his military career. All that was missing were children crying. That, at least, had added a human quality to the devastation. Even a sense of hope; children cried when they came into the world. The base was simply black and white and dead.

Caught between two guns, the Naval Health Clinic had taken a far greater hit than any other location. As pieces of wall had been blasted out, they tore down other chunks, leaving maws that saw to underlying pipes and structure. Not just windows but window frames had been blown out.

"She's on the top floor, back side," Mann said as they approached.

Williams's eyes drifted up into the darkness. The only lights that were on there were the firefly beams of work lights. The two officers entered. Mann's limp was more pronounced than it had been in her office; if she was in pain, she did not show it; if the hurried walk had been difficult, she did not lose a step on Williams.

Because this was the captain's command, she led the way up the stairs. They stepped over serpentine extension cords that had been run from intact outlets, the lanterns hung conveniently on whatever was handy—including holes punched in the walls.

Mann led the way down the hall to Sophia Hamill's room. The outer wall was intact, and a working room light was on inside. A corpsman was on the opposite side of the bed, kneeling.

Mann had intended to ask how she was but had no voice. The medic turned and rose as they entered. It must to have appeared to the young man that they were angry, the way they had charged into the room.

"Captain," he said, neglecting to salute. "I—I know there are wounded, but I thought—"

"You did the right thing, Mr. Madison," Mann said.

The captain and Williams had turned the corner of the bed, looked down. Sophia was sitting with her back to the gunmetal night table, the bed on her right, her knees drawn to her chin. Her hair glistened oddly in the light, and she was staring ahead, breathing heavily. The woman did not acknowledge the new arrivals.

"Is she injured?" Mann asked the medic.

"No, Captain. Not physically."

"Give us a moment alone."

"Of course, Captain . . . Admiral."

The young man left, and Mann squatted beside Sophia. Williams remained a few steps back, not wanting to crowd the patient.

"Mrs. Hamill, can you hear me?" Mann said quietly. "It's all right. You're safe."

"Glass," she murmured. "It was . . . raining glass."

"That's over now," the captain said. "May I brush it from your hair?"

Sophia did not reply. Mann raised a hand slowly, without menace, and lightly touched the woman's long, black hair. As best she could, she brushed the crystalline fragments free. They sounded like the dying hiss of Fourth of July sparklers as they hit the tile floor.

As they stood there, Williams received a text from Matt Berry.

ONI went into Stroud house. Explosion, all believed dead. No word from Stroud.

He did not pass the information on to Mann. Not then. He copied the message and sent it to Breen, then looked down at the woman. There was compassion behind his eyes but rising hate in his heart. He wanted Stroud and his team. He stopped short of the vulgar bravado he would have felt in his youth. *I will gut that monster.* This was a formidable enemy who had planned so much, from the perfectly executed attacks and getaways to the automated death here and in Germantown.

But there was still enough of the naval academy lieutenant left that as soon as he was done here, Williams wanted to go after the Black Order in a way that would take the strut out of the man, distract him just enough to give Black Wasp an opening.

First, though, he had a job here. Still maintaining a distance—as he had from so many servicemen and -women suffering post-traumatic stress—he crouched and smiled at the patient.

"Mrs. Hamill—Sophia—it's Chase Williams. Do you remember me?"

Her eyes continued to look ahead, seeing nothing or the past or the attack—he had no way of knowing.

"I was a friend of your husband. I knew Atlas."

The eyes did not move, but the lids flickered.

"It's cold on the floor. How would it be if we helped you back into bed?"

Captain Mann had finished brushing the woman's hair and rose slowly. She went to the other side of the bed and removed the pillowcase, then carefully bundled the blanket—so as not to disturb the woman—and shook out the glass particles.

"Atlas," Sophia said as her brow knit slightly. "Bed."

The admiral got a sense of why she had been sedated. She was still in that moment. He did not dare to agitate her with talk or efforts at explanation she would not process. Remaining low, he eased toward her.

"That was a different bed," Williams said softly. "It's cold, and you're shivering. Come with me. You're safe here."

Taking her shoulders gently in his hands, he guided the woman to her feet. She rose without resisting, looking and seeing nothing that was present. Whether it was the drugs or the trauma or both, she had the appearance of a sleepwalker.

With the help of Captain Mann, Williams eased Sophia into the bed. She was compliant, blinking now with confusion, her lips trembling from the cold. The two covered her, and Mann called the medic back into the room. He had been down the hall, assisting others.

"If the others can spare you, stay with her," the captain said.

"There's not much for me to do," the corpsman admitted. "The EMTs are better equipped for this. Captain, do we have any idea how this happened?"

She nodded.

The young man's face hardened. It wasn't like Commander

Brandon's face; this was stone-hard anger. "If you don't mind, I suggest fixed bayonets, and I volunteer."

"So would we all," she replied.

As the officers left and returned to the car, Williams gave Mann the update about the ONI. She took it without reaction. Williams recognized this too; she had reached her fill of reacting to atrocities.

Slipping behind the wheel, Captain Mann asked, "Where are we going?"

"Free Library," he said. "First I want to see if Stroud contacts the president. Second, I want to know where my team is. As much as we both want to take Stroud down, I have to take him at his word."

"About the war?"

"More than a war," Williams said. "I don't know whether his soldiers figure in his endgame or whether he has something else in mind."

"Such as?"

Williams thought back to the text Berry had sent about the drug traffickers who moved through Pennsylvania. Their money gave them access to weapons of mass destruction.

"I don't know," Williams acknowledged. "But before we confront him, we have to be prepared that he may escalate to a level we have not yet seen."

"Nothing," Matt Berry told Williams. "Abso-goddamn-lutely *nothing* from that lunatic. I haven't called because I don't have a damn thing to say."

"Who's riding this?" Williams asked.

"Here? Just the president and me, and we're just figuring out what to say to the nation at eight. Angie and Wright are out spinning 'mishandling' to the press, the ONI has kicked this back to us, Trevor is off resigning, and the other agencies *and* local law enforcement have pounced like wolves, ramping up their own ideas, attack plans, and responses—frankly, it's a disaster. Just as that devious monster Stroud intended."

"And now he's gone to ground," Williams guessed.

"That's right. Like a snake or a mole. God only knows what his next move will be. Where are you?"

"Headed from the NSA back to downtown. We saw Sophia Hamill; she's alive but near comatose. Does anyone have any thoughts about what's next?"

"Nothing good. The president spoke with the head of Centro Nacional de Inteligencia about Los Verdugos. General Director de la Vega said the CNI thinks 'the executioners' have got everything from anthrax to sarin gas to freaking plutonium stashed in the mountains of Jalisco, Michoacán, and Colima."

"But they've never *sold* those, as far as we know," Williams said.

"We're thinking, and de la Vega agrees, that they may have made a onetime exception to get something they don't have. The Black Order may have swapped them dark web know-how for overkill. A cartel with weapons, mass destruction capabilities, and tech makes them kings of all they survey."

"So it could be any of that, all of that, or none of that . . . and anywhere," Williams said.

"Chase, I hate to say it—but we may have to bend on this one. A lot. I don't know how this got here so fast without us getting a whiff of it—but it did."

Williams understood. But he had no intention of surrendering to the Black Order. That was not what the U.S. Navy did.

"Are you in the room with the president?" the admiral asked.

"I am."

"Put this on speaker?"

"Okay. Go."

"Mr. President? Black Wasp thinks they have a strong lead on a Western Pennsylvania base, and I know where Stroud is. If we feel we can take them all down, in tandem, we have to try."

"He may have other assets he hasn't used yet. More cells."

"I'm not so sure," Williams said. "He told you he wants to build an army. That makes it sound like he only has a platoon right now."

"Regarding personnel, maybe. Matt told you what they may have access to."

"Yes, sir. Plutonium 239 has a half-life of about twenty-four thousand years. Too long to be under their heel."

The president snickered at that. "Thank you for putting things in perspective, Director Williams." The commander in chief was thoughtful for a moment. "I do not want to give the nation false hope, but I also refuse to plant lack of trust in our armed forces, and a failure of resolve, that will bear fruit for generations. If you think you can get the job done, then I have to put my trust—and prayers—on that."

"That and something that has not failed us in two hundred and fifty years."

"Which is?"

Williams replied, "Divine providence."

CHAPTER TWENTY-FOUR

Dover, Delaware
January 16, 7:45 p.m.

The AFB contingent of Black Wasp was about to go airborne in a navy Bell UH-1Y Venom. They were studying the networked National Reconnaissance Office files when Williams called Breen with news about the ONI misfire and the radio silence from Stroud. The team had not yet put on their headphones, and the other two heard Breen's side of the call.

"We heard about Germantown, and I'm not surprised about the Black Order going quiet," the major said. "The pathology of vigilante justice is to create fear in the dark. Kill, retreat, and give law enforcement no chance to negotiate. The target isn't the police or the administration, it's the citizenry."

"Which is why we are going to find these psychos and torch them," Rivette said.

"I'll have to hear it from the White House, but I'm tired of waiting," Williams said. "What's your flying time?"

"Hour and fifteen to Tussey Mountain. We've got 3D satellite recon from the GEDI satellite showing the cabins, have isolated three that have the land and privacy Black Order would require, as well as other critical strategic assets. We'll see what we can determine from the air."

"They'll know you're coming."

"That's the plan," Breen said.

There was a delay as the team shifted to internal communications and the helicopter took off. The admiral knew what the team was feeling physically: the rapid ascent, the sense of physical buoyancy, the irresistible mental and emotional countdown to action. He felt a small charge go off in his own gut as the hoped-for showdown began, a jolt as grave and exhilarating as when he went off into the unknown. For that reason, and for lack of other options, Williams did not argue the tactic Breen had presented.

Once the Venom was airborne, the admiral said that he and Captain Mann would be going to the Free Library—to observe, at least for now.

"Stroud has lost his home base," the admiral said. "Unless the store is rigged, we have to hope he has nowhere else to go."

"There's that basement he mentioned, where they do their home monitoring."

"Unless, what, a half dozen or so employees are also in on this, someone might have noticed incendiary devices or whatever other horror the Black Order might conceive. No. The library is a sensible safe house with a selection of potential hostages."

"And they will come to him," Breen said. "Anyone who knows Stroud will wonder why he isn't in Germantown with firefighters."

It was known to war planners as the Alamo Stratagem. Preserve your assets for offense by making people come to you. Breen suspected that a unit comprised in part or in whole of former military would be familiar with it.

"There is one other possibility that concerns me," Breen went on. "If one of those two bases falls, the other resorts to a different strategy—one of mutual assured destruction."

"Hamilton, there is a very narrow corridor leading to a good resolution, and I pray we find it," Williams said. "Depending on what you find, and when, I'll wait to hear before we go in."

Grace had taken the lead of communicating with the flight deck while Breen was on the call. The major continued to let her.

"When we reach the target area, I want to track the main roads, watching traffic headed both directions," she told the flight crew over the headset. "We are looking for persons who are likely to be heavily armed and willing to use those arms."

Rivette said, "We're packing .50-caliber and 7.62 machine guns, door mounted, ready to rock. Maybe we should've had the 70mm rocket add-ons."

"There could be wives and children in a compound," Grace said. "If there are, that's all the media will remember."

"That means door by door," Rivette said.

"We've got to find the place first," she reminded him. "One challenge at a time."

The woman spoke with finality, and neither Breen nor Rivette pressed her. The strength of Black Wasp was not only in its numbers but its individuals. Rivette seemed satisfied as long as he got to see action.

Breen, frankly, was content as long as he did not have to decide just now.

Community.

Routine.

In times of trial, and there had been many in his life, Chuck Boyd found comfort in the familiar and in the company of those he loved or worked with. The two were often one and the same.

The day had been rocked by horror wider and deeper than any human could process. The murder of Mayor Tom Albert was the most personal and hit the hardest. The police had already come and gone, collecting his office computer to see if there had been any threats on his life. They also took the names and addresses of all the clients he had been working with at the Office of Adult Education. A politician acquired a lot of enemies, but disappointed job seekers were their main focus. They also wanted the names and addresses of everyone Mayor Albert worked with at the library.

The shocking destruction of Burton Stroud's home was another horror, especially because the man had not answered calls or texts and for all anyone knew was inside the house when it was consumed by what witnesses described as a "fireball."

Stroud was not at his store, but Boyd hoped that he had gone somewhere else—perhaps to dinner. He did not know who the man's friends were; Stroud was dauntingly private about that part of his life. But Boyd felt there was a chance that he was with one of them when it happened, had stayed with them.

Boyd was able to put his arms around that hope and set

about to lean on community and routine to deal with the death of Albert. There were the former mayor's personal effects to collect at the office, and that was where Boyd went.

Fitzpatrick was just leaving for the night. While sharing disbelief with him at the front door, Boyd was surprised to learn that Burton Stroud was upstairs.

"Left and came back," the guard told him. "Seemed pretty agitated. I guess we found out why."

"Thank God," Boyd said.

His heart rising, the OAE director had hurried up the marble staircase, taking two steps at a time, pulling himself along with the mahogany banister. He was already perspiring, having overdressed for the cold. He reached the second floor, breathless, smiling in spite of everything as he hurried down the corridor—not too fast, not so that he would panic anyone who was still up here—until he reached the OAE office.

The six-panel door was unlocked, and he entered respectfully, aware that Stroud had suffered an incredible loss. The businessman was behind his desk, as usual. He appeared to be calm, as usual. He did not look up when Boyd entered—also as usual. The director heard the gentle tap of computer keys as he hung up his scarf and overcoat. He did not intend to stay long, would not have removed them except to make a bit of noise, perhaps to get a response so he could measure the man's state of mind.

"Eventful day," Stroud said without looking up.

"I . . . was hoping I'd find you here, Burton."

"Thank you. I'm actually trying to resolve some issues,

Chuck. Insurance issues." His mouth twisted a little as he said that.

"Certainly, yes. I wanted to gather Tom's things for his wife."

"Very kind."

Stroud's eyes were still on the computer. He was clearly disinterested in conversation. Still moving quietly, Boyd went to Albert's desk.

"Sorry, Burton, but I want you to know that the police asked for the names of everyone who worked here."

"Of course they did."

"I know you value your privacy—"

"They would have come in any event," Stroud said. "About my home."

"Yes."

Stroud finished typing and regarded the other man. The businessman's eyes seemed flat to Boyd—understandably, although the dead gaze was mildly unnerving.

"Is there anything I can do for you?" Boyd asked.

"There is," Stroud said. "I have a videoconference coming up—about all of this, you understand. If I can have privacy for that?"

"By all means. Certainly. I'll get what I came for and leave you."

Boyd was not insulted. In fact, Stroud seemed surprisingly serene for a man who had just lost his home.

The director returned to the front of the office, to Albert's desk, and began collecting whatever notes and doodles and mementos the police had left behind. He carefully tucked them into his shoulder bag and put on his coat.

"Good night, Burton. Please. If there's anything I can do?"

"I will let you know. Thank you, Chuck."

Boyd departed. As he walked along the corridor and down the stairs, he had a feeling of unease. Not about Stroud, per se—if he had wanted help, he would have asked for it—but about the way he had said one word.

Insurance.

The night watchman, Eloise May, had just come on. Boyd had helped get her into criminology classes at the University of Pennsylvania; she seemed a little more watchful than usual.

The woman smiled bravely as he approached. Everyone was like that, the living dead, going through motions with whatever grit they could muster.

"Good evening, Mr. Boyd. Is there anything I can do for you?"

"Thanks, no. I think we're all struggling."

"Fitz told me that Mr. Stroud is upstairs. The poor man."

"He seemed to have it together," Boyd said. He started toward the exit, then stopped, hesitated. "You know what? I'm going to the break room. You have my number?"

She held up a clipboard.

"Good. If Mr. Stroud comes down and seems like he needs anything, let me know."

"Police are still talking to folks down there."

"I saw them earlier, told them what I could about the

mayor." He smiled reassuringly. "If I hear anything that might help your studies, I'll let you know."

The woman smiled back. "You're a good man, Mr. Boyd. The kind who gave the City of Brotherly Love its name."

He turned and went down the staircase to have a vending machine dinner and wait.

Tussey Mountain was a popular ski destination, but there was roughly a decade during the 1960s and '70s when the publicly funded slopes were idled by budgetary cutbacks. At that time, areas were opened for development to defray some of the debt. Those lots remained in private hands when the resort itself was taken private.

That was the time, and the area, when the Stroud family could have built there. She felt better about the decision to come here; one more piece in the Black Order puzzle had a possible answer.

It was dark in the passenger bay as Breen and Rivette looked out the windows with night vision glasses. The configuration in the multi-role cabin was two rows of benches. The men were in the forward bench, watching the north-south sides. Grace was behind them and had spent the last half hour of the flight with her tablet angled away from her teammates so they would not be blinded. She was looking through old images from the Global Ecosystem Dynamics Investigation satellite. NASA's three lasers were designed to collect vital information about biomass and carbon in forests—but the 3D imaging also captured residential sites.

There were ten billion laser observations. Fortunately, she

had been able to narrow her research area to two and a half miles of "high potential" terrain. She was looking for structures on a lot of land and heavy tree cover, even though the branches would be bare now.

Taikinys had not specified the route he had taken to deliver guns, but he had told the ONI that the cartels stuck to back roads because of the number of road accidents on the nation's highways.

"*They're careful drivers,*" he had reported. "*They have to be.*"

They also preferred to travel at night when there were fewer cars around and the limited resources of law enforcement stayed close to the resort and residential areas, where the winter entertainment consisted of heavy drinking.

The Mt. Nittany Expressway afforded the directest passage through the region. The only other major routes were interconnected routes that passed through this particular region to and from Earlystown Road. The expressway, Route 322, was the one the helicopter was following at a height of fifteen hundred feet.

The world was quiet and dark below. The day had been near to freezing, and whatever snow had covered the road as sun-melt had refrozen. Grace could only imagine what they were thinking on the flight deck. They did not know what the mission was or what their passengers were looking for. That was not the kind of military operation they would be accustomed to.

"Major, bend in the road—coming up on your nine o'clock," Rivette said suddenly. "Vehicle on the side of the road."

Breen swung his goggles in that direction. It took him a

moment to find what Rivette was referring to. There was a car parked just off the shoulder, roughly twenty feet from a thickly wooded area to the south. With the lights off, the object looked like a large, green-gray rock.

"You don't go dark to walk the dog," Rivette said.

"Could be Los Verdugos," Grace suggested.

"That'd be a caravan," Rivette said. "I've watched those guys roll into town. Never travel fewer than two, usually three cars."

"Worth a look," Breen said. He pressed the button on the mic that wirelessly engaged the flight deck. "Captain Singer, let's take a closer look at the car parked—five o'clock now, northeast side. One pass, circle back, then another."

"Roger that."

The Venom nosed down and banked in that direction, dropping half of its height in thirty seconds as it swung toward the parked car. It looked to Breen like a Jeep Wrangler. No one and nothing moved as the Venom made its first crossing. When the helicopter swept back for its second run, the occupants had already gotten out and were running toward the trees.

"You don't run if you got nothing to hide," Rivette said.

Grace was digging deeper than that. This close to what she believed was the Black Order headquarters, motorists did not get out unless they had someplace to go.

"Set us down!" the woman barked into her mic after checking her maps.

"On the road?"

"*On the road!*"

"We're gonna spend time we don't have," Rivette said. "You sure?"

She removed her helmet and cocked her head toward the tablet. "Those woods are for bow hunters. And I think Mrs. Hamill got it wrong when she told Nathan her husband was tracking bear. The next intersection is Bear Meadow Road. There are farms here. He was probably sharing what he *saw*."

"Well, damn," Rivette said.

While Breen continued to watch, the lance corporal tore off his goggles and helmet, and armed himself from his grip. The three were all rocking gently as the Venom fought a sudden side wind. A few yards from the ground, the rotors kicked up snow, dusting the icy particles all around.

Breen lowered his glasses. "Can't see anything now. They went into the woods. If they're Black Order, they may only be going as far as the trees and calling for backup."

"You said they'd come to us, Major," Rivette said.

"They're under cover, you're not," Breen said. "And more may come silently, with one or more bows."

"If they left the car running, we can drive in after them," Rivette said.

"They didn't, but we'll deploy from the driver's side," Grace said. She turned to Breen. "You take off; the floods are all on us. Follow their retreat."

"Air cover too," Rivette said. "This close to home, there may be reinforcements."

Breen gave a thumbs-up, and Rivette nodded involuntarily

as the helicopter thudded to a landing and skidded several feet on the sloping, icy road. The two Black Wasps left their helmets and comm sets on to stay in contact with Breen. They pulled on tactical weather gloves and went to the door. Breen slid it open, and the two eased out onto the icy asphalt.

Gray Kirby pushed the terrified Jackson Poole ahead of him as they ran through the woods. The snow cover was not deep, but it was hard, and with each footfall the earth seemed to grab them.

At least it will be the same for whoever they *are,* he thought.

Kirby was not surprised that the tech wizard had panicked. He was not even annoyed. As in business, he was prepared for most eventualities. When Poole panicked and bolted, Kirby briefly considered leaving him and driving on the short way to the Homestead. But the chopper would likely have followed the car.

And this situation also presented opportunities: it drew the enemy out, gave him an opportunity to find out who they were and relay that information to Stroud.

As soon as they were in the trees, Poole in the front, legs heavy from flight, Kirby pushed him behind a chestnut oak.

"I'm sorry, Gray! I'm—"

"*Quiet.*"

Poole stopped speaking as much from what Kirby had said as what he did. The man drew his Maxim 9. With the other hand, he took his cell phone from the outside pocket and pressed the button for the Homestead.

Sarno answered.

"We are in the woods on foot about three hundred yards

past camera four," Kirby said. "Hostile helo landed, two occupants in pursuit."

"You armed?"

"Maxim, fully loaded, seventeen plus one."

"Let the boss know. We're coming."

Sarno hung up, and Kirby turned his attention to the chopper. They were shining a spotlight on him; that, plus the sound of the rotors, made it impossible for him to see or hear any pursuit. That was the bad news. The good news: to get him, the enemy would have to run in that same light.

While he waited, Kirby dictated a text to Stroud:

Navy chopper landed at Homestead perimeter. K&P on foot. Occupants in pursuit. S&D coming.

Stroud's reply was immediate:

Will handle. Stay safe.

CHAPTER TWENTY-FIVE

The White House, Washington, D.C.
January 16, 8:58 p.m.

The president did not feel bad about his speech. Not as bad as he felt about his helplessness to protect the nation. It was not that the response had been misguided, but no government could play catch-up to fleet-footed enemies who had mined the nation with horrific plots.

Midkiff had expressed his sorrow and condolences, went through the usual litany about not bowing to terrorists, shared that they believed this was the work of ultranationalists, and vowed that despite the loss of the navy team in Germantown they would bring the enemy to heel.

It sounded tough, if not reassuring. Now he had to make that happen, and Op-Center was the only option.

The text from Breen had been encouraging; the silence from Williams less so. And the call from Burton Stroud was devastating.

The president had spoken in the East Room instead of the Oval Office. He wanted reporters present, even though he would not be taking questions. There were optics involved; he wanted to project active engagement, be on his feet, not seated serenely amidst the trappings of an office. After the cameras went off, the president stayed to answer a few questions off the record, using every variation he could think of for "That's something I cannot discuss." He could not discuss what he did not know.

After nearly an hour he had returned to the Oval Office with only Matt Berry. The press secretary and his team had gone to Off the Record for a drink. Harward, Angie, and the rest of Midkiff's trusted core team—Kim, Hewlett, key members of Congress on whose second term coattails they had ridden in, then out—were looking for answers in their own way. Not just solutions about how to stop the Black Order but how to fix the country when this was done. Trust in all federal and local intelligence and law enforcement systems had been shattered. Midkiff did not need instant polling and social media algorithms to tell him that. He saw it in every face he looked at.

Except that of Matt Berry. The man was going to ride this horse into the ground—not just belief in Chase Williams and Black Wasp but support for the president's belief in Op-Center.

Until the call from Stroud. The president put it on speaker.

"Go ahead, Mr. Stroud." Midkiff heard the ever-serene voice of Natalie Cannon, who was still at her post.

"You have a team—some kind of team—in Western Pennsylvania. Recall them at once or they will die along with hundreds of others."

Midkiff was watching Berry, who was watching his tablet. Berry held up a finger.

"Also call off the dog who is sniffing at my heels," Stroud added.

"I wonder, Mr. Stroud," Midkiff said. "Whose arsenal is going to run out first?"

Stroud snickered. "Yours. You will quite literally be history, and neither the public nor Wright will have the stomach to continue. Not after tonight."

"What's tonight?" the president asked, not expecting an answer but needing time. "Public transportation? A university?"

"Back off or you'll find out."

Berry approached the president's desk and turned his tablet around. Midkiff read the text from Major Breen.

Wasp pursuing enemy toward what we believe is HQ. I am in Venom ready to lend support.

Black Wasp on the ground, Williams on Stroud's doorstep. Chase's words about legacy were still in the president's head: not what the nation thought of him but how it regarded itself in years to come.

"Mr. Stroud," Midkiff said, "I will not do as you ask."

The caller hung up. Midkiff replaced the receiver. He was still looking at Berry.

"Either we believe in the team or we do not," the president said.

The Oval Office was always too hot in the winter, and the deputy chief of staff was perspiring—but not, Midkiff suspected, from the heat.

"I believe they can end this," Berry replied. "What I do not want to imagine is what it will cost."

The president nodded and, sitting back, waited for divine providence or hell—or both—to be revealed.

Ann Ellen Mann did not want to waste any time in thought, mourning, or indecision. As she drove through the thin evening traffic, in a city possessed by fear and mourning, only one thing mattered: ending the Black Order's terror operations, whatever the price.

Williams had other matters to concern him. Breen had copied him on the text to the president. The admiral's first response was pride; the war was finally to become two-sided, and the boots on the ground belonged to Black Wasp. That same news put a weight in his heart. For all their drilling, for all their skills, nothing was guaranteed.

Outnumbered and facing God knows what . . . again.

But this was the work Black Wasp did, and they would not want it any other way. He said a short prayer. Then he updated Berry and turned to his part in the fight.

"What's the plan?" Mann asked as they turned onto North Nineteenth Street, headed toward the library.

"Just been thinking about that. When we get inside, I'll go see Stroud. I'm also going to call you. Answer and leave the line open, but mute your side. If he says anything actionable, call the cops." He pointed ahead as Vine Street came into view. "They're already here, probably talking to people about Mayor Albert."

They parked in a handicapped spot—it was the first time Captain Mann had ever used one—and went inside.

"What if he won't see you?" Mann asked.

"I'll get a police escort," he said as they approached Eloise.

"I'm sorry, we're closed—"

"Official business. Admiral Chase Williams to see Mr. Stroud."

"Oh. Is he expecting you?"

"I believe he is."

"And you, ma'am?"

"I'll wait here, thank you."

The guard picked up the phone on the desk, called his extension. She announced the admiral.

"Yes, Mr. Stroud," she said and hung up. "Second floor, turn left, end of the corridor."

"Thank you," Williams said.

When Williams left, Eloise turned to Captain Mann. "Are you both from that naval station here in town?"

"I'm the commander," Mann said, choking up for the first time.

"I am so sorry," the guard said. "I'm studying criminology. If there's anything I can do, please let me know."

"Thank you." Mann's gaze followed Williams up the staircase. "I will surely let you know."

Upon hitting the ground, Grace dashed toward the abandoned car, Rivette right behind her.

Grace slammed against the driver's side of the Wrangler, followed by Rivette. "Don't count on the Venom opening up on them. By the time they run it past Dover—"

"I was thinking red tape. It's bow hunting only here."

The lance corporal was not joking. The request from the flight deck would get passed along and hit the wall of armed domestic protocols.

"Let's make it a nonissue," Grace said. She was nearer to the back of the Jeep and crept in that direction. "We go in on my mark—you cover me."

"Taliban Guzargah Overrun Reversal, Scenario Three," he confirmed, referring to the appropriate drill while thinking, *We really need shorthand for those.*

Even as the two spoke, the Venom rose. The wide cone of white moved from the intervening field to the woods, and the rotor wash caused snow to once again obscure the area.

"Go!" Grace said after easing around the back, waiting for Rivette to get in position behind her, then running in, bent low.

The crunch of the ice-covered snow was lost in the sound of the Venom. Grace looked ahead, seeking their quarry, trying to distinguish them from the moving shadows of the trees. She pushed ahead even as Rivette lost ground, his Sig Sauer raised and ready and watching for a target, his light assault boots failing to provide necessary traction.

Grace turned suddenly, and in the same movement grabbed Rivette's legs below the knees. She took him down backward, shielding him as a series of shots cracked overhead.

Even as he fell, the lance corporal was looking ahead. He

saw the three flashing bursts, returned two rounds, saw dark splinters fly in the light of the Venom.

Two figures ran deeper into the woods.

"Go, my ten o'clock!" he shouted.

Grace was already scrambling back to her feet and giving chase. Rivette was only a few heartbeats behind her. Without breaking stride, she circled an arm and pointed up before entering the woods. The chopper saw her signal and rose, casting the area in an artificial twilight—but, more importantly, reducing the noise. She listened for the trudge of boots as she started through the trees.

"Only one of them fired," Rivette said.

Grace had noticed that too and nodded. They could have set up a cross fire. Only one of them might be armed.

As the Venom ascended, she listened, heard two sets of feet, labored breathing. She motioned Rivette to the right while she angled left. The trees were thickening, and she left her companion behind as she sped ahead in a serpentine pattern. She was centered, low, her arms moving ahead and snaking around each tree to help her ease around them without breaking stride.

Hearing footfalls nearby, she stopped, punched the ground with both fists, and scooped up snow. She continued ahead, sliding from tree to tree while she formed a snowball. The Shaolin art of distraction: judging the overhead light, she heaved the projectile eye level through a space in the trees.

The man with the gun fired two shots.

A moment later, to her right, a single shot cracked from

Rivette's 9mm. There was a moan, a shape fell to her left about ten yards ahead, and someone cried out to the right. From their training, the Black Wasps knew to take the target nearest them. Grace went for the man with the gun. Rivette knew to cover her.

The downed man moved, his shape wavering in the unsteady glow from above. She continued to run toward him even as he swung his weapon in her direction. The instant he had locked his arms, a shot echoed through the trees.

It had come from Rivette. The target's arms slackened, and the gun hit the snow. As soon as Grace was beside him, Rivette continued after his quarry.

Grace heard her partner's footsteps—and then she heard others. The lieutenant whistled, partly to let Rivette know where she was and partly to draw fire. The man on the ground was dead, but she threw his gun behind her anyway as she bolted toward the nearest tree. She heard crunching footfalls and took the last few feet by jumping into a somersault, knowing the ice cover would give and drop her farther. The top of her helmet barely cleared the aerial turn. Even as she rolled ahead, something whizzed by where her head had been.

The bow hunter had arrived. Grace was angry that, by habit, she had left her throwing stars back at Fort Belvoir; Army Special Forces frowned on unorthodoxy.

Heading to the nearest tree, a fat oak, Grace climbed some six feet. She moved up swiftly, using buoyancy training—neutralizing her weight by allowing her fingers to do the work, not by tensing her arm and shoulder muscles. As soon as she was in position, she put her tongue to the top of her mouth and widened her mouth; snake breath to maximize breathing without making a sound.

The enemy approached cautiously, bow at the ready. Ordinarily, Grace would have dropped down behind her and thrown a choke hold—elbow to the throat, other hand to the back of her head pushing forward. That would have cut off air and blood flow and caused unconsciousness in just a few seconds. But the woman had taken the time to put on a thick scarf.

Grace stood on a single branch, pivoting at the knees to watch the woman move to and then under the tree. Bark fell from underfoot, and the bow turned upward.

The Black Wasp swore and dropped sooner than she had anticipated. It was not optimal, they were slightly at angles, but a high kick pushed the bow away and allowed Grace to move closer. She managed to grab one end and then the other end of the scarf. There was no time to pull them tight and choke her; the lieutenant dropped to both knees, dropping the woman onto her back. The bow and arrow fell on the other side and, releasing the scarf, Grace placed her left knee on the woman's chest with all her weight behind it. Then she leaned over, grabbed the arrow in her right hand, and drove it hard into her open hand.

The woman hissed painfully as the tip penetrated sinew and grazed bone, then shrieked as Grace rose, leaned on the carbon-fiber shaft, and staked it deeper into the cold ground.

The woman craned to her right side, tried to reach the arrow.

"Stay," the lieutenant warned as she took the bow and flung it back toward the clearing.

Grace whistled again. Then she rolled the woman onto her shoulder, the tug on her ruined palm causing her to cry out. The lieutenant had zero sympathy for the woman as she grabbed a pair of arrows from the quiver. Holding them like a pair of sai—her short fighting tridents—she moved wide in the direction the woman had come.

Behind her, Dee Dee Allen did not remain still. Screaming inside her throat, she put her heels to the ground, reached over, and grabbed the shaft of the arrow that had pinned her to the earth. The stainless steel–aluminum broadhead tip had gone in with crude force, not the power of a bowstring, and had cut an ugly wound.

Unable to muster the strength to pull the arrow out, Dee Dee arched her back so her shoulders were on the cold snow, pressed her left palm down until it reached solid ground, then raised her hand along the bloody shaft. When it reached the fletching she closed her trembling fingers around it and pulled up and to the side. The pain was murderous as she clapped her teeth together and continued to raise her arm, and in a few moments of anguish that sent lightning pain from her skull to her heel, she was free.

When they separated, Rivette knew that Grace knew to watch where she moved; he could easily mistake her for the enemy.

There was no mistaking his immediate target, a man slapping back and forth between the trees, panting, hunched over in a desperate effort to gain forward momentum.

Rivette let him run as he took a position behind a tree and covered Grace. Once her opponent was put down, the lance corporal continued running. His target had announced his location with a wail when his companion was shot. Rivette marked the location and ran for it, listening not only for anyone coming from a forward position but to any electronic communications that might come through to his quarry.

There was nothing. The man was slumping now, wheezing across snows given a ghostly, ivory pallor by the hovering Venom. Rivette caught up to the man, grabbed the back of his collar, and swung him against the nearest tree.

"Don't!" the man cried. "I haven't done anything!"

"Yeah, you did," Rivette said. "I recognize your voice from the van, dirt. You asshole!"

"I didn't actually *hurt* anyone!"

"Shut up!"

The lance corporal turned the man around. Jackson Poole had drawn a pocketknife, held it tremulously before him. Rivette slapped it away and put the gun to his chest. Poole shivered, and his knees gave out. Rivette pulled him back up and put the gun back over the man's heart. His prisoner raised both hands temple-high.

"Don't shoot!"

"How many of you are out here and where?"

"I don't know!"

Rivette moved the gun to the man's left eye. "Mister, this tree will be wearing most of your head unless you suddenly don't *not* know!"

The lance corporal gave the man a moment to retch. As Poole hacked out lunch, they heard a woman scream, once and then again more forcefully. Rivette prayed it was not Grace. A moment later, he heard her whistle and relaxed—but not much.

"I got a better idea, scumbag. You take me to your HQ." He pulled the man from the tree, spun him around, put the gun in his back. "Move!"

Poole started walking, then stopped.

Rivette had heard it too—footsteps on the crusted snow. He leaned close to the man's ear.

"*Call him!*" he whispered.

Poole did not need a second invitation. "Sarno! Here!"

"Sarno" was not stupid enough to respond.

Neither were the individuals whose footsteps Rivette heard coming from his right.

CHAPTER TWENTY-SIX

Philadelphia, Pennsylvania
January 16, 9:09 p.m.

Williams walked into the Office of Adult Education expecting to find precisely what he did: a man in control of himself, sitting at a computer.

Stroud looked up with an expression of serenity that Williams found unnerving. Terrorists he had faced were intense, focused, angry, bitter—a litany of hostile purpose. Not this man.

"I am impressed," Stroud said. "You left everyone behind to get this far."

"It's time to give this up, Mr. Stroud."

"'Mister'? Gracious in victory, like Grant to Lee or Eisenhower to Dönitz. We will agree to disagree about our situation." The man returned to his computer. "Who are you? I don't mean your name, I mean your affiliation."

"The police are downstairs. Will you come with me, or do we have them come up?"

"Neither." He finished typing and looked up again. His hand was on the keypad, finger raised above it. "I've just armed several barrels of sarin gas. One tap—even if I'm shot, my finger will fall—and hundreds, perhaps thousands, will die. It's a heavy gas, as you probably know. It will sink into the SEPTA system and from there into countless basements."

Williams did not show the revulsion he felt. "Why? You'll be taken."

"I have allies."

"In Pennsylvania—Tussey Mountain? They're under siege as we speak."

The information, though slightly premature, had the desired effect. Keeping his right finger on the keypad and his eyes on Williams, Stroud used his left hand to access a file on the computer—the video security system outside the Homestead. He listened for a moment and thought he heard the sound of a rotor. He glanced at the screen, saw a shifting glow in the distance. His expression soured slightly.

"It does not matter," Stroud said. "This is about something far bigger than I am. There will be a trial. I will make a case that is worth dying for, the preserving of the character of America."

The admiral was thinking, not listening. Stroud did not seem to feel his plan could be foiled, either physically or electronically. Williams considered the previous attacks. Tactically perfect but with nothing pre-placed except at the NSA. There, they had obviously infected the command system of the guns.

Where else did they have access like that? There were no naval facilities with a direct link to the SEPTA subway system.

Williams's eyes drifted to the window. It took a moment, but then it came to him. He smiled. "That's one of your alarms."

Stroud followed his gaze, said nothing. His finger did not move—but Williams knew that he had to be very careful about what he said.

"Mr. Stroud, you donated a security system to the library, installed it. You obviously volunteer your time. Was that generosity sincere?"

"Do I strike you as insincere, Admiral?"

"No. I'm just looking to see if there is more to you than just the Black Order."

"What can be 'more' than having a purpose in life?"

"What I have witnessed these many hours is not purpose."

"No, that's leverage. The purpose is to keep alive a beacon that has burned for centuries, a light that the small-minded tribalists are trying to douse. I have purpose, Admiral. I am America." He looked dismissively at the admiral. "I'm being judged by a man who wears a uniform that announces murderous intent."

"I didn't come up here armed."

Stroud's eyes looked the admiral over. "You didn't, did you. Why?"

"No one else needs to die."

"Says the man who is attacking my people!" Stroud yelled.

"Mr. Stroud, there are methods other than killing. In 1918, the Austrians and Italians fostered peace by dropping leaflets from warplanes instead of bombs."

"Another historian," Stroud said, without naming Gray Kirby. "People have stopped listening. Or reading."

"Nonetheless, I have to believe you want peace—"

"I want obedience."

"Fine. Don't release the gas downstairs. Let me be your hostage."

Stroud's expression fell deeper into darkness. His eyes lowered slightly, regarded Williams's right hand.

"You clever, stupid son of a bitch," Stroud said and lowered his finger, hard.

The Bluetooth in her ear, listening to the conversation, Captain Mann had been ahead of Williams on this. She had seen countless ASPs—Absentee Spark Personnel—in Afghanistan. It could be something as simple as a trip wire in a doorway, as relatively sophisticated as a cell phone call detonating remote explosives, or a computer controlling a drone. Stroud had positioned someone to trigger this latest attack, just as he had at the NSA. Only in this case the ASP was himself. Here, now.

Where would he—could he—hide gas adjacent to a subway stop? Or kill hundreds locally during the day? Why is he here*?*

Mann turned urgently to Eloise. "Who knows this building really well?"

"You mean who's here, at this hour?"

"Yes—this is urgent!"

"That would be Mr. Boyd, I guess."

"Where is he?"

"In the break room, in the basement—"

"Call him now! Tell him I'm coming, to meet me. Then get the police to evacuate the building!" Mann was already hurrying toward the stairs.

"Evacuate?"

"Yes, immediately!" she said over her shoulder. "There may be a poison gas attack!"

"You can tell them yourself down there—"

"No time to be questioned! *Do it!*"

Eloise was confused but looked up Boyd's cell number and called him, told him to watch for a navy captain on her way down. Then she punched in 911.

Mann walked as fast as she was able, ducking low as she descended the stairs, her eyes searching for a man who would be looking for her. A middle-aged man stepped into the corridor, holding a coffee cup.

"Mr. Boyd?" she asked.

"Yes?"

"Where would Burton Stroud have wired your security system? We believe he did the same thing he did to my base—wired it to kill."

It took a moment for everything she had said to register.

"Stroud?"

"There isn't time to explain—"

"That's what's off with him. Is he involved with what's happening?"

"He's behind it," she said as she reached the floor. "There's gas hidden, probably in this building. Where could that be?"

"He did all that work in the electrical room."

"Take me."

Boyd turned toward a door at the end of the corridor. "That leads to the subbasement where all the electrical panels are. It may be locked."

He tried the knob; it did not move. Boyd turned to her, his expression grave.

"We'll have to find the night janitor—"

"No time," Mann said. "Police—someone with a gun."

"There are two detectives in the break room, talking to—"

She turned and started running down the hallway, ignoring her limp, shouting, "Police! Anyone there?"

A plainclothes detective and a policewoman emerged from the room.

"We just got the call," the detective said. "Is this for real?"

"Yes! Sarin gas! We've got to open a goddamn door!"

"Metal plate?"

"I don't know—"

"Find a key in case we can't shoot the thing open," the detective said to his companion as he ran forward.

Breen had watched the battle unfold in silence—until now.

"Total of three converging on Rivette, one from the north, two from the east," he said. "Copy?"

"Copy," Grace said.

"Copy," Rivette said in a barely audible voice.

The lance corporal and his prisoner were a single blob under the bare tree limbs. The major did not know if Rivette intended to use the man as a shield, but he could not afford to stay as he was.

Breen had his answer a moment later. Rivette and his prisoner separated. As the major watched, the captive flew forward into a tree, then flopped to the ground.

Good man, Breen thought. He could have shot him.

"Man to your north is nearest—"

"I've got him," Grace said.

"Three o'clock."

"I see him."

"Jaz, due east at two o'clock and four o'clock."

"Yeah," the lance corporal said. "And time's up."

Grace was crouched low like a tiger as she closed on her target. Though the man would certainly have a gun, his attention would be on Rivette. She considered asking Breen to kill the light; they had drilled in the dark. But then he could not be their eyes above.

"Grace, figure on north fifteen yards and now moving in your direction—"

"He probably heard the woman."

"She's up!"

"Where?"

"Behind, coming toward you. She's got her bow!"

The woman would have trouble drawing accurately, but even an inaccurate hit could kill or cause her to move in a way that made her a target for the other attacker. Swearing, Grace turned and retraced her steps. She saw the woman moments later.

The woman was hunched to her injured side, leaning on a tree. The bow was in her wounded hand, the bloody arrow in the other. She was trying to load it.

Stand down, Grace thought as she picked up her pace.

"Joseph!" Dee Dee cried out, almost in triumph. "Come!"

Grace heard crunching behind her. She threw herself behind a tree as a shot kicked up snow where she had been standing.

"Hurry! She doesn't have a gun!" Dee Dee shouted.

There was no choice now. The lieutenant ran forward, reached Dee Dee while the woman was still trying to arm herself, and pushed one of the arrows into the soft tissue of her right leg, just below the belly. The woman bent over, crying, and fell forward. The bow dropped, and Grace scooped it up. She was not confident in her ability to draw it, but that was not her plan. She ran back, saw the gunman approaching, got behind a tree as a pair of rounds whizzed by.

"Major, is Jaz okay?" she asked, knowing Rivette might not be able to answer.

"He's got cover."

"Kill the light and pull back."

Breen did not ask why. A moment later the woods went dark. At once, Grace crouched, removed the glove from her right hand, and laid the bow on the ice. She pushed it down so it cracked the ice. Then she held one end in her bare hand and waited. She was breathing hard and did not seek to disguise that fact. She wanted the attacker to know where she was.

As the sound of the rotors retreated, Grace could clearly hear the woman moaning behind her and the crunch of feet on ice a few feet ahead—

Dammit.

He was coming the wrong way around the tree. She needed him to come from the south, not the north. If he knew these woods, he knew that animals would have fled from the "hunters" moving through. She was low on options. He would shoot at any movement.

She put her left cheek against the icy bark near the south side of the oak. She relaxed everything but the hand holding the bow. That was the only part of her that would need to move. What she needed now was to hear.

"Hey, jerk!" she said.

A moment later the footfalls continued from the south.

Grace closed her eyes. She was listening but, more than that, she was feeling for the movement of the bow. With each step, it shifted slightly. When he reached the tree, the bow shifted, the way it would if someone had stepped on the far end—

The lieutenant shoved the bow forward along the snow. It came free of his boot, leaving his foot between the string and the lower limb. She pivoted fast and hard at the waist, pulling the bow with her. She had the fleeting sense that the oak was a great cello as the string drew cracked sounds from the bark. There were two sounds: a surprised cough from the man's throat and the discharge of his weapon, both occurring as he fell backward.

Grace had already discarded the bow and launched herself forward. The lingering smell of the gun was to the left; she went right. Still on his back, he fired a second and third shot immediately, blindly toward his feet. Grace was not there. She was on his other side. With a big, counterclockwise rotation of her right arm, she brought a hammer fist hard across the bridge of his nose, shattering it and the right eye socket.

The man screamed, tried to turn, to raise his gun. But she

hit him with a second swing, cracking more suborbital bone, blinding him with blood and damage to the eye.

Both arms writhed, not with purpose but with pain.

"Target down. Lights on," she said.

The chopper lit up the woods, and she took the gun, tossed it, and looked to the east, where two figures were weaving around tulip poplars, converging on an oak some twenty yards from her.

His back to the tree, a lump of coward semiconscious at his feet before him, Rivette had drawn both weapons now. His Sig Sauer was in his right hand, the Colt .45 in his left. He was alert to every sound, not for proximity—he knew where the two were headed—but for any click or creaking that might tell him what they carried. He wondered if one of the men was the knife fighter who had gone berserk in Atlanta. He did not take that skill lightly; at this distance, a thrown knife was as lethal as a bullet. But he would show a different stance as he approached. The other stalker, a possible demolitions expert, was not likely to blow anything up. Not this near, where shrapnel from a blasted tree could be deadly to all.

In the dark, the two had approached very, very cautiously. Rivette judged them to be about ten yards away. Then the lights came back on.

"Major—give me shadows," Rivette whispered.

Breen understood. He directed the helicopter east. At once, elongated black shapes appeared on the snow, spilling west. A moment later, having suddenly recognized their predicament, the shadows stopped moving.

Rivette slid down with his back against the tree.

The shadows started to move again. The way the coward was heaped, Rivette had more room on his right than his left. He readied himself with little movements of his back as he prepared to move—

Still low, the lance corporal pushed off the tree. He came out firing, shooting low, putting two rounds from the Sig Sauer in the legs of the man; a big knife flew but passed a foot too high. Even as the man screamed and fell, Rivette threw his right shoulder against the tree, moving in its shadow, and circled toward the south. The other man was moving round the tree to where the coward lay. He did not make it. The Colt barked twice, and the man's right hip and knee shattered in twin splashes of blood.

"Crap!" Rivette cried.

The man *was* carrying a grenade, a Ruchnaya Granata Oboronitel'naya. The small defensive grenade would have limited its killing radius to Rivette's side of the tree. It rolled from the hand of the fallen man, the pin popping free, the countdown of five seconds begun.

"Grace, down!" Rivette shouted.

The wounded man tried to roll away, and Rivette moved to put the oak between himself and ground zero as the small, circular RGO detonated. The explosion rang through Rivette's helmet, the tree was struck with a series of angry *snicks,* and the man who had been holding it screamed as metal fragments tore into him.

The cries lasted only slightly longer than the yellowish flash.

And then, save for the rotor and the muted cries of the wounded, the woods went silent.

Rivette turned to the man on the ground, squatted beside him, and rolled him faceup. The man's eyes were half-shut.

"Hey, you," the lance corporal said. "Can you hear me?"

The man nodded weakly.

"Five clowns down out here, plus you. There more?"

The head shook once.

"I don't have to shoot you somewhere to find out if that's the truth, do I?"

"That's . . . all. Six."

"You get that, Major?"

"I got it. I'll let the admiral know."

Still listening to Williams on her Bluetooth, Captain Mann heard the admiral drawing information from Stroud, stalling, even trying to change the man's mind. She was grateful for the time but knew it was finite.

While she made her way back to the subbasement, the captain checked the SEPTA stops on her phone. The nearest was several blocks away, Race Vine, on the southeast side of the library.

When Mann arrived, Chuck Boyd was pulling hard on the door with a crowbar. He jerked his head behind him as he pulled.

"Utility room," he said.

"Good man," the officer said.

The jamb cracked, the door opened, and the three of them

ran in, followed by the policewoman. Boyd found the light switch. A room the size of a small movie theater was illuminated in fluorescent white. The concrete floor was crowded with crates, stacks of books covered with tarps, barrels of oil for generators, and construction and janitorial equipment. There were two electrical boxes with large metal switches on the outside. Overhead were insulated conduits for water, ventilation, heat.

"What are we looking for?" the detective asked.

"There's some kind of remote trigger—probably close to the gas, wherever that's stored."

"Not a lot to go on."

Just then, Mann heard Stroud swear. Time had run out.

It was an instinct that had cost her something in Afghanistan—an instinct to act rather than be acted upon. Inactivity was tantamount to death. Do something wrong, but do *something.*

The action she chose arose from something Commander Brandon had said to her: "If we had been able to kill the power." Pivoting to her right, she grabbed the two switches on the electrical boxes and yanked them down. At once, the entire library went dark and mechanically silent. Emergency lights came on almost immediately; there were muffled voices from above, but locally Mann did not hear anything in the unnatural silence. She did not know whether Stroud's proposed attack should be a hiss or a rushing of air; but there was nothing.

"I don't know if that stopped anything, but keep looking!" she said.

Phone flashlights came on, and Captain Mann followed

hers toward the southeast, probing with the light for whatever installations Stroud had made here. Moving around the boxes and old furniture, ducking under pipes, she came to several wall panels that had Stroud labels. They looked like fuse boxes, with cables and wires running this way and that.

"Over here!" she said.

The others converged on the spot where Mann was shining her light.

"Let me check under the hood," Boyd said. He went to one of the boxes and opened it.

The policewoman joined him, her own light stabbing around inside. It stopped on a small disc.

"There," she said. "A wireless connection leading"—she moved her light outside the box along the wall to a thick orange feeder tube—"to that." She walked toward an oil burner, tracked the tube to a water utility duct. A hole had been cut, allowing the cable to enter the iron pipe. "From the basement into the sewer."

"So where's the gas?" Mann asked.

"My guess is behind the burner," the policewoman said. "There's insulation back there—no one would have any reason to go there unless the burner died."

The detective walked to the wall-mounted box and unplugged the wireless unit.

"I think we can restore power now," he said.

The lights came back on in the OAE office. Both men had remained where they were, Williams watching his opponent's expression. To his surprise, Stroud had gone blank.

Two messages arrived, almost simultaneously. The first was a text from Breen.

Six enemy stopped

The second was Captain Mann, who came on the open line.

"I think we stopped it," she said. "Pulled the wireless plug."

"Thank you," Williams said. "Send the police up. I'll meet you in the lobby."

The men continued to face one another as the sound of forced air returned.

"My team?" Stroud asked.

"Six down. I don't have a detailed status report."

"They would have died rather than be taken."

"Perhaps they did."

Stroud's finger was still pressing on the pad. He was pushing so hard the tip was white. He lifted it and pressed another button, one that erased the contents of the laptop. He shut the lid.

"You doomed our nation, Admiral," Stroud said gravely.

"We're pretty resilient. I'm hoping we'll be okay."

"You're naïve, you lack sight let alone vision. I'll have to live with failure, but you'll have to live with what you've done."

There were fast, heavy footsteps in the corridor behind them. A moment later Philadelphia police officers entered the room. One stood in the doorway, one by the front of the desk, and one behind Burton Stroud.

Stroud rose. "Fortunately, I still have a voice. And you have given me the platform to use it."

Chuck Boyd arrived, breathless and with searching eyes. He told police who he was and was permitted to enter his office. There was nothing he had to retrieve; he only wanted to look at Burton Stroud. What he saw, standing behind the desk, was a man he had admired, had trusted, had *thanked*. Stroud was now ethically naked, revealed as a creature of cold contempt who had slain dozens, including his fellow volunteer Tom Albert.

Boyd stared for a moment into the man's unrepentant eyes. His own eyes damp, his mouth quivering, the OAE director lingered only a moment. He wanted the felon to witness, in at least one human face, exactly what he had accomplished.

Mann arrived then, and Boyd made way for her. He turned, finding an anchor in silent prayer; he thanked the God who had given him the humanity, the compassion, that made him stay behind this night.

Stepping into the room, Mann explained who she was and what Burton Stroud had done. The businessman did not deny the allegations and was taken away. Williams was asked to identify his role in the matter.

"I have a call to make," the admiral replied. "I believe President Midkiff is waiting for it."

CHAPTER TWENTY-SEVEN

Naval Support Activity, Philadelphia, Pennsylvania
January 16, 11:11 p.m.

"I'm proud of you," Berry told Williams over the phone. "What you and the team did—I'm just freakin' *proud.* So is the president. He'll tell you later. He's busy getting ready for a midnight press conference. It may be a first—I don't know. I don't care. I am just so damn impressed *and* grateful."

"Thanks," Williams replied.

Williams and Captain Mann had left the library and gone directly to NSA Philadelphia, where they were met by a contingent of Philadelphia PD officers and brass. The president had called to explain the highly secretive nature of the operation to the mayor of Philadelphia, and the mayor communicated this to the chief of police.

The police complied but were not happy to be reduced to jailers and chauffeurs in their own jurisdiction.

To avoid reporters, Captain Mann was allowed to furnish a statement in her office. Williams was present, though apart from information generally and informally given to Deputy Commissioner Larry Church, Williams was not cited by name.

While impressed with the deeds and independent action of the two naval officers, the deputy commissioner expressed dismay that the federal government had not involved the PPD at any point. Before leaving, the law enforcement veteran faced Williams.

"What I heard here is that you saved the citizenry by seconds, and very few of them," Church said. "That's impressive. It was also reckless. We could have shaved time off that."

"That was not my wish, sir," Williams assured him. "It was also not my call."

The men parted amiably. Before leaving, Church turned back.

"By the way—we found a Stroud van in the Drexel University parking lot. We've had it towed to our garage. Our team will be going over it for evidence. We'll be sure to let Washington know what we find."

Williams smiled.

Local restaurants had sent over food for recovery workers, and some of that was brought to Mann and Williams while they awaited the arrival of the helicopter carrying Breen, Grace, and Rivette.

A second presidential call had been placed to Brigadier General Eugenie Bundonis, instructing her to provide the Black Wasps with any support they required, to extend all privileges, and then to pass them through to NSA Philadelphia without undue delay or debrief. The three had remained on-site until Air Mobility Command could ferry personnel from Dover to take charge of the prisoners, tend to the wounded—who had been given triage by the Venom crew—and secure the site.

The Black Wasps had already located Black Order headquarters a few hundred yards from the combat zone, a quaint log cabin that was the unassuming entrance to hell. They went in with the strike team, which had been briefed about the automated guns at NSA Philadelphia. The squad looked for concealed personnel and both mechanical and electronic booby traps as they pushed deeper into the compound. They used flashlights rather than internal light switches, any one of which could have been a trigger.

"Looks like they were ready for a siege," Rivette remarked when they came upon the carefully stacked and organized stores of food, water, and weapons.

"Or an assault," Grace said, pointing to drums of sarin gas.

A stencil near the bottom read, GAS VENENOSO. There was no doubt where that had originated.

"How would you feel about getting those killers next?" Rivette said with uncharacteristic gravity.

Grace did not answer. She did not have to.

By the time the team had choppered into NSA Philadelphia, word had spread about what had happened in Philadelphia and in the western part of the state. Workers sifting through the ruin of the buildings paused to look at—and in some cases salute—the anonymous warriors as they moved past.

They were reunited in Captain Mann's office. Briefed by

Williams while they were en route, Breen had already informed the other two about the commander's role in the action.

"I read about your career on the trip over," Grace said. "It's an honor to meet you."

The captain replied with a tight-lipped smile. For her, this was not a day of triumph but of terrible loss.

The new arrivals washed and changed into workout clothes from the quartermaster. With Black Wasp informality, they pulled chairs around in Captain Breen's office, treated the officer as an equal partner, and settled down for pizza.

"How is Mrs. Hamill?" Breen asked.

"She was airlifted to Jefferson Health," Captain Mann said. "I spoke with the lead physician. Physically, she's fine, but it's going to be a long road to recovery."

"What about the dirtbags from the woods?" Rivette asked.

"They're at Dover, the living and the dead."

"It's sad," Breen remarked. "Now that the fighting is done, the jurisdictional battle begins. It will be a year or more before any one of these people sees the inside of a courtroom."

"Enough time for the public to move on to the next thing," Williams said.

"Including us?" Rivette asked. "We got a new president coming in just about three days now."

"I don't think so," Williams said. "Sadly, this is the kind of day from which job security is built. In fact, seeing as how this played out in his home state, I'm hoping that President Wright will have no objection to expanding our team." Williams regarded Captain Mann. "If the officer is willing."

"The officer is honored and grateful," Mann said. "If the admiral can wait until NSA is back on its feet—along with its commander—it's something we should discuss."

"The admiral is willing," Williams said.

While Mann arranged for Black Wasp to be flown back to Fort Belvoir, Williams went to an empty office at the base HQ to videoconference with the president and Matt Berry.

There was, in the admiral's experience, a unique start to the call: no one spoke. Williams and Berry were waiting for Midkiff, but the exhausted commander in chief just sat for a long, long moment.

"Hell of a day. Hell of a mission," the president said at last. He shook his head and looked down, then up. "Thanks to you, Admiral, it's a hell of an exit. I have to admit it isn't easy to feel gratitude after what this has cost, but I do."

"That's the price of war," Williams said. "But I thank you for the sentiment and for your trust, sir. Not just on this but across the board. And I've asked Captain Mann to join us. She was exemplary."

"Did she accept?"

"With humility and gratitude."

The president shook his head. "Curious how that all went."

"You don't just mean today, sir."

"No, no—bringing Op-Center back from the dead to save us." He laughed.

"I don't even want to think of the bigger message in that."

Williams did not mind the sentiment; it was refreshing

to hear. His eyes shifted to Berry. "Not a bad exit for you, either."

"Oh, I won't soon forget this, and yes, it'll give me street cred in my new position. Though I'm waiting for the contrarian voices to start their chorus of 'How could they have let this happen on their watch?'"

The president thought for a moment, then slapped his hands on his desk. "I have a press conference." He regarded Williams as he stood. "Chase, John Wright is a different breed. You know that. But with all his public posturing about charity for all—mostly at government expense—he's going to need someone vigilant to watch his back."

"We'll be there," Williams said.

The president thanked him again, and Berry sighed into the camera. "Jesus, Chase. It kind of does make you believe in a higher power."

"Always have," Williams replied.

"I know. We'll have to have a long talk about that, but some other time. I want to go over the president's opening remarks with him, and you have a flight, I understand."

"Yeah. See you tomorrow."

"Oh, and before I go, I want to talk to you about this Jackson Poole your team captured."

"What about him?"

"Air force has him and will debrief him. He's like a German rocket scientist. Before I leave, I want access to what he knows."

Berry ended the call, and Chase Williams sat alone for a

moment in the still office as the commotion of Americans helping Americans banged and shouted outside.

After everything they had been through, after this vicious strike at the national heart, it was a sound that filled him with pride, faith, and most important of all:

Hope.